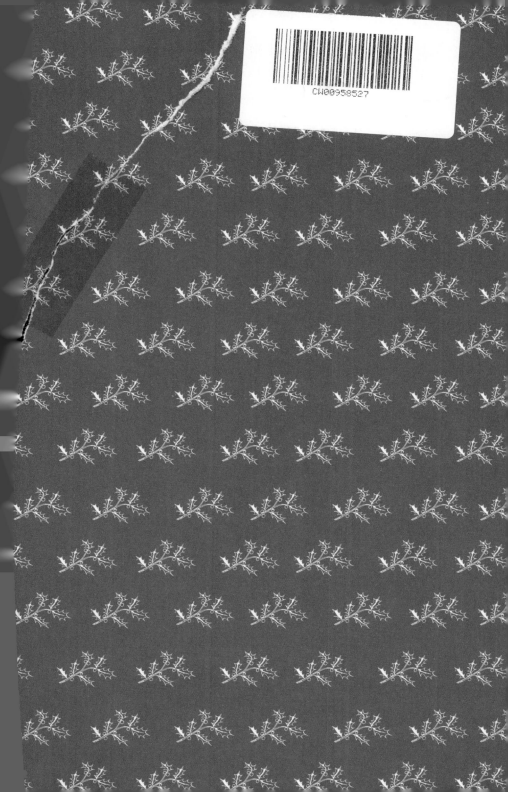

CONTENTS

CHRISTMAS DIARIES

CHRISTMAS CAROLING

CHRISTMAS WITH THE FAMILY

EX LIBRIS

VINTAGE CLASSICS

ROUND THE CHRISTMAS FIRE:
FESTIVE STORIES

A Selection of Seasonal Writings

Truman Capote, John Cheever, Charles Dickens,
Stella Gibbons, Kenneth Grahame,
George & Weedon Grossmith, O. Henry,
M. R. James, Laurie Lee, Nancy Mitford,
E. Nesbit, Damon Runyon, Dylan Thomas,
Sue Townsend, Edith Wharton, P. G. Wodehouse

VINTAGE BOOKS
LONDON

Published by Vintage 2013

2 4 6 8 10 9 7 5 3 1

Illustrations copyright © Emily Sutton 2013

The acknowledgements page at the end of the book should be seen
as an extension of this copyright page.

Vintage
Random House, 20 Vauxhall Bridge Road,
London SW1V 2SA

www.vintage-classics.info

Addresses for companies within The Random House Group Limited can be found at:
www.randomhouse.co.uk/offices.htm

The Random House Group Limited Reg. No. 954009

A CIP catalogue record for this book
is available from the British Library

ISBN 9780099577072

The Random House Group Limited supports the Forest Stewardship Council® (FSC®),
the leading international forest-certification organisation. Our books carrying the FSC
label are printed on FSC®-certified paper. FSC is the only forest-certification
scheme supported by the leading environmental organisations, including Greenpeace.
Our paper procurement policy can be found at www.randomhouse.co.uk/environment

Typeset in Fournier MT by Palimpsest Book Production Limited,
Falkirk, Stirlingshire

Printed and bound in Germany
by GGP Media GmbH, Pößneck

CHRISTMAS GIFTS

CHRISTMAS DINNERS

LAST CHRISTMAS

CHRISTMAS CHILLS:
GHOST STORIES
FOR CHRISTMAS EVE

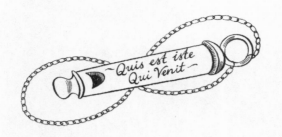

'OH, WHISTLE AND I'LL COME TO YOU, MY LAD' *BY* M. R. JAMES

Montague Rhodes James was born on 1 August 1862 near Bury St Edmunds. He studied at Eton and King's College, Cambridge, where he was eventually elected Fellow. In 1918 he became Provost of Eton. He was a renowned medievalist and biblical scholar, and published works on palaeography, antiquarianism, bibliography and history. However, he remains best known for his ghost stories, which were published in several collections, including *Ghost Stories of an Antiquary* (1904), *A Thin Ghost and Other Stories* (1919), *A Warning to the Curious* (1925) and a collected edition in 1931. M. R. James never married and died on 12 June 1936.

'I SUPPOSE you will be getting away pretty soon, now Full term is over, Professor,' said a person not in the story to the Professor of Ontography, soon after they had sat down next to each other at a feast in the hospitable hall of St James's College.

The Professor was young, neat, and precise in speech.

'Yes,' he said; 'my friends have been making me take up golf this term, and I mean to go to the East Coast – in point of fact to Burnstow – (I dare say you know it) for a week or ten days, to improve my game. I hope to get off tomorrow.'

'Oh, Parkins,' said his neighbour on the other side, 'if you are going to Burnstow, I wish you would look at the site of the Templars' preceptory, and let me know if you think it would be any good to have a dig there in the summer.'

It was, as you might suppose, a person of antiquarian pursuits who said this, but, since he merely appears in this prologue, there is no need to give his entitlements.

'Certainly,' said Parkins, the Professor: 'if you will describe to me whereabouts the site is, I will do my best to give you an idea of the lie of the land when I get back; or I could write to you about it, if you would tell me where you are likely to be.'

'Don't trouble to do that, thanks. It's only that I'm thinking of taking my family in that direction in the Long, and it occurred to me that, as very few of the English preceptories have ever been properly planned, I might have an opportunity of doing something useful on off-days.'

The Professor rather sniffed at the idea that planning out a preceptory could be described as useful. His neighbour continued:

'The site – I doubt if there is anything showing above ground – must be down quite close to the beach now. The sea has encroached tremendously, as you know, all along that bit of coast. I should think, from the map, that it must be about three-quarters of a mile from the Globe Inn, at the north end of the town. Where are you going to stay?'

'Well, *at* the Globe Inn, as a matter of fact,' said Parkins; 'I have engaged a room there. I couldn't get in anywhere else; most of the lodging-houses are shut up in winter, it seems; and, as it is, they tell me that the only room of any size I can have is really a double-bedded one, and that they haven't a corner in which to store the other bed, and so on. But I must have a fairly large room, for I am taking some books down, and mean to do a bit of work; and though I don't quite fancy having an empty bed – not to speak of two – in what I may call for the time being my study, I suppose I can manage to rough it for the short time I shall be there.'

'Do you call having an extra bed in your room roughing it, Parkins?' said a bluff person opposite. 'Look here, I shall come down and occupy it for a bit; it'll be company for you.'

The Professor quivered, but managed to laugh in a courteous manner.

'By all means, Rogers; there's nothing I should like better. But I'm afraid you would find it rather dull; you don't play golf, do you?'

'No, thank Heaven!' said rude Mr Rogers.

'Well, you see, when I'm not writing I shall most likely be out on the links, and that, as I say, would be rather dull for you, I'm afraid.'

'Oh, I don't know! There's certain to be somebody I know in the place; but, of course, if you don't want me, speak the word, Parkins; I shan't be offended. Truth, as you always tell us, is never offensive.'

Parkins was, indeed, scrupulously polite and strictly truthful. It is to be feared that Mr Rogers sometimes practised upon his knowledge of these characteristics. In Parkins's breast there was a conflict now raging, which for a moment or two did not allow him to answer. That interval being over, he said:

'Well, if you want the exact truth, Rogers, I was considering whether the room I speak of would really be large enough to accommodate us both comfortably; and also whether (mind, I shouldn't have said this if you hadn't pressed me) you would not constitute something in the nature of a hindrance to my work.'

Rogers laughed loudly.

'Well done, Parkins!' he said. 'It's all right. I promise not to interrupt your work; don't you disturb yourself about that. No, I won't come if you don't want me; but I thought I should do so nicely to keep the ghosts off.' Here he might have been seen to wink and to nudge his next neighbour. Parkins might also have been seen to become pink. 'I beg pardon, Parkins,' Rogers continued; 'I oughtn't to have said that. I forgot you didn't like levity on these topics.'

'Well,' Parkins said, 'as you have mentioned the matter, I freely own that I do *not* like careless talk about what you call ghosts. A man in my position,' he went on, raising his voice a little, 'cannot, I find, be too careful about appearing to sanction the current beliefs on such subjects. As you know, Rogers, or as you ought to know; for I think I have never concealed my views —'

'No, you certainly have not, old man,' put in Rogers *sotto voce*.

'– I hold that any semblance, any appearance of concession to the view that such things might exist is equivalent to a renunciation of all that I hold most sacred. But I'm afraid I have not succeeded in securing your attention.'

'Your *undivided* attention, was what Dr Blimber actually *said*,'* Rogers interrupted, with every appearance of an earnest desire for accuracy. 'But I beg your pardon, Parkins; I'm stopping you.'

'No, not at all,' said Parkins. 'I don't remember Blimber; perhaps he was before my time. But I needn't go on. I'm sure you know what I mean.'

'Yes, yes,' said Rogers, rather hastily – 'just so. We'll go into it fully at Burnstow, or somewhere.'

In repeating the above dialogue I have tried to give the impression which it made on me, that Parkins was something of an old woman – rather hen-like, perhaps, in his little ways; totally destitute, alas! of the sense of humour, but at the same time dauntless and sincere in his convictions, and a man deserving of the greatest respect. Whether or not the reader has gathered so much, that was the character which Parkins had.

On the following day Parkins did, as he had hoped, succeed in getting away from his college, and in arriving at Burnstow. He was made welcome at the Globe Inn, was safely installed in the large double-bedded room of which we have heard, and was able before retiring to rest to arrange his materials for work in apple-pie order upon a commodious table which occupied the outer end of the room, and was surrounded on three sides by windows looking out seaward; that is to say, the central window

---

* Mr Rogers was wrong, *vide Dombey and Son*, Chapter xii.

looked straight out to sea, and those on the left and right commanded prospects along the shore to the north and south respectively. On the south you saw the village of Burnstow. On the north no houses were to be seen, but only the beach and the low cliff backing it. Immediately in front was a strip – not considerable – of rough grass, dotted with old anchors, capstans, and so forth; then a broad path; then the beach. Whatever may have been the original distance between the Globe Inn and the sea, not more than sixty yards now separated them.

The rest of the population of the inn was, of course, a golfing one, and included few elements that call for a special description. The most conspicuous figure was, perhaps, that of an *ancien militaire*, secretary of a London club, and possessed of a voice of incredible strength, and of views of a pronouncedly Protestant type. These were apt to find utterance after his attendance upon the ministrations of the Vicar, an estimable man with inclinations towards a picturesque ritual, which he gallantly kept down as far as he could out of deference to East Anglian tradition.

Professor Parkins, one of whose principal characteristics was pluck, spent the greater part of the day following his arrival at Burnstow in what he had called improving his game, in company with this Colonel Wilson: and during the afternoon – whether the process of improvement were to blame or not, I am not sure – the Colonel's demeanour assumed a colouring so lurid that even Parkins jibbed at the thought of walking home with him from the links. He determined, after a short and furtive look at that bristling moustache and those incarnadined features, that it would be wiser to allow the influences of tea and tobacco to do what they could with the Colonel before the dinner-hour should render a meeting inevitable.

'I might walk home tonight along the beach,' he reflected – 'yes, and take a look – there will be light enough for that – at the ruins of which Disney was talking. I don't exactly know where they are, by the way; but I expect I can hardly help stumbling on them.'

This he accomplished, I may say, in the most literal sense, for in picking his way from the links to the shingle beach his foot caught, partly in a gorse-root and partly in a biggish stone, and over he went. When he got up and surveyed his surroundings, he found himself in a patch of somewhat broken ground covered with small depressions and mounds. These latter, when he came to examine them, proved to be simply masses of flints embedded in mortar and grown over with turf. He must, he quite rightly concluded, be on the site of the preceptory he had promised to look at. It seemed not unlikely to reward the spade of the explorer; enough of the foundations was probably left at no great depth to throw a good deal of light on the general plan. He remembered vaguely that the Templars, to whom this site had belonged, were in the habit of building round churches, and he thought a particular series of the humps or mounds near him did appear to be arranged in something of a circular form. Few people can resist the temptation to try a little amateur research in a department quite outside their own, if only for the satisfaction of showing how successful they would have been had they only taken it up seriously. Our Professor, however, if he felt something of this mean desire, was also truly anxious to oblige Mr Disney. So he paced with care the circular area he had noticed, and wrote down its rough dimensions in his pocket-book. Then he proceeded to examine an oblong eminence which lay east of the centre of the circle, and seemed to his thinking likely to be the base of a platform or altar. At one end of it, the northern, a patch of the turf was gone – removed by some boy or other creature *ferae naturae*. It might, he thought, be as well to probe the soil here for evidences of masonry, and he took out his knife and began scraping away the earth. And now followed another little discovery: a portion of soil fell inward as he scraped, and disclosed a small cavity. He lighted one match after another to help him to see of what nature the hole was, but the wind was too strong for them all. By tapping and scratching the sides with his knife, however, he was able to make out that it must be an artificial hole in masonry. It was rectangular, and the sides, top, and bottom, if not actually plastered, were smooth and regular. Of course it was empty. No! As he withdrew the knife he heard a metallic clink, and when he introduced his hand it met with a cylindrical object lying on the floor of the hole. Naturally enough, he picked it up, and when he brought it into the light, now fast fading, he could see that it, too, was of man's making – a metal tube about four inches long, and evidently of some considerable age.

By the time Parkins had made sure that there was nothing else in this odd receptacle, it was too late and too dark for him to think of undertaking any further search. What he had done had proved so unexpectedly interesting that he determined to sacrifice a little more of the daylight on the morrow to archaeology. The object which he now had safe in his pocket was bound to be of some slight value at least, he felt sure.

Bleak and solemn was the view on which he took a last look before starting homeward. A faint yellow light in the west showed the links, on which a few figures moving towards the club-house were still visible, the squat martello tower, the lights of Aldsey village, the pale ribbon of sands intersected at intervals by black wooden groynes, the dim and murmuring sea. The wind was bitter from the north, but was at his back when he set out for the Globe. He quickly rattled and clashed through the shingle and gained the sand, upon which, but for the groynes which had to be got over every few yards, the going was both good and quiet. One last look behind, to measure the distance he had made since leaving the ruined Templars' church, showed him a prospect of company on his walk, in the shape of a rather indistinct personage, who seemed to be making great efforts to catch up with him, but made little, if any, progress. I mean that there was an appearance of running about his movements, but that the distance between him and Parkins did not seem materially to lessen. So, at least, Parkins thought, and decided that he almost certainly did not know him, and that it would be absurd to wait until he came up. For all that, company, he began to think, would really be very welcome on that lonely shore, if only you could choose your companion. In his unenlightened days he had read of meetings in such places which even now would hardly bear thinking of. He went on thinking of them, however, until he reached home, and particularly of one which catches most people's fancy at some time of their childhood. 'Now I saw in my dream that Christian had gone but a very little way when he saw a foul fiend coming over the field to meet him.' 'What should I do now,' he thought, 'if I looked back and caught sight of a black figure sharply defined against the yellow sky, and saw that it had horns and wings? I wonder whether I should stand or run for it. Luckily, the gentleman behind is not of that kind, and he seems to be about as far off now as when I saw him first. Well, at this rate he won't get his dinner as soon as I shall; and, dear me! it's within a quarter of an hour of the time now. I must run!'

Parkins had, in fact, very little time for dressing. When he met the Colonel at dinner, Peace – or as much of her as that gentleman could manage – reigned once more in the military bosom; nor was she put to flight in the hours of bridge that followed dinner, for Parkins was a more than respectable player. When, therefore, he retired towards twelve o'clock, he felt that he had spent his evening in quite a satisfactory way, and that, even for so long as a fortnight or three weeks, life at the Globe would be supportable under similar conditions – 'especially,' thought he, 'if I go on improving my game.'

As he went along the passages he met the boots of the Globe, who stopped and said:

'Beg your pardon, sir, but as I was a-brushing your coat just now there was somethink fell out of the pocket. I put it on your chest of drawers, sir, in your room, sir – a piece of a pipe or somethink of that, sir. Thank you, sir. You'll find it on your chest of drawers, sir – yes, sir. Good night, sir.'

The speech served to remind Parkins of his little discovery of that afternoon. It was with some considerable curiosity that he turned it over by the light of his candles. It was of bronze, he now saw, and was shaped very much after the manner of the modern dog-whistle; in fact it was – yes, certainly it was – actually no more nor less than a whistle. He put it to his lips, but it was quite full of a fine, caked-up sand or earth, which would not yield to knocking, but must be loosened with a knife. Tidy as ever in his habits, Parkins cleared out the earth on to a piece of paper, and took the latter to the window to empty it out. The night was clear and bright, as he saw when he had opened the casement, and he stopped for an instant to look at the sea and note a belated wanderer stationed on the shore in front of the inn. Then he shut the window, a little surprised at the late hours people kept at Burnstow, and took his whistle to the light again. Why, surely there were marks on it, and not merely marks, but letters! A very little rubbing rendered the deeply-cut inscription quite legible, but the Professor had to confess, after some earnest thought, that the meaning of it was as obscure to him as the writing on the wall to Belshazzar. There were legends both on the front and on the back of the whistle. The one read thus:

FUR **FLA** **BIS**
        PLE

The other:

⚜ QUIS EST ISTE QUI UENIT ⚜

'I ought to be able to make it out,' he thought; 'but I suppose I am a little rusty in my Latin. When I come to think of it, I don't believe I even know the word for a whistle. The long one does seem simple enough. It ought to mean, "Who is this who is coming?" Well, the best way to find out is evidently to whistle for him.'

He blew tentatively and stopped suddenly, startled and yet pleased at the note he had elicited. It had a quality of infinite distance in it, and, soft as it was, he somehow felt it must be audible for miles round. It was a sound, too, that seemed to have the power (which many scents possess) of forming pictures in the brain. He saw quite clearly for a moment a vision of a wide, dark expanse at night, with a fresh wind blowing and in the midst a lonely figure – how employed, he could not tell. Perhaps he would have seen more had not the picture been broken by the sudden surge of a gust of wind against his casement, so sudden that it made him look up, just in time to see the white glint of a sea-bird's wing somewhere outside the dark panes.

The sound of the whistle had so fascinated him that he could not help trying it once more, this time more boldly. The note was little, if at all, louder than before, and repetition broke the illusion – no picture followed, as he had half hoped it might. 'But what is this? Goodness! what force the wind can get up in a few minutes! What a tremendous gust! There! I knew that window-fastening was no use! Ah! I thought so – both candles out. It's enough to tear the room to pieces.'

The first thing was to get the window shut. While you might count twenty Parkins was struggling with the small casement, and felt almost as if he were pushing back a sturdy burglar, so strong was the pressure. It slackened all at once, and the window banged to and latched itself. Now to relight the candles and see what damage, if any, had been done. No, nothing seemed amiss; no glass even was broken in the casement. But the noise had evidently roused at least one member of the household: the Colonel was to be heard stumping in his stockinged feet on the floor above, and growling.

Quickly as it had risen, the wind did not fall at once. On it went, moaning and rushing past the house, at times rising to a cry so desolate that, as Parkins disinterestedly said, it might have made fanciful people feel quite uncomfortable; even the unimaginative, he thought after a quarter of an hour, might be happier without it.

Whether it was the wind, or the excitement of golf, or of the researches in the preceptory that kept Parkins awake, he was not sure. Awake he remained, in any case, long enough to fancy (as I am afraid I often do myself under such conditions) that he was the victim of all manner of fatal disorders: he would lie counting the beats of his heart, convinced that it was going to stop work every moment, and would entertain grave suspicions of his lungs, brain, liver, etc. – suspicions which he was sure would be dispelled by the return of daylight, but which until then refused to be put aside. He found a little vicarious comfort in the idea that someone else was in the same boat. A near neighbour (in the darkness it was not easy to tell his direction) was tossing and rustling in his bed, too.

The next stage was that Parkins shut his eyes and determined to give sleep every chance. Here again over-excitement asserted itself in another form – that of making pictures. *Experto crede*, pictures do come to the closed eyes of one trying to sleep, and are often so little to his taste that he must open his eyes and disperse them.

Parkins's experience on this occasion was a very distressing one. He found that the picture which presented itself to him was continuous. When he opened his eyes, of course, it went; but when he shut them once more it framed itself afresh, and acted itself out again, neither quicker nor slower than before. What he saw was this: A long stretch of shore – shingle edged by sand, and intersected at short intervals with black groynes running down to the water – a scene, in fact, so like that of his afternoon's walk that, in the absence of any landmark, it could not be distinguished therefrom. The light was obscure, conveying an impression of gathering storm, late winter evening, and slight cold rain. On this bleak stage at first no actor was visible. Then, in the distance, a bobbing black object appeared; a moment more, and it was a man running, jumping, clambering over the groynes, and every few seconds looking eagerly back. The nearer he came the more obvious it was that he was not only anxious, but even terribly frightened, though his face was not to be distinguished. He was, moreover, almost at the end of his strength. On he came; each successive obstacle seemed to cause him more difficulty than the last. 'Will he get over this next one?' thought Parkins; 'it seems a little higher than the others.' Yes; half-climbing, half throwing himself, he did get over, and fell all in a heap on the other side (the side nearest to the spectator). There, as if really unable to get up again, he remained crouching under the groyne, looking up in an attitude of painful anxiety.

So far no cause whatever for the fear of the runner had been shown; but now there began to be seen, far up the shore, a little flicker of something light-coloured moving to and fro with great swiftness and irregularity. Rapidly growing larger, it, too, declared itself as a figure in pale, fluttering draperies, ill-defined. There was something about its motion which made Parkins very unwilling to see it at close quarters. It would stop, raise arms, bow itself toward the sand, then run stooping across the beach to the water-edge and back again; and then, rising upright, once more continue its course forward at a speed that was startling and terrifying. The moment came when the pursuer was hovering about from left to right only a few yards beyond the groyne where the runner lay in hiding. After two or three ineffectual castings hither and thither it came to a stop, stood upright, with arms raised high, and then darted straight forward towards the groyne.

It was at this point that Parkins always failed in his resolution to keep his eyes shut. With many misgivings as to incipient failure of eyesight, over-worked brain, excessive smoking, and so on, he finally resigned himself to light his candle, get out a book, and pass the night waking, rather than be tormented by this persistent panorama, which he saw clearly enough could only be a morbid reflection of his walk and his thoughts on that very day.

The scraping of match on box and the glare of light must have startled some creatures of the night – rats or what not – which he heard scurry across the floor from the side of his bed with much rustling. Dear, dear! the match is out! Fool that it is! But the second one burnt better, and a candle and book were duly procured, over which Parkins pored till sleep of a wholesome kind came upon him, and that in no long space. For about the first time in his orderly and prudent life he forgot to blow out the candle, and when he was called next morning at eight there was still a flicker in the socket and a sad mess of guttered grease on the top of the little table.

After breakfast he was in his room, putting the finishing

touches to his golfing costume – fortune had again allotted the Colonel to him for a partner – when one of the maids came in.

'Oh, if you please,' she said, 'would you like any extra blankets on your bed, sir?'

'Ah! thank you,' said Parkins. 'Yes, I think I should like one. It seems likely to turn rather colder.'

In a very short time the maid was back with the blanket.

'Which bed should I put it on, sir?' she asked.

'What? Why, that one – the one I slept in last night,' he said, pointing to it.

'Oh yes! I beg your pardon, sir, but you seemed to have tried both of 'em; leastways, we had to make 'em both up this morning.'

'Really? How very absurd!' said Parkins. 'I certainly never touched the other, except to lay some things on it. Did it actually seem to have been slept in?'

'Oh, yes, sir!' said the maid. 'Why, all the things was crumpled and throwed about all ways, if you'll excuse me, sir – quite as if anyone 'adn't passed but a very poor night, sir.'

'Dear me,' said Parkins. 'Well, I may have disordered it more than I thought when I unpacked my things. I'm very sorry to have given you the extra trouble, I'm sure. I expect a friend of mine soon, by the way – a gentleman from Cambridge – to come and occupy it for a night or two. That will be all right, I suppose, won't it?'

'Oh yes, to be sure, sir. Thank you, sir. It's no trouble, I'm sure,' said the maid, and departed to giggle with her colleagues.

Parkins set forth, with a stern determination to improve his game.

I am glad to be able to report that he succeeded so far in this enterprise that the Colonel, who had been rather repining at the prospect of a second day's play in his company, became quite chatty as the morning advanced; and his voice boomed out over the flats, as certain also of our own minor poets have said, 'like some great bourdon in a minster tower'.

'Extraordinary wind, that, we had last night,' he said. 'In my old home we should have said someone had been whistling for it.'

'Should you, indeed!' said Parkins. 'Is there a superstition of that kind still current in your part of the country?'

'I don't know about superstition,' said the Colonel. 'They believe in it all over Denmark and Norway, as well as on the Yorkshire coast; and my experience is, mind you, that there's generally something at the bottom of what these country-folk hold to, and have held to for generations. But it's your drive' (or whatever it might have been: the golfing reader will have to imagine appropriate digressions at the proper intervals).

When conversation was resumed, Parkins said, with a slight hesitancy:

'Apropos of what you were saying just now, Colonel, I think I ought to tell you that my own views on such subjects are very strong. I am, in fact, a convinced disbeliever in what is called the "supernatural".'

'What!' said the Colonel, 'do you mean to tell me you don't believe in second-sight, or ghosts, or anything of that kind?'

'In nothing whatever of that kind,' returned Parkins firmly.

'Well,' said the Colonel, 'but it appears to me at that rate, sir, that you must be little better than a Sadducee.'

Parkins was on the point of answering that, in his opinion, the Sadducees were the most sensible persons he had ever read of in the Old Testament; but, feeling some doubt as to whether much mention of them was to be found in that work, he preferred to laugh the accusation off.

'Perhaps I am,' he said; 'but – Here, give me my cleek, boy!

– Excuse me one moment, Colonel.' A short interval. 'Now, as to whistling for the wind, let me give you my theory about it. The laws which govern winds are really not at all perfectly known – to fisher-folk and such, of course, not known at all. A man or woman of eccentric habits, perhaps, or a stranger, is seen repeatedly on the beach at some unusual hour, and is heard whistling. Soon afterwards a violent wind rises; a man who could read the sky perfectly or who possessed a barometer could have foretold that it would. The simple people of a fishing-village have no barometers, and only a few rough rules for prophesying weather. What more natural than that the eccentric personage I postulated should be regarded as having raised the wind, or that he or she should clutch eagerly at the reputation of being able to do so? Now, take last night's wind: as it happens, I myself was whistling. I blew a whistle twice, and the wind seemed to come absolutely in answer to my call. If anyone had seen me –'

The audience had been a little restive under this harangue, and Parkins had, I fear, fallen somewhat into the tone of a lecturer; but at the last sentence the Colonel stopped.

'Whistling, were you?' he said. 'And what sort of whistle did you use? Play this stroke first.' Interval.

'About that whistle you were asking, Colonel. It's rather a curious one. I have it in my – No; I see I've left it in my room. As a matter of fact, I found it yesterday.'

And then Parkins narrated the manner of his discovery of the whistle, upon hearing which the Colonel grunted, and opined that, in Parkins's place, he should himself be careful about using a thing that had belonged to a set of Papists, of whom, speaking generally, it might be affirmed that you never knew what they might not have been up to. From this topic he diverged to the enormities of the Vicar, who had given notice on the previous Sunday that Friday would be the Feast of St Thomas the Apostle, and that there would be service at eleven o'clock in the church. This and other similar proceedings constituted in the Colonel's view a strong presumption that the Vicar was a concealed Papist, if not a Jesuit; and Parkins, who could not very readily follow the Colonel in this region, did not disagree with him. In fact, they got on so well together in the morning that there was no talk on either side of their separating after lunch.

Both continued to play well during the afternoon, or, at least, well enough to make them forget everything else until the light began to fail them. Not until then did Parkins remember that he had meant to do some more investigating at the preceptory; but it was of no great importance, he reflected. One day was as good as another; he might as well go home with the Colonel.

As they turned the corner of the house, the Colonel was almost knocked down by a boy who rushed into him at the very top of his speed, and then, instead of running away, remained hanging on to him and panting. The first words of the warrior were naturally those of reproof and objurgation, but he very quickly discerned that the boy was almost speechless with fright. Inquiries were useless at first. When the boy got his breath he began to howl, and still clung to the Colonel's legs. He was at last detached, but continued to howl.

'What in the world is the matter with you? What have you been up to? What have you seen?' said the two men.

'Ow, I seen it wive at me out of the winder,' wailed the boy, 'and I don't like it.'

'What window?' said the irritated Colonel. 'Come, pull yourself together, my boy.'

'The front winder it was, at the 'otel,' said the boy.

At this point Parkins was in favour of sending the boy home, but the Colonel refused; he wanted to get to the bottom of it, he said; it was most dangerous to give a boy such a fright as this one had had, and if it turned out that people had been playing jokes, they should suffer for it in some way. And by a series of questions he made out this story. The boy had been playing about on the grass in front of the Globe with some others; then they had gone home to their teas, and he was just going, when he happened to look up at the front winder and see it a-wiving at him. *It* seemed to be a figure of some sort, in white as far as he knew – couldn't see its face; but it wived at him, and it warn't a right thing – not to say not a right person. Was there a light in the room? No, he didn't think to look if there was a light. Which was the window? Was it the top one or the second one? The seckind one it was – the big winder what got two little uns at the sides.

'Very well, my boy,' said the Colonel, after a few more questions. 'You run away home now. I expect it was some person trying to give you a start. Another time, like a brave English boy, you just throw a stone – well, no, not that exactly, but you go and speak to the waiter, or to Mr Simpson, the landlord, and – yes – and say that I advised you to do so.'

The boy's face expressed some of the doubt he felt as to the likelihood of Mr Simpson's lending a favourable ear to his complaint, but the Colonel did not appear to perceive this, and went on:

'And here's a sixpence – no, I see it's a shilling – and you be off home, and don't think any more about it.'

The youth hurried off with agitated thanks, and the Colonel and Parkins went round to the front of the Globe and reconnoitred. There was only one window answering to the description they had been hearing.

'Well, that's curious,' said Parkins; 'it's evidently my window the lad was talking about. Will you come up for a moment, Colonel Wilson? We ought to be able to see if anyone has been taking liberties in my room.'

They were soon in the passage, and Parkins made as if to

open the door. Then he stopped and felt in his pockets.

'This is more serious than I thought,' was his next remark. 'I remember now that before I started this morning I locked the door. It is locked now, and, what is more, here is the key.' And he held it up. 'Now,' he went on, 'if the servants are in the habit of going into one's room during the day when one is away, I can only say that – well, that I don't approve of it at all.' Conscious of a somewhat weak climax, he busied himself in opening the door (which was indeed locked) and in lighting candles. 'No,' he said, 'nothing seems disturbed.'

'Except your bed,' put in the Colonel.

'Excuse me, that isn't my bed,' said Parkins. 'I don't use that one. But it does look as if someone has been playing tricks with it.'

It certainly did: the clothes were bundled up and twisted together in a most tortuous confusion. Parkins pondered.

'That must be it,' he said at last: 'I disordered the clothes last night in unpacking, and they haven't made it since. Perhaps they came in to make it, and that boy saw them through the window; and then they were called away and locked the door after them. Yes, I think that must be it.'

'Well, ring and ask,' said the Colonel, and this appealed to Parkins as practical.

The maid appeared, and, to make a long story short, deposed that she had made the bed in the morning when the gentleman was in the room, and hadn't been there since. No, she hadn't no other key. Mr Simpson he kep' the keys; he'd be able to tell the gentleman if anyone had been up.

This was a puzzle. Investigation showed that nothing of value had been taken, and Parkins remembered the disposition of the small objects on tables and so forth well enough to be pretty sure that no pranks had been played with them. Mr and Mrs

Simpson furthermore agreed that neither of them had given the duplicate key of the room to any person whatever during the day. Nor could Parkins, fair-minded man as he was, detect anything in the demeanour of master, mistress, or maid that indicated guilt. He was much more inclined to think that the boy had been imposing on the Colonel.

The latter was unwontedly silent and pensive at dinner and throughout the evening. When he bade good night to Parkins, he murmured in a gruff undertone:

'You know where I am if you want me during the night.'

'Why, yes, thank you, Colonel Wilson, I think I do; but there isn't much prospect of my disturbing you, I hope. By the way,' he added, 'did I show you that old whistle I spoke of? I think not. Well, here it is.'

The Colonel turned it over gingerly in the light of the candle.

'Can you make anything of the inscription?' asked Parkins, as he took it back.

'No, not in this light. What do you mean to do with it?'

'Oh, well, when I get back to Cambridge I shall submit it to some of the archaeologists there, and see what they think of it; and very likely, if they consider it worth having, I may present it to one of the museums.'

''M!' said the Colonel. 'Well, you may be right. All I know is that, if it were mine, I should chuck it straight into the sea. It's no use talking, I'm well aware, but I expect that with you it's a case of live and learn. I hope so, I'm sure, and I wish you a good night.'

He turned away leaving Parkins in act to speak at the bottom of the stair, and soon each was in his own bedroom.

By some unfortunate accident, there were neither blinds nor curtains to the windows of the Professor's room. The previous night he had thought little of this, but tonight there seemed every prospect of a bright moon rising to shine directly on his bed, and probably wake him later on. When he noticed this he was a good deal annoyed, but, with an ingenuity which I can only envy, he succeeded in rigging up, with the help of a railway-rug, some safety-pins, and a stick and umbrella, a screen which, if it only held together, would completely keep the moonlight off his bed. And shortly afterwards he was comfortably in that bed. When he had read a somewhat solid work long enough to produce a decided wish for sleep, he cast a drowsy glance round the room, blew out the candle, and fell back upon the pillow.

He must have slept soundly for an hour or more, when a sudden clatter shook him up in a most unwelcome manner. In a moment he realised what had happened: his carefully-constructed screen had given way, and a very bright frosty moon was shining directly on his face. This was highly annoying. Could he possibly get up and reconstruct the screen? or could he manage to sleep if he did not?

For some minutes he lay and pondered over the possibilities; then he turned over sharply, and with all his eyes open lay breathlessly listening. There had been a movement, he was sure, in the empty bed on the opposite side of the room. Tomorrow he would have it moved, for there must be rats or something playing about in it. It was quiet now. No! the commotion began again. There was a rustling and shaking: surely more than any rat could cause.

I can figure to myself something of the Professor's bewilderment and horror, for I have in a dream thirty years back seen the same thing happen; but the reader will hardly, perhaps, imagine how dreadful it was to him to see a figure suddenly sit up in what he had known was an empty bed. He was out of his own bed in one bound, and made a dash towards the window, where lay his only weapon, the stick with which he had propped his screen. This was, as it turned out, the worst thing he could have done, because the personage in the empty bed, with a sudden smooth motion, slipped from the bed and took up a position, with outspread arms, between the two beds, and in front of the door. Parkins watched it in a horrid perplexity. Somehow, the idea of getting past it and escaping through the door was intolerable to him; he could not have borne – he didn't know why – to touch it; and as for its touching him, he would sooner dash himself through the window than have that happen. It stood for the moment in a band of dark shadow, and he had not seen what its face was like. Now it began to move, in a stooping posture, and all at once the spectator realised, with some horror and some relief, that it must be blind, for it seemed to feel about it with its muffled arms in a groping and random fashion. Turning half away from him, it became suddenly conscious of the bed he had just left, and darted towards it, and bent over and felt the pillows in a way which made Parkins shudder as he had never in his life thought it possible. In a very few moments it seemed to know that the bed was empty, and then, moving forward into the area of light and facing the window, it showed for the first time what manner of thing it was.

Parkins, who very much dislikes being questioned about it, did once describe something of it in my hearing, and I gathered that what he chiefly remembers about it is a horrible, an intensely horrible, face *of crumbled linen*. What expression he read upon it he could not or would not tell, but that the fear of it went nigh to maddening him is certain.

But he was not at leisure to watch it for long. With formidable quickness it moved into the middle of the room, and, as it groped and waved, one corner of its draperies swept across Parkins's face. He could not – though he knew how perilous a sound was – he could not keep back a cry of disgust, and this gave the searcher an instant clue. It leapt towards him upon the instant, and the next moment he was half-way through the window backwards, uttering cry upon cry at the utmost pitch of his voice, and the linen face was thrust close into his own. At this, almost the last possible second, deliverance came, as you will have guessed: the Colonel burst the door open, and was just in time to see the dreadful group at the window. When he reached the figures only one was left. Parkins sank forward into the room in a faint, and before him on the floor lay a tumbled heap of bedclothes.

Colonel Wilson asked no questions, but busied himself in keeping everyone else out of the room and in getting Parkins back to his bed; and himself, wrapped in a rug, occupied the other bed for the rest of the night. Early on the next day Rogers arrived, more welcome than he would have been a day before, and the three of them held a very long consultation in the Professor's room. At the end of it the Colonel left the hotel door carrying a small object between his finger and thumb, which he cast as far into the sea as a very brawny arm could send it. Later on the smoke of a burning ascended from the back premises of the Globe.

Exactly what explanation was patched up for the staff and visitors at the hotel I must confess I do not recollect. The Professor was somehow cleared of the ready suspicion of delirium tremens, and the hotel of the reputation of a troubled house.

There is not much question as to what would have happened to Parkins if the Colonel had not intervened when he did. He would either have fallen out of the window or else lost his wits. But it is not so evident what more the creature that came in answer to the whistle could have done than frighten. There seemed to be absolutely nothing material about it save the bedclothes of which it had made itself a body. The Colonel, who remembered a not very dissimilar occurrence in India, was of opinion that if Parkins had closed with it it could really have done very little, and that its one power was that of frightening. The whole thing, he said, served to confirm his opinion of the Church of Rome.

There is really nothing more to tell, but, as you may imagine, the Professor's views on certain points are less clear cut than they used to be. His nerves, too, have suffered: he cannot even now see a surplice hanging on a door quite unmoved, and the spectacle of a scarecrow in a field late on a winter afternoon has cost him more than one sleepless night.

AFTERWARD
BY EDITH WHARTON

Edith Wharton was born on 24 January 1862 in New York. She was educated in both America and Europe. In 1899 she published her first work, a collection of stories called *The Greater Inclination*, followed by her first novel, *The Touchstone*. She wrote many other works including home decoration manuals, short stories and her famous novels *The House of Mirth* (1905), *Ethan Frome* (1911), *The Custom of the Country* (1913) and *The Age of Innocence* (1920). She lived in France from 1907 and was made a Chevalier of the Legion of Honour in 1916 for her work helping refugees during the war. Edith Wharton died on 11 August 1937.

I

'OH, THERE *is* one, of course, but you'll never know it.'

The assertion, laughingly flung out six months earlier in a bright June garden, came back to Mary Boyne with a sharp perception of its latent significance as she stood, in the December dusk, waiting for the lamps to be brought into the library.

The words had been spoken by their friend Alida Stair, as they sat at tea on her lawn at Pangbourne, in reference to the very house of which the library in question was the central, the pivotal 'feature.' Mary Boyne and her husband, in quest of a country place in one of the southern or south-western counties, had, on their arrival in England, carried their problem straight to Alida Stair, who had successfully solved it in her own case; but it was not until they had rejected, almost capriciously, several practical and judicious suggestions that she threw it out: 'Well, there's Lyng, in Dorsetshire. It belongs to Hugo's cousins, and you can get it for a song.'

The reasons she gave for its being obtainable on these terms – its remoteness from a station, its lack of electric light, hot-water pipes, and other vulgar necessities – were exactly those pleading in its favour with two romantic Americans perversely in search of the economic drawbacks which were associated, in their tradition, with unusual architectural felicities.

'I should never believe I was living in an old house unless I was thoroughly uncomfortable,' Ned Boyne, the more extravagant of the two, had jocosely insisted; 'the least hint of "convenience" would make me think it had been bought out of an exhibition, with the pieces numbered, and set up again.' And they had proceeded to enumerate, with humorous precision, their various suspicions and exactions, refusing to believe that the house their cousin recommended was *really* Tudor till they learned it had no heating system, or that the village church was literally in the grounds till she assured them of the deplorable uncertainty of the water supply.

'It's too uncomfortable to be true!' Edward Boyne had continued to exult as the avowal of each disadvantage was successively wrung from her; but he had cut short his rhapsody to ask, with a sudden relapse to distrust: 'And the ghost? You've been concealing from us the fact that there is no ghost!'

Mary, at the moment, had laughed with him, yet almost with her laugh, being possessed of several sets of independent perceptions, had noted a sudden flatness of tone in Alida's answering hilarity.

'Oh, Dorsetshire's full of ghosts, you know.'

'Yes, yes; but that won't do. I don't want to have to drive ten miles to see somebody else's ghost. I want one of my own on the premises. *Is* there a ghost at Lyng?'

His rejoinder had made Alida laugh again, and it was then that she had flung back tantalizingly: 'Oh, there *is* one, of course, but you'll never know it.'

'Never know it?' Boyne pulled her up. 'But what in the world constitutes a ghost except the fact of its being known for one?'

'I can't say. But that's the story.'

'That there's a ghost, but that nobody knows it's a ghost?'

'Well — not till afterward, at any rate.'

'Till afterward?'

'Not till long, long afterward.'

'But if it's once been identified as an unearthly visitant, why hasn't its signalement been handed down in the family? How has it managed to preserve its incognito?'

Alida could only shake her head. 'Don't ask me. But it has.'

'And then suddenly –' Mary spoke up as if from some cavernous depth of divination – 'suddenly, long afterward, one says to one's self, "*That was it?*"'

She was oddly startled at the sepulchral sound with which her question fell on the banter of the other two, and she saw the shadow of the same surprise flit across Alida's clear pupils. 'I suppose so. One just has to wait.'

'Oh, hang waiting!' Ned broke in. 'Life's too short for a ghost who can only be enjoyed in retrospect. Can't we do better than that, Mary?'

But it turned out that in the event they were not destined to, for within three months of their conversation with Mrs Stair they were established at Lyng, and the life they had yearned for to the point of planning it out in all its daily details had actually begun for them.

It was to sit, in the thick December dusk, by just such a wide-hooded fireplace, under just such black oak rafters, with the sense that beyond the mullioned panes the downs were darkening to a deeper solitude: it was for the ultimate indulgence in such sensations that Mary Boyne had endured for nearly fourteen years the soul-deadening ugliness of the Middle West, and that Boyne had ground on doggedly at his engineering till, with a suddenness that still made her blink, the prodigious windfall of the Blue Star Mine had put them at a stroke in possession of life and the leisure to taste it. They had never for a moment meant their new state to be one of idleness; but they meant to give themselves only to harmonious activities. She had her vision of painting and gardening (against a background of grey walls), he dreamed of the production of his long-planned book on the 'Economic Basis of Culture'; and with such absorbing work ahead no existence could be too sequestered; they could not get far enough from the world, or plunge deep enough into the past.

Dorsetshire had attracted them from the first by a semblance of remoteness out of all proportion to its geographical position. But to the Boynes it was one of the ever-recurring wonders of the whole incredibly compressed island – a nest of counties, as they put it – that for the production of its effects so little of a given quality went so far: that so few miles made a distance, and so short a distance a difference.

'It's that,' Ned had once enthusiastically explained, 'that gives such depth to their effects, such relief to their least contrasts. They've been able to lay the butter so thick on every exquisite mouthful.'

The butter had certainly been laid on thick at Lyng: the old grey house, hidden under a shoulder of the downs, had almost all the finer marks of commerce with a protracted past. The mere fact that it was neither large nor exceptional made it, to the Boynes, abound the more richly in its special sense – the sense of having been for centuries a deep, dim reservoir of life. The life had probably not been of the most vivid order: for long periods, no doubt, it had fallen as noiselessly into the past as the quiet drizzle of autumn fell, hour after hour, into the green fish-pond between the yews; but these back-waters of existence sometimes breed, in their sluggish depths, strange acuities of emotion, and Mary Boyne had felt from the first the occasional brush of an intenser memory.

The feeling had never been stronger than on the December

afternoon when, waiting in the library for the belated lamps, she rose from her seat and stood among the shadows of the hearth. Her husband had gone off, after luncheon, for one of his long tramps on the downs. She had noticed of late that he preferred to be unaccompanied on these occasions; and, in the tried security of their personal relations, had been driven to conclude that his book was bothering him, and that he needed the afternoons to turn over in solitude the problems left from the morning's work. Certainly the book was not going as smoothly as she had imagined it would, and the lines of perplexity between his eyes had never been there in his engineering days. Then he had often looked fagged to the verge of illness, but the native demon of 'worry' had never branded his brow. Yet the few pages he had so far read to her – the introduction, and a synopsis of the opening chapter – gave evidences of a firm possession of his subject, and a deepening confidence in his powers.

The fact threw her into deeper perplexity, since, now that he had done with 'business' and its disturbing contingencies, the one other possible element of anxiety was eliminated. Unless it were his health, then? But physically he had gained since they had come to Dorsetshire, grown robuster, ruddier, and fresher-eyed. It was only within a week that she had felt in him the indefinable change that made her restless in his absence, and as tongue-tied in his presence as though it were *she* who had a secret to keep from him!

The thought that there *was* a secret somewhere between them struck her with a sudden smart rap of wonder, and she looked about her down the dim, long room.

'Can it be the house?' she mused.

The room itself might have been full of secrets. They seemed to be piling themselves up, as evening fell, like the layers and layers of velvet shadow dropping from the low ceiling, the dusky walls of books, the smoke-blurred sculpture of the hooded hearth.

'Why, of course – the house is haunted!' she reflected.

The ghost – Alida's imperceptible ghost – after figuring largely in the banter of their first month or two at Lyng, had been gradually discarded as too ineffectual for imaginative use. Mary had, indeed, as became the tenant of a haunted house, made the customary inquiries among her few rural neighbours, but, beyond a vague, 'They du say so, Ma'am,' the villagers had nothing to impart. The elusive spectre had apparently never had sufficient identity for a legend to crystallize about it, and after a time the Boynes had laughingly set the matter down to their profit-and-loss account, agreeing that Lyng was one of the few houses good enough in itself to dispense with super-natural enhancements.

'And I suppose, poor, ineffectual demon, that's why it beats its beautiful wings in vain in the void,' Mary had laughingly concluded.

'Or, rather,' Ned answered, in the same strain, 'why, amid so much that's ghostly, it can never affirm its separate existence as *the* ghost.' And thereupon their invisible housemate had finally dropped out of their references, which were numerous enough to make them promptly unaware of the loss.

Now, as she stood on the hearth, the subject of their earlier curiosity revived in her with a new sense of its meaning – a sense gradually acquired through close daily contact with the scene of the lurking mystery. It was the house itself, of course, that possessed the ghost-seeing faculty, that communed visually but secretly with its own past; and if one could only get into close enough communion with the house, one might surprise its secret, and acquire the ghost-sight on one's own account. Perhaps, in

his long solitary hours in this very room, where she never tres-
passed till the afternoon, her husband *had* acquired it already, and
was silently carrying the dread weight of whatever it had revealed
to him. Mary was too well-versed in the code of the spectral
world not to know that one could not talk about the ghosts one
saw: to do so was almost as great a breach of good breeding as
to name a lady in a club. But this explanation did not really satisfy
her. 'What, after all, except for the fun of the frisson,' she reflected,
'would he really care for any of their old ghosts?' And thence
she was thrown back once more on the fundamental dilemma:
the fact that one's greater or less susceptibility to spectral influences had no particular bearing on the case, since, when one *did*
see a ghost at Lyng, one did not know it.

'Not till long afterward,' Alida Stair had said. Well, supposing
Ned *had* seen one when they first came, and had known only
within the last week what had happened to him? More and more
under the spell of the hour, she threw back her searching
thoughts to the early days of their tenancy, but at first only to
recall a gay confusion of unpacking, settling, arranging of
books, and calling to each other from remote corners of the
house as treasure after treasure of their habitation revealed itself
to them. It was in this particular connection that she presently
recalled a certain soft afternoon of the previous October, when,
passing from the first rapturous flurry of exploration to a
detailed inspection of the old house, she had pressed (like a
novel heroine) a panel that opened at her touch, on a narrow
flight of stairs leading to an unsuspected flat ledge of the roof
– the roof which, from below, seemed to slope away on all sides
too abruptly for any but practised feet to scale.

The view from this hidden coign was enchanting, and she had
flown down to snatch Ned from his papers and give him the
freedom of her discovery. She remembered still how, standing

on the narrow ledge, he had passed his arm about her while their gaze flew to the long, tossed horizon-line of the downs, and then dropped contentedly back to trace the arabesque of yew hedges about the fish-pond, and the shadow of the cedar on the lawn.

'And now the other way,' he had said, gently turning her about within his arm; and closely pressed to him, she had absorbed, like some long, satisfying draft, the picture of the grey-walled court, the squat lions on the gates, and the lime avenue reaching up to the highroad under the downs.

It was just then, while they gazed and held each other, that she had felt his arm relax, and heard a sharp 'Hullo!' that made her turn to glance at him.

Distinctly, yes, she now recalled she had seen, as she glanced, a shadow of anxiety, of perplexity, rather, fall across his face; and, following his eyes, had beheld the figure of a man – a man in loose, greyish clothes, as it appeared to her – who was sauntering down the lime-avenue to the court with the tentative gait of a stranger seeking his way. Her short-sighted eyes had given her but a blurred impression of slightness and greyness, with something foreign, or at least un-local, in the cut of the figure or its garb; but her husband had apparently seen more – seen enough to make him push past her with a sharp 'Wait!' and dash down the twisting stairs without pausing to give her a hand for the descent.

A slight tendency to dizziness obliged her, after a provisional clutch at the chimney against which they had been leaning, to follow him down more cautiously; and when she had reached the attic landing she paused again for a less definite reason, leaning over the oak banister to strain her eyes through the silence of the brown, sun-flecked depths below. She lingered there till, somewhere in those depths, she heard the closing of a door; then, mechanically impelled, she went down the shallow flights of steps till she reached the lower hall.

The front door stood open on the mild sunlight of the court, and hall and court were empty. The library door was open, too, and after listening in vain for any sound of voices within, she quickly crossed the threshold, and found her husband alone, vaguely fingering the papers on his desk.

He looked up, as if surprised at her precipitate entrance, but the shadow of anxiety had passed from his face, leaving it even, as she fancied, a little brighter and clearer than usual.

'What was it? Who was it?' she asked.

'Who?' he repeated, with the surprise still all on his side.

'The man we saw coming toward the house.'

He seemed honestly to reflect. 'The man? Why, I thought I saw Peters; I dashed after him to say a word about the stable-drains, but he had disappeared before I could get down.'

'Disappeared? Why, he seemed to be walking so slowly when we saw him.'

Boyne shrugged his shoulders. 'So I thought; but he must have got up steam in the interval. What do you say to our trying a scramble up Meldon Steep before sunset?'

That was all. At the time the occurrence had been less than nothing, had, indeed, been immediately obliterated by the magic of their first vision from Meldon Steep, a height which they had dreamed of climbing ever since they had first seen its bare spine heaving itself above the low roof of Lyng. Doubtless it was the mere fact of the other incident's having occurred on the very day of their ascent to Meldon that had kept it stored away in the unconscious fold of association from which it now emerged; for in itself it had no mark of the portentous. At the moment there could have been nothing more natural than that Ned should dash himself from the roof in the pursuit of dila-tory tradesmen. It was the period when they were always on the watch for one or the other of the specialists employed about the place; always lying in wait for them, and dashing out at them with questions, reproaches, or reminders. And certainly in the distance the grey figure had looked like Peters.

Yet now, as she reviewed the rapid scene, she felt her husband's explanation of it to have been invalidated by the look of anxiety on his face. Why had the familiar appearance of Peters made him anxious? Why, above all, if it was of such prime necessity to confer with that authority on the subject of the stable-drains, had the failure to find him produced such a look of relief? Mary could not say that any one of these considerations had occurred to her at the time, yet, from the promptness with which they now marshalled themselves at her summons, she had a sudden sense that they must all along have been there, waiting their hour.

II

WEARY WITH her thoughts, she moved toward the window. The library was now completely dark, and she was surprised to see how much faint light the outer world still held.

As she peered out into it across the court, a figure shaped itself in the tapering perspective of bare lines: it looked a mere blot of deeper grey in the greyness, and for an instant, as it moved toward her, her heart thumped to the thought, 'It's the ghost!'

She had time, in that long instant, to feel suddenly that the man of whom, two months earlier, she had a brief distant vision from the roof was now, at his predestined hour, about to reveal himself as *not* having been Peters; and her spirit sank under the impending fear of the disclosure. But almost with the next tick of the clock the ambiguous figure, gaining substance and character, showed itself even to her weak sight as her husband's; and she turned away to meet him, as he entered, with the confession of her folly.

'It's really too absurd,' she laughed out from the threshold, 'but I never *can* remember!'

'Remember what?' Boyne questioned as they drew together.

'That when one sees the Lyng ghost one never knows it.'

Her hand was on his sleeve, and he kept it there, but with no response in his gesture or in the lines of his fagged, preoccupied face.

'Did you think you'd seen it?' he asked, after an appreciable interval.

'Why, I actually took *you* for it, my dear, in my mad determination to spot it!'

'Me – just now?' His arm dropped away, and he turned from her with a faint echo of her laugh. 'Really, dearest, you'd better give it up, if that's the best you can do.'

'Yes, I give it up – I give it up. Have *you*?' she asked, turning round on him abruptly.

The parlour-maid had entered with letters and a lamp, and the light struck up into Boyne's face as he bent above the tray she presented.

'Have *you*?' Mary perversely insisted, when the servant had disappeared on her errand of illumination.

'Have I what?' he rejoined absently, the light bringing out the sharp stamp of worry between his brows as he turned over the letters.

'Given up trying to see the ghost.' Her heart beat a little at the experiment she was making.

Her husband, laying his letters aside, moved away into the shadow of the hearth.

'I never tried,' he said, tearing open the wrapper of a newspaper.

'Well, of course,' Mary persisted, 'the exasperating thing is that there's no use trying, since one can't be sure till so long afterward.'

He was unfolding the paper as if he had hardly heard her; but after a pause, during which the sheets rustled spasmodically between his hands, he lifted his head to say abruptly, 'Have you any idea *how long*?'

Mary had sunk into a low chair beside the fireplace. From her seat she looked up, startled, at her husband's profile, which was darkly projected against the circle of lamplight.

'No; none. Have YOU?' she retorted, repeating her former phrase with an added keenness of intention.

Boyne crumpled the paper into a bunch, and then inconsequently turned back with it toward the lamp.

'Lord, no! I only meant,' he explained, with a faint tinge of impatience, 'is there any legend, any tradition, as to that?'

'Not that I know of,' she answered; but the impulse to add, 'What makes you ask?' was checked by the reappearance of the parlour-maid with tea and a second lamp.

With the dispersal of shadows, and the repetition of the daily domestic office, Mary Boyne felt herself less oppressed by that sense of something mutely imminent which had darkened her solitary afternoon. For a few moments she gave herself silently to the details of her task, and when she looked up from it she was struck to the point of bewilderment by the change in her husband's face. He had seated himself near the farther lamp, and was absorbed in the perusal of his letters; but was it something he had found in them, or merely the shifting of her own point of view, that had restored his features to their normal aspect? The longer she looked, the more definitely the change affirmed itself. The lines of painful tension had vanished, and such traces of fatigue as lingered were of the kind easily attributable to steady mental effort. He glanced up, as if drawn by her gaze, and met her eyes with a smile.

'I'm dying for my tea, you know; and here's a letter for you,' he said.

She took the letter he held out in exchange for the cup she proffered him, and, returning to her seat, broke the seal with the languid gesture of the reader whose interests are all enclosed in the circle of one cherished presence.

Her next conscious motion was that of starting to her feet, the letter falling to them as she rose, while she held out to her husband a long newspaper clipping.

'Ned! What's this? What does it mean?'

He had risen at the same instant, almost as if hearing her cry before she uttered it; and for a perceptible space of time he and she studied each other, like adversaries watching for an advantage, across the space between her chair and his desk.

'What's what? You fairly made me jump!' Boyne said at length, moving toward her with a sudden, half-exasperated laugh. The shadow of apprehension was on his face again, not now a look of fixed foreboding, but a shifting vigilance of lips and eyes that gave her the sense of his feeling himself invisibly surrounded.

Her hand shook so that she could hardly give him the clipping.

'This article – from the *Waukesha Sentinel* – that a man named Elwell has brought suit against you – that there was something wrong about the Blue Star Mine. I can't understand more than half.'

They continued to face each other as she spoke, and to her astonishment, she saw that her words had the almost immediate effect of dissipating the strained watchfulness of his look.

'Oh, *that*!' He glanced down the printed slip, and then folded it with the gesture of one who handles something harmless and familiar. 'What's the matter with you this afternoon, Mary? I thought you'd got bad news.'

She stood before him with her indefinable terror subsiding slowly under the reassuring touch of his composure.

'You knew about this, then – it's all right?'

'Certainly I knew about it; and it's all right.'

'But what *is* it? I don't understand. What does this man accuse you of?'

'Oh, pretty nearly every crime in the calendar.' Boyne had tossed the clipping down, and thrown himself comfortably into an arm-chair near the fire. 'Do you want to hear the story? It's not particularly interesting – just a squabble over interests in the Blue Star.'

'But who is this Elwell? I don't know the name.'

'Oh, he's a fellow I put into it – gave him a hand up. I told you all about him at the time.'

'I daresay. I must have forgotten.' Vainly she strained back among her memories. 'But if you helped him, why does he make this return?'

'Oh, probably some shyster lawyer got hold of him and talked him over. It's all rather technical and complicated. I thought that kind of thing bored you.'

His wife felt a sting of compunction. Theoretically, she deprecated the American wife's detachment from her husband's professional interests, but in practice she had always found it difficult to fix her attention on Boyne's report of the transactions in which his varied interests involved him. Besides, she had felt from the first that, in a community where the amenities of living could be obtained only at the cost of efforts as arduous as her husband's professional labours, such brief leisure as they could command should be used as an escape from immediate preoccupations, a flight to the life they always dreamed of living. Once or twice, now that this new life had actually drawn its magic circle about them, she had asked herself if she had done right; but hitherto such conjectures had been no more than the retrospective excursions of an active fancy. Now, for the first time, it startled her a little to find how little she knew of the material foundation on which her happiness was built.

She glanced again at her husband, and was reassured by the composure of his face; yet she felt the need of more definite grounds for her reassurance.

'But doesn't this suit worry you? Why have you never spoken to me about it?'

He answered both questions at once: 'I didn't speak of it at first because it *did* worry me – annoyed me, rather. But it's all ancient history now. Your correspondent must have got hold of a back number of the *Sentinel*.'

She felt a quick thrill of relief. 'You mean it's over? He's lost his case?'

There was a just perceptible delay in Boyne's reply. 'The suit's been withdrawn – that's all.'

But she persisted, as if to exonerate herself from the inward charge of being too easily put off. 'Withdrawn because he saw he had no chance?'

'Oh, he had no chance,' Boyne answered.

She was still struggling with a dimly felt perplexity at the back of her thoughts.

'How long ago was it withdrawn?'

He paused, as if with a slight return of his former uncertainty. 'I've just had the news now; but I've been expecting it.'

'Just now – in one of your letters?'

'Yes; in one of my letters.'

She made no answer, and was aware only, after a short interval of waiting, that he had risen, and strolling across the room, had placed himself on the sofa at her side. She felt him, as he did so, pass an arm about her, she felt his hand seek hers and clasp it, and turning slowly, drawn by the warmth of his cheek, she met the smiling clearness of his eyes.

'It's all right – it's all right?' she questioned, through the flood of her dissolving doubts; and 'I give you my word it never was righter!' he laughed back at her, holding her close.

III

O NE OF the strangest things she was afterward to recall out of all the next day's incredible strangeness was the sudden and complete recovery of her sense of security.

It was in the air when she woke in her low-ceilinged, dusky room; it accompanied her down-stairs to the breakfast-table, flashed out at her from the fire, and re-duplicated itself brightly from the flanks of the urn and the sturdy flutings of the Georgian teapot. It was as if, in some roundabout way, all her diffused apprehensions of the previous day, with their moment of sharp concentration about the newspaper article – as if this dim questioning of the future, and startled return upon the past – had between them liquidated the arrears of some haunting moral obligation. If she had indeed been careless of her husband's affairs, it was, her new state seemed to prove, because her faith in him instinctively justified such carelessness; and his right to her faith had overwhelmingly affirmed itself in the very face of menace and suspicion. She had never seen him more untroubled, more naturally and unconsciously in possession of himself, than after the cross-examination to which she had subjected him: it was almost as if he had been aware of her lurking doubts, and had wanted the air cleared as much as she did.

It was as clear, thank Heaven! as the bright outer light that surprised her almost with a touch of summer when she issued from the house for her daily round of the gardens. She had left Boyne at his desk, indulging herself, as she passed the library door, by a last peep at his quiet face, where he bent, pipe in his mouth, above his papers, and now she had her own morning's task to perform. The task involved on such charmed winter days almost as much delighted loitering about the different quarters of her demesne as if spring were already at work on shrubs and borders. There were such inexhaustible possibilities still before her, such opportunities to bring out the latent graces of the old place, without a single irreverent touch of alteration, that the winter months were all too short to plan what spring and autumn executed. And her recovered sense of safety gave, on this particular morning, a peculiar zest to her progress through the sweet, still place. She went first to the kitchen-garden, where the espaliered pear-trees drew complicated patterns on the walls, and pigeons were fluttering and preening about the silvery-slated roof of their cot. There was something wrong about the piping of the hot-house, and she was expecting an authority from Dorchester, who was to drive out between trains and make a diagnosis of the boiler. But when she dipped into the damp heat of the greenhouses, among the spiced scents and waxy pinks and reds of old-fashioned exotics – even the flora of Lyng was in the note! – she learned that the great man had not arrived, and the day being too rare to waste in an artificial atmosphere, she came out again and paced slowly along the springy turf of the bowling-green to the gardens behind the house. At their farther end rose a grass terrace, commanding, over the fish-pond and the yew hedges, a view of the long house-front, with its twisted chimney-stacks and the blue shadows of its roof angles, all drenched in the pale gold moisture of the air.

Seen thus, across the level tracery of the yews, under the suffused, mild light, it sent her, from its open windows and hospitably smoking chimneys, the look of some warm human presence, of a mind slowly ripened on a sunny wall of experience. She had never before had so deep a sense of her intimacy with it, such a conviction that its secrets were all beneficent, kept, as they said to children, 'for one's good,' so complete a trust in its power to gather up her life and Ned's into the harmonious pattern of the long, long story it sat there weaving in the sun.

She heard steps behind her, and turned, expecting to see the gardener, accompanied by the engineer from Dorchester. But only one figure was in sight, that of a youngish, slightly built man, who, for reasons she could not on the spot have specified, did not remotely resemble her preconceived notion of an authority on hot-house boilers. The newcomer, on seeing her, lifted his hat, and paused with the air of a gentleman – perhaps a traveller – desirous of having it immediately known that his intrusion is involuntary. The local fame of Lyng occasionally attracted the more intelligent sight-seer, and Mary half-expected to see the stranger dissemble a camera, or justify his presence by producing it. But he made no gesture of any sort, and after a moment she asked, in a tone responding to the courteous deprecation of his attitude: 'Is there any one you wish to see?'

'I came to see Mr Boyne,' he replied. His intonation, rather than his accent, was faintly American, and Mary, at the familiar note, looked at him more closely. The brim of his soft felt hat cast a shade on his face, which, thus obscured, wore to her short-sighted gaze a look of seriousness, as of a person arriving 'on business,' and civilly but firmly aware of his rights.

Past experience had made Mary equally sensible to such claims; but she was jealous of her husband's morning hours, and doubtful of his having given any one the right to intrude on them.

'Have you an appointment with Mr Boyne?' she asked.

He hesitated, as if unprepared for the question.

'Not exactly an appointment,' he replied.

'Then I'm afraid, this being his working-time, that he can't receive you now. Will you give me a message, or come back later?'

The visitor, again lifting his hat, briefly replied that he would come back later, and walked away, as if to regain the front of the house. As his figure receded down the walk between the yew hedges, Mary saw him pause and look up an instant at the peaceful house-front bathed in faint winter sunshine; and it struck her, with a tardy touch of compunction, that it would have been more humane to ask if he had come from a distance, and to offer, in that case, to inquire if her husband could receive him. But as the thought occurred to her he passed out of sight behind a pyramidal yew, and at the same moment her attention was distracted by the approach of the gardener, attended by the bearded pepper-and-salt figure of the boiler-maker from Dorchester.

The encounter with this authority led to such far-reaching issues that they resulted in his finding it expedient to ignore his train, and beguiled Mary into spending the remainder of the morning in absorbed confabulation among the greenhouses. She was startled to find, when the colloquy ended, that it was nearly luncheon-time, and she half expected, as she hurried back to the house, to see her husband coming out to meet her. But she found no one in the court but an under-gardener raking the gravel, and the hall, when she entered it, was so silent that she guessed Boyne to be still at work behind the closed door of the library.

Not wishing to disturb him, she turned into the drawing-room, and there, at her writing-table, lost herself in renewed calculations of the outlay to which the morning's conference had committed her. The knowledge that she could permit herself such follies had not yet lost its novelty; and somehow, in contrast to the vague apprehensions of the previous days, it now seemed an element of her recovered security, of the sense that, as Ned had said, things in general had never been 'righter.'

She was still luxuriating in a lavish play of figures when the parlour-maid, from the threshold, roused her with a dubiously worded inquiry as to the expediency of serving luncheon. It was one of their jokes that Trimmle announced luncheon as if she were divulging a state secret, and Mary, intent upon her papers, merely murmured an absent-minded assent.

She felt Trimmle wavering expressively on the threshold as if in rebuke of such offhand acquiescence; then her retreating steps sounded down the passage, and Mary, pushing away her papers, crossed the hall, and went to the library door. It was still closed, and she wavered in her turn, disliking to disturb her husband, yet anxious that he should not exceed his normal measure of work. As she stood there, balancing her impulses, the esoteric Trimmle returned with the announcement of luncheon, and Mary, thus impelled, opened the door and went into the library.

Boyne was not at his desk, and she peered about her, expecting to discover him at the book-shelves, somewhere down the length of the room; but her call brought no response, and gradually it became clear to her that he was not in the library.

She turned back to the parlour-maid.

'Mr Boyne must be upstairs. Please tell him that luncheon is ready.'

The parlour-maid appeared to hesitate between the obvious duty of obeying orders and an equally obvious conviction of the foolishness of the injunction laid upon her. The struggle resulted in her saying doubtfully, 'If you please, Madam, Mr Boyne's not upstairs.'

'Not in his room? Are you sure?'

'I'm sure, Madam.'

Mary consulted the clock. 'Where is he, then?'

'He's gone out,' Trimmle announced, with the superior air of one who has respectfully waited for the question that a well-ordered mind would have first propounded.

Mary's previous conjecture had been right, then. Boyne must have gone to the gardens to meet her, and since she had missed him, it was clear that he had taken the shorter way by the south door, instead of going round to the court. She crossed the hall to the glass portal opening directly on the yew garden, but the parlour-maid, after another moment of inner conflict, decided to bring out recklessly, 'Please, Madam, Mr Boyne didn't go that way.'

Mary turned back. 'Where *did* he go? And when?'

'He went out of the front door, up the drive, Madam.' It was a matter of principle with Trimmle never to answer more than one question at a time.

'Up the drive? At this hour?' Mary went to the door herself, and glanced across the court through the long tunnel of bare limes. But its perspective was as empty as when she had scanned it on entering the house.

'Did Mr Boyne leave no message?' she asked.

Trimmle seemed to surrender herself to a last struggle with the forces of chaos.

'No, Madam. He just went out with the gentleman.'

'The gentleman? What gentleman?' Mary wheeled about, as if to front this new factor.

'The gentleman who called, Madam,' said Trimmle, resignedly.

'When did a gentleman call? Do explain yourself, Trimmle!'

Only the fact that Mary was very hungry, and that she wanted to consult her husband about the greenhouses, would have caused her to lay so unusual an injunction on her attendant; and even now she was detached enough to note in Trimmle's eye the dawning defiance of the respectful subordinate who has been pressed too hard.

'I couldn't exactly say the hour, Madam, because I didn't let the gentleman in,' she replied, with the air of magnanimously ignoring the irregularity of her mistress's course.

'You didn't let him in?'

'No, Madam. When the bell rang I was dressing, and Agnes –'

'Go and ask Agnes, then,' Mary interjected. Trimmle still wore her look of patient magnanimity. 'Agnes would not know, Madam, for she had unfortunately burnt her hand in trying the wick of the new lamp from town –' Trimmle, as Mary was aware, had always been opposed to the new lamp – 'and so Mrs Dockett sent the kitchen-maid instead.'

Mary looked again at the clock. 'It's after two! Go and ask the kitchen-maid if Mr Boyne left any word.'

She went into luncheon without waiting, and Trimmle presently brought her there the kitchen-maid's statement that the gentleman had called about one o'clock, that Mr Boyne had gone out with him without leaving any message. The kitchen-maid did not even know the caller's name, for he had written it on a slip of paper, which he had folded and handed to her, with the injunction to deliver it at once to Mr Boyne.

Mary finished her luncheon, still wondering, and when it was over, and Trimmle had brought the coffee to the drawing-room, her wonder had deepened to a first faint tinge of disquietude. It was unlike Boyne to absent himself without explanation at so unwonted an hour, and the difficulty of identifying the visitor whose summons he had apparently obeyed made his disappearance the more unaccountable. Mary Boyne's experience as the wife of a busy engineer, subject to sudden calls and compelled to keep irregular hours, had trained her to the philosophic acceptance of surprises; but since Boyne's withdrawal from business he had adopted a Benedictine regularity of life. As if to make up for the dispersed and agitated years, with their 'stand-up' lunches and dinners rattled down to the joltings of the dining-car, he cultivated the last refinements of punctuality and monotony, discouraging his wife's fancy for the unexpected; and declaring that to a delicate taste there were infinite gradations of pleasure in the fixed recurrences of habit.

Still, since no life can completely defend itself from the unforeseen, it was evident that all Boyne's precautions would sooner or later prove unavailable, and Mary concluded that he had cut short a tiresome visit by walking with his caller to the station, or at least accompanying him for part of the way.

This conclusion relieved her from farther preoccupation, and she went out herself to take up her conference with the gardener. Thence she walked to the village post-office, a mile or so away; and when she turned toward home, the early twilight was setting in.

She had taken a foot-path across the downs, and as Boyne, meanwhile, had probably returned from the station by the high-road, there was little likelihood of their meeting on the way. She felt sure, however, of his having reached the house before her; so sure that, when she entered it herself, without even pausing to inquire of Trimmle, she made directly for the library. But the library was still empty, and with an unwonted precision of visual memory she immediately observed that the papers on her husband's desk lay precisely as they had lain when she had gone in to call him to luncheon.

Then of a sudden she was seized by a vague dread of the unknown. She had closed the door behind her on entering, and as she stood alone in the long, silent, shadowy room, her dread seemed to take shape and sound, to be there audibly breathing and lurking among the shadows. Her short-sighted eyes strained through them, half-discerning an actual presence, something aloof, that watched and knew; and in the recoil from that intangible propinquity she threw herself suddenly on the bell-rope and gave it a desperate pull.

The long, quavering summons brought Trimmle in precipitately with a lamp, and Mary breathed again at this sobering reappearance of the usual.

'You may bring tea if Mr Boyne is in,' she said, to justify her ring.

'Very well, Madam. But Mr Boyne is not in,' said Trimmle, putting down the lamp.

'Not in? You mean he's come back and gone out again?'

'No, Madam. He's never been back.'

The dread stirred again, and Mary knew that now it had her fast.

'Not since he went out with – the gentleman?'

'Not since he went out with the gentleman.'

'But who *was* the gentleman?' Mary gasped out, with the sharp note of someone trying to be heard through a confusion of meaningless noises.

'That I couldn't say, Madam.' Trimmle, standing there by

the lamp, seemed suddenly to grow less round and rosy, as though eclipsed by the same creeping shade of apprehension.

'But the kitchen-maid knows – wasn't it the kitchen-maid who let him in?'

'She doesn't know either, Madam, for he wrote his name on a folded paper.'

Mary, through her agitation, was aware that they were both designating the unknown visitor by a vague pronoun, instead of the conventional formula which, till then, had kept their allusions within the bounds of custom. And at the same moment her mind caught at the suggestion of the folded paper.

'But he must have a name! Where is the paper?'

She moved to the desk, and began to turn over the scattered documents that littered it. The first that caught her eye was an unfinished letter in her husband's hand, with his pen lying across it, as though dropped there at a sudden summons.

'My dear Parvis' – who was Parvis? – 'I have just received your letter announcing Elwell's death, and while I suppose there is now no farther risk of trouble, it might be safer –'

She tossed the sheet aside, and continued her search; but no folded paper was discoverable among the letters and pages of manuscript which had been swept together in a promiscuous heap, as if by a hurried or a startled gesture.

'But the kitchen-maid *saw* him. Send her here,' she commanded, wondering at her dullness in not thinking sooner of so simple a solution.

Trimmle, at the behest, vanished in a flash, as if thankful to be out of the room, and when she reappeared, conducting the agitated underling, Mary had regained her self-possession, and had her questions pat.

The gentleman was a stranger, yes – that she understood. But what had he said? And, above all, what had he looked like?

The first question was easily enough answered, for the discon-
certing reason that he had said so little – had merely asked for
Mr Boyne, and, scribbling something on a bit of paper, had
requested that it should at once be carried in to him.

'Then you don't know what he wrote? You're not sure it *was*
his name?'

The kitchen-maid was not sure, but supposed it was, since
he had written it in answer to her inquiry as to whom she should
announce.

'And when you carried the paper in to Mr Boyne, what did
he say?'

The kitchen-maid did not think that Mr Boyne had said
anything, but she could not be sure, for just as she had handed
him the paper and he was opening it, she had become aware
that the visitor had followed her into the library, and she had
slipped out, leaving the two gentlemen together.

'But then, if you left them in the library, how do you know
that they went out of the house?'

This question plunged the witness into momentary inarticu-
lateness, from which she was rescued by Trimmle, who, by
means of ingenious circumlocutions, elicited the statement that
before she could cross the hall to the back passage she had heard
the gentlemen behind her, and had seen them go out of the
front door together.

'Then, if you saw the gentleman twice, you must be able to
tell me what he looked like.'

But with this final challenge to her powers of expression it
became clear that the limit of the kitchen-maid's endurance had
been reached. The obligation of going to the front door to
'show in' a visitor was in itself so subversive of the fundamental
order of things that it had thrown her faculties into hopeless
disarray, and she could only stammer out, after various panting

efforts at evocation, 'His hat, mum, was different-like, as you might say —'

'Different? How different?' Mary flashed out at her, her own mind, in the same instant, leaping back to an image left on it that morning, but temporarily lost under layers of subsequent impressions.

'His hat had a wide brim, you mean? and his face was pale — a youngish face?' Mary pressed her, with a white-lipped intensity of interrogation. But if the kitchen-maid found any adequate answer to this challenge, it was swept away for her listener down the rushing current of her own convictions. The stranger — the stranger in the garden! Why had Mary not thought of him before? She needed no one now to tell her that it was he who had called for her husband and gone away with him. But who was he, and why had Boyne obeyed his call?

IV

IT LEAPED out at her suddenly, like a grin out of the dark, that they had often called England so little — 'such a confoundedly hard place to get lost in.'

A confoundedly hard place to get lost in! That had been her husband's phrase. And now, with the whole machinery of official investigation sweeping its flash-lights from shore to shore, and across the dividing straits; now, with Boyne's name blazing from the walls of every town and village, his portrait (how that wrung her!) hawked up and down the country like the image of a hunted criminal; now the little compact, populous island, so policed, surveyed, and administered, revealed itself as a Sphinx-like guardian of abysmal mysteries, staring back into his wife's anguished eyes as if with the malicious joy of knowing something they would never know!

In the fortnight since Boyne's disappearance there had been no word of him, no trace of his movements. Even the usual misleading reports that raise expectancy in tortured bosoms had been few and fleeting. No one but the bewildered kitchen-maid had seen him leave the house, and no one else had seen 'the gentleman' who accompanied him. All inquiries in the neighbourhood failed to elicit the memory of a stranger's presence that day in the neighbourhood of Lyng. And no one had met Edward Boyne, either alone or in company, in any of the neighbouring villages, or on the road across the downs, or at either of the local railway-stations. The sunny English noon had swallowed him as completely as if he had gone out into Cimmerian night.

Mary, while every external means of investigation was working at its highest pressure, had ransacked her husband's papers for any trace of antecedent complications, of entanglements or obligations unknown to her that might throw a faint ray into the darkness. But if any such had existed in the background of Boyne's life, they had disappeared as completely as the slip of paper on which the visitor had written his name. There remained no possible thread of guidance except – if it were indeed an exception – the letter which Boyne had apparently been in the act of writing when he received his mysterious summons. That letter, read and reread by his wife, and submitted by her to the police, yielded little enough for conjecture to feed on.

'I have just heard of Elwell's death, and while I suppose there is now no farther risk of trouble, it might be safer –' That was all. The 'risk of trouble' was easily explained by the newspaper clipping which had apprised Mary of the suit brought against her husband by one of his associates in the Blue Star enterprise. The only new information conveyed in the letter was the fact of its showing Boyne, when he wrote it, to be still apprehensive of the results of the suit, though he had assured his wife that it had been withdrawn, and though the letter itself declared that the plaintiff was dead. It took several weeks of exhaustive cabling to fix the identity of the 'Parvis' to whom the fragmentary communication was addressed, but even after these inquiries had shown him to be a Waukesha lawyer, no new facts concerning the Elwell suit were elicited. He appeared to have had no direct concern in it, but to have been conversant with the facts merely as an acquaintance, and possible intermediary; and he declared himself unable to divine with what object Boyne intended to seek his assistance.

This negative information, sole fruit of the first fortnight's feverish search, was not increased by a jot during the slow weeks that followed. Mary knew that the investigations were still being carried on, but she had a vague sense of their gradually slackening, as the actual march of time seemed to slacken. It was as though the days, flying horror-struck from the shrouded image of the one inscrutable day, gained assurance as the distance lengthened, till at last they fell back into their normal gait. And so with the human imaginations at work on the dark event. No doubt it occupied them still, but week by week and hour by hour it grew less absorbing, took up less space, was slowly but inevitably crowded out of the foreground of consciousness by the new problems perpetually bubbling up from the vaporous caldron of human experience.

Even Mary Boyne's consciousness gradually felt the same

lowering of velocity. It still swayed with the incessant oscilla-
tions of conjecture; but they were slower, more rhythmical in
their beat. There were moments of overwhelming lassitude
when, like the victim of some poison which leaves the brain
clear, but holds the body motionless, she saw herself domesti-
cated with the Horror, accepting its perpetual presence as one
of the fixed conditions of life.

These moments lengthened into hours and days, till she
passed into a phase of stolid acquiescence. She watched the
familiar routine of life with the incurious eye of a savage on
whom the meaningless processes of civilization make but the
faintest impression. She had come to regard herself as part of
the routine, a spoke of the wheel, revolving with its motion;
she felt almost like the furniture of the room in which she sat,
an insensate object to be dusted and pushed about with the
chairs and tables. And this deepening apathy held her fast at
Lyng, in spite of the urgent entreaties of friends and the usual
medical recommendation of 'change'. Her friends supposed
that her refusal to move was inspired by the belief that her
husband would one day return to the spot from which he had
vanished, and a beautiful legend grew up about this imaginary
state of waiting. But in reality she had no such belief: the depths
of anguish inclosing her were no longer lighted by flashes of
hope. She was sure that Boyne would never come back, that he
had gone out of her sight as completely as if Death itself had
waited that day on the threshold. She had even renounced, one
by one, the various theories as to his disappearance which had
been advanced by the press, the police, and her own agonized
imagination. In sheer lassitude her mind turned from these
alternatives of horror, and sank back into the blank fact that
he was gone.

No, she would never know what had become of him – no

one would ever know. But the house *knew*; the library in which she spent her long, lonely evenings knew. For it was here that the last scene had been enacted, here that the stranger had come, and spoken the word which had caused Boyne to rise and follow him. The floor she trod had felt his tread; the books on the shelves had seen his face; and there were moments when the intense consciousness of the old, dusky walls seemed about to break out into some audible revelation of their secret. But the revelation never came, and she knew it would never come. Lyng was not one of the garrulous old houses that betray the secrets entrusted to them. Its very legend proved that it had always been the mute accomplice, the incorruptible custodian of the mysteries it had surprised. And Mary Boyne, sitting face to face with its portentous silence, felt the futility of seeking to break it by any human means.

V

'I DON'T say it *wasn't* straight, yet don't say it *was* straight. It was business.'

Mary, at the words, lifted her head with a start, and looked intently at the speaker.

When, half an hour before, a card with 'Mr Parvis' on it had been brought up to her, she had been immediately aware that the name had been a part of her consciousness ever since she had read it at the head of Boyne's unfinished letter. In the library she had found awaiting her a small neutral-tinted man with a bald head and gold eye-glasses, and it sent a strange tremor through her to know that this was the person to whom her husband's last known thought had been directed.

Parvis, civilly, but without vain preamble – in the manner of a man who has his watch in his hand – had set forth the object of his visit. He had 'run over' to England on business, and finding himself in the neighbourhood of Dorchester, had not wished to leave it without paying his respects to Mrs Boyne; without asking her, if the occasion offered, what she meant to do about Bob Elwell's family.

The words touched the spring of some obscure dread in Mary's bosom. Did her visitor, after all, know what Boyne had meant by his unfinished phrase? She asked for an elucidation of his question, and noticed at once that he seemed surprised at her continued ignorance of the subject. Was it possible that she really knew as little as she said?

'I know nothing – you must tell me,' she faltered out; and her visitor thereupon proceeded to unfold his story. It threw, even to her confused perceptions, and imperfectly initiated vision, a lurid glare on the whole hazy episode of the Blue Star Mine. Her husband had made his money in that brilliant speculation at the cost of 'getting ahead' of some one less alert to seize the chance; the victim of his ingenuity was young Robert Elwell, who had 'put him on' to the Blue Star scheme.

Parvis, at Mary's first startled cry, had thrown her a sobering glance through his impartial glasses.

'Bob Elwell wasn't smart enough, that's all; if he had been, he might have turned round and served Boyne the same way. It's the kind of thing that happens every day in business. I guess it's what the scientists call the survival of the fittest,' said Mr Parvis, evidently pleased with the aptness of his analogy.

Mary felt a physical shrinking from the next question she

tried to frame; it was as though the words on her lips had a taste that nauseated her.

'But then – you accuse my husband of doing something dishonourable?'

Mr Parvis surveyed the question dispassionately. 'Oh, no, I don't. I don't even say it wasn't straight.' He glanced up and down the long lines of books, as if one of them might have supplied him with the definition he sought. 'I don't say it *wasn't* straight, and yet I don't say it *was* straight. It was business.' After all, no definition in his category could be more comprehensive than that.

Mary sat staring at him with a look of terror. He seemed to her like the indifferent, implacable emissary of some dark, formless power.

'But Mr Elwell's lawyers apparently did not take your view, since I suppose the suit was withdrawn by their advice.'

'Oh, yes, they knew he hadn't a leg to stand on, technically. It was when they advised him to withdraw the suit that he got desperate. You see, he'd borrowed most of the money he lost in the Blue Star, and he was up a tree. That's why he shot himself when they told him he had no show.'

The horror was sweeping over Mary in great, deafening waves.

'He shot himself? He killed himself because of *that*?'

'Well, he didn't kill himself, exactly. He dragged on two months before he died.' Parvis emitted the statement as unemotionally as a gramophone grinding out its 'record.'

'You mean that he tried to kill himself, and failed? And tried again?'

'Oh, he didn't have to try again,' said Parvis, grimly.

They sat opposite each other in silence, he swinging his eyeglass thoughtfully about his finger, she, motionless, her arms stretched along her knees in an attitude of rigid tension.

'But if you knew all this,' she began at length, hardly able to force her voice above a whisper, 'how is it that when I wrote you at the time of my husband's disappearance you said you didn't understand his letter?'

Parvis received this without perceptible discomfiture. 'Why, I didn't understand it – strictly speaking. And it wasn't the time to talk about it, if I had. The Elwell business was settled when the suit was withdrawn. Nothing I could have told you would have helped you to find your husband.'

Mary continued to scrutinize him. 'Then why are you telling me now?'

Still Parvis did not hesitate. 'Well, to begin with, I supposed you knew more than you appear to – I mean about the circumstances of Elwell's death. And then people are talking of it now; the whole matter's been raked up again. And I thought, if you didn't know, you ought to.'

She remained silent, and he continued: 'You see, it's only come out lately what a bad state Elwell's affairs were in. His wife's a proud woman, and she fought on as long as she could, going out to work, and taking sewing at home, when she got too sick – something with the heart, I believe. But she had his bedridden mother to look after, and the children, and she broke down under it, and finally had to ask for help. That attracted attention to the case, and the papers took it up, and a subscription was started. Everybody out there liked Bob Elwell, and most of the prominent names in the place are down on the list, and people began to wonder why –'

Parvis broke off to fumble in an inner pocket. 'Here,' he continued, 'here's an account of the whole thing from the *Sentinel* – a little sensational, of course. But I guess you'd better look it over.'

He held out a newspaper to Mary, who unfolded it slowly, remembering, as she did so, the evening when, in that same room, the perusal of a clipping from the *Sentinel* had first shaken the depths of her security.

As she opened the paper, her eyes, shrinking from the glaring headlines, 'Widow of Boyne's Victim Forced to Appeal for Aid,' ran down the column of text to two portraits inserted in it. The first was her husband's, taken from a photograph made the year they had come to England. It was the picture of him that she liked best, the one that stood on the writing-table upstairs in her bedroom. As the eyes in the photograph met hers, she felt it would be impossible to read what was said of him, and closed her lids with the sharpness of the pain.

'I thought if you felt disposed to put your name down –' she heard Parvis continue.

She opened her eyes with an effort, and they fell on the other portrait. It was that of a youngish man, slightly built, in rough clothes, with features somewhat blurred by the shadow of a projecting hat-brim. Where had she seen that outline before? She stared at it confusedly, her heart hammering in her throat and ears. Then she gave a cry.

'This is the man – the man who came for my husband!'

She heard Parvis start to his feet, and was dimly aware that she had slipped backward into the corner of the sofa, and that he was bending above her in alarm. With an intense effort she straightened herself, and reached out for the paper, which she had dropped.

'It's the man! I should know him anywhere!' she cried in a voice that sounded in her own ears like a scream.

Parvis's voice seemed to come to her from far off, down endless, fog-muffled windings.

'Mrs Boyne, you're not very well. Shall I call somebody? Shall I get a glass of water?'

'No, no, no!' She threw herself toward him, her hand frantically clenching the newspaper. 'I tell you, it's the man! I *know* him! He spoke to me in the garden!'

Parvis took the journal from her, directing his glasses to the portrait. 'It can't be, Mrs Boyne. It's Robert Elwell.'

'Robert Elwell?' Her white stare seemed to travel into space. 'Then it was Robert Elwell who came for him.'

'Came for Boyne? The day he went away?' Parvis's voice dropped as hers rose. He bent over, laying a fraternal hand on her, as if to coax her gently back into her seat. 'Why, Elwell was dead! Don't you remember?'

Mary sat with her eyes fixed on the picture, unconscious of what he was saying.

'Don't you remember Boyne's unfinished letter to me – the one you found on his desk that day? It was written just after he'd heard of Elwell's death.' She noticed an odd shake in Parvis's unemotional voice. 'Surely you remember that!' he urged her.

Yes, she remembered: that was the profoundest horror of it. Elwell had died the day before her husband's disappearance; and this was Elwell's portrait; and it was the portrait of the man who had spoken to her in the garden. She lifted her head and looked slowly about the library. The library could have borne witness that it was also the portrait of the man who had come in that day to call Boyne from his unfinished letter. Through the misty surgings of her brain she heard the faint boom of half-forgotten words – words spoken by Alida Stair on the lawn at Pangbourne before Boyne and his wife had ever seen the house at Lyng, or had imagined that they might one day live there.

'This was the man who spoke to me,' she repeated.

She looked again at Parvis. He was trying to conceal his disturbance under what he imagined to be an expression of indulgent commiseration; but the edges of his lips were blue. 'He thinks me mad; but I'm not mad,' she reflected; and suddenly there flashed upon her a way of justifying her strange affirmation.

She sat quiet, controlling the quiver of her lips, and waiting till she could trust her voice to keep its habitual level; then she said, looking straight at Parvis: 'Will you answer me one question, please? When was it that Robert Elwell tried to kill himself?'

'When – when?' Parvis stammered.

'Yes; the date. Please try to remember.'

She saw that he was growing still more afraid of her. 'I have a reason,' she insisted gently.

'Yes, yes. Only I can't remember. About two months before, I should say.'

'I want the date,' she repeated.

Parvis picked up the newspaper. 'We might see here,' he said, still humouring her. He ran his eyes down the page. 'Here it is. Last October – the –'

She caught the words from him. 'The 20th, wasn't it?'

With a sharp look at her, he verified. 'Yes, the 20th. Then you *did* know?'

'I know now.' Her white stare continued to travel past him. 'Sunday, the 20th – that was the day he came first.'

Parvis's voice was almost inaudible. 'Came *here* first?'

'Yes.'

'You saw him twice, then?'

'Yes, twice.' She breathed it at him with dilated eyes. 'He came first on the 20th of October. I remember the date because it was the day we went up Meldon Steep for the first time.' She felt a faint gasp of inward laughter at the thought that but for that she might have forgotten.

Parvis continued to scrutinize her, as if trying to intercept her gaze.

'We saw him from the roof,' she went on. 'He came down the lime avenue toward the house. He was dressed just as he is in that picture. My husband saw him first. He was frightened, and ran down ahead of me; but there was no one there. He had vanished.'

'Elwell had vanished?' Parvis faltered.

'Yes.' Their two whispers seemed to grope for each other. 'I couldn't think what had happened. I see now. He *tried* to come then; but he wasn't dead enough – he couldn't reach us. He had to wait for two months; and then he came back again – and Ned went with him.'

She nodded at Parvis with the look of triumph of a child who has successfully worked out a difficult puzzle. But suddenly she lifted her hands with a desperate gesture, pressing them to her bursting temples.

'Oh, my God! I sent him to Ned – I told him where to go! I sent him to this room!' she screamed out.

She felt the walls of the room rush toward her, like inward falling ruins; and she heard Parvis, a long way off, as if through the ruins, crying to her, and struggling to get at her. But she was numb to his touch, she did not know what he was saying. Through the tumult she heard but one clear note, the voice of Alida Stair, speaking on the lawn at Pangbourne.

'You won't know till afterward,' it said. 'You won't know till long, long afterward.'

THE YULETIDE SPIRIT

JEEVES AND THE YULE-TIDE SPIRIT *BY* P. G. WODEHOUSE

The author of almost a hundred books and the creator of Jeeves, Blandings Castle, Psmith, Ukridge, Uncle Fred and Mr Mulliner, P. G. Wodehouse was born in 1881 and educated at Dulwich College. After two years with the Hong Kong and Shanghai Bank he became a full-time writer, contributing to a variety of periodicals including *Punch* and the *Globe*. He married in 1914. As well as his novels and short stories, he wrote lyrics for musical comedies with Guy Bolton and Jerome Kern, and at one stage had five musicals running simultaneously on Broadway. His time in Hollywood also provided much source material for fiction.

At the age of 93, in the New Year's Honours List of 1975, he received a long-overdue knighthood, only to die on St Valentine's Day some forty-five days later.

THE LETTER arrived on the morning of the sixteenth. I was pushing a bit of breakfast into the Wooster face at the moment and, feeling fairly well-fortified with coffee and kippers, I decided to break the news to Jeeves without delay. As Shakespeare says, if you're going to do a thing you might just as well pop right at it and get it over. The man would be disappointed, of course, and possibly even chagrined: but, dash it all, a splash of disappointment here and there does a fellow good. Makes him realize that life is stern and life is earnest.

'Oh, Jeeves,' I said.

'Sir?'

'We have here a communication from Lady Wickham. She has written inviting me to Skeldings for the festives. So you will see about bunging the necessaries together. We repair thither on the twenty-third. Plenty of white ties, Jeeves, also a few hearty country suits for use in the daytime. We shall be there some little time, I expect.'

There was a pause. I could feel he was directing a frosty gaze at me, but I dug into the marmalade and refused to meet it.

'I thought I understood you to say, sir, that you proposed to visit Monte Carlo immediately after Christmas.'

'I know. But that's all off. Plans changed.'

'Very good, sir.'

At this point the telephone bell rang, tiding over very nicely what had threatened to be an awkward moment. Jeeves unhooked the receiver.

'Yes? . . . Yes, madam . . . Very good, madam. Here is Mr Wooster.' He handed me the instrument. 'Mrs Spenser Gregson, sir.'

You know, every now and then I can't help feeling that Jeeves is losing his grip. In his prime it would have been with him the work of a moment to have told Aunt Agatha that I was not at home. I gave him one of those reproachful glances, and took the machine.

'Hullo?' I said. 'Yes? Hullo? Hullo? Bertie speaking. Hullo? Hullo? Hullo?'

'Don't keep on saying Hullo,' yipped the old relative in her customary curt manner. 'You're not a parrot. Sometimes I wish you were, because then you might have a little sense.'

Quite the wrong sort of tone to adopt towards a fellow in the early morning, of course, but what can one do?

'Bertie, Lady Wickham tells me she has invited you to Skeldings for Christmas. Are you going?'

'Rather!'

'Well, mind you behave yourself. Lady Wickham is an old friend of mine.'

I was in no mood for this sort of thing over the telephone. Face to face, I'm not saying, but at the end of a wire, no.

'I shall naturally endeavour, Aunt Agatha,' I replied stiffly, 'to conduct myself in a manner befitting an English gentleman paying a visit –'

'What did you say? Speak up. I can't hear.'

'I said Right-ho.'

'Oh? Well, mind you do. And there's another reason why I particularly wish you to be as little of an imbecile as you can manage while at Skeldings. Sir Roderick Glossop will be there.'

'What!'

'Don't bellow like that. You nearly deafened me.'

'Did you say Sir Roderick Glossop?'

'I did.'

'You don't mean Tuppy Glossop?'

'I mean Sir Roderick Glossop. Which was my reason for saying Sir Roderick Glossop. Now, Bertie, I want you to listen to me attentively. Are you there?'

'Yes. Still here.'

'Well, then, listen. I have at last succeeded, after incredible difficulty, and in face of all the evidence, in almost persuading Sir Roderick that you are not actually insane. He is prepared to suspend judgement until he has seen you once more. On your behaviour at Skeldings, therefore —'

But I had hung up the receiver. Shaken. That's what I was. S. to the core.

Stop me if I've told you this before: but, in case you don't know, let me just mention the facts in the matter of this Glossop. He was a formidable old bird with a bald head and out-size eyebrows, by profession a loony-doctor. How it happened, I couldn't tell you to this day, but I once got engaged to his daughter, Honoria, a ghastly dynamic exhibit who read Nietzsche and had a laugh like waves breaking on a stern and rock-bound coast. The fixture was scratched owing to events occurring which convinced the old boy that I was off my napper; and since then he has always had my name at the top of his list of 'Loonies I have Lunched With'.

It seemed to me that even at Christmas time, with all the peace on earth and goodwill towards men that there is knocking about at that season, a reunion with this bloke was likely to be tough going. If I hadn't had more than one particularly good reason for wanting to go to Skeldings, I'd have called the thing off.

'Jeeves,' I said, all of a twitter, 'do you know what? Sir Roderick Glossop is going to be at Lady Wickham's.'

'Very good, sir. If you have finished breakfast, I will clear away.'

Cold and haughty. No symp. None of the rallying-round spirit which one likes to see. As I had anticipated, the information that we were not going to Monte Carlo had got in amongst him. There is a keen sporting streak in Jeeves, and I knew he had been looking forward to a little flutter at the tables.

We Woosters can wear the mask. I ignored his lack of decent feeling.

'Do so, Jeeves,' I said proudly, 'and with all convenient speed.'

Relations continued pretty fairly strained all through the rest of the week. There was a frigid detachment in the way the man brought me my dollop of tea in the mornings. Going down to Skeldings in the car on the afternoon of the twenty-third, he was aloof and reserved. And before dinner on the first night of my visit he put the studs in my dress-shirt in what I can only call a marked manner. The whole thing was extremely painful, and it seemed to me, as I lay in bed on the morning of the twenty-fourth, that the only step to take was to put the whole facts of the case before him and trust to his native good sense to effect an understanding.

I was feeling considerably in the pink that morning. Everything had gone like a breeze. My hostess, Lady Wickham, was a beaky female built far too closely on the lines of my Aunt Agatha for comfort, but she had seemed matey enough on my arrival. Her daughter, Roberta, had welcomed me with a warmth which, I'm bound to say, had set the old heart-strings fluttering a bit. And Sir Roderick, in the brief moment we had had together, appeared to have let the Yule Tide Spirit soak into him to the most amazing extent. When he saw me, his mouth sort of flickered at one corner, which I took to be his idea of smiling, and he said 'Ha, young man!' Not particularly chummily, but he said it: and my view was that it practically amounted to the lion lying down with the lamb.

So, all in all, life at this juncture seemed pretty well all to the mustard, and I decided to tell Jeeves exactly how matters stood.

'Jeeves,' I said, as he appeared with the steaming.

'Sir?'

'Touching on this business of our being here, I would like to say a few words of explanation. I consider that you have a right to the facts.'

'Sir?'

'I'm afraid scratching that Monte Carlo trip has been a bit of a jar for you, Jeeves.'

'Not at all, sir.'

'Oh, yes, it has. The heart was set on wintering in the world's good old Plague Spot, I know. I saw your eye light up when I said we were due for a visit there. You snorted a bit and your fingers twitched. I know, I know. And now that there has been a change of programme the iron has entered into your soul.'

'Not at all, sir.'

'Oh, yes, it has. I've seen it. Very well, then, what I wish to impress upon you, Jeeves, is that I have not been actuated in this matter by any mere idle whim. It was through no light and airy caprice that I accepted this invitation to Lady Wickham's. I have been angling for it for weeks, prompted by many considerations. In the first place, does one get the Yule-tide spirit at a spot like Monte Carlo?'

'Does one desire the Yule-tide spirit, sir?'

'Certainly one does. I am all for it. Well, that's one thing. Now here's another. It was imperative that I should come to Skeldings for Christmas, Jeeves, because I knew that young Tuppy Glossop was going to be here.'

'Sir Roderick Glossop, sir?'

'His nephew. You may have observed hanging about the place a fellow with light hair and a Cheshire-cat grin. That is Tuppy, and I have been anxious for some time to get to grips with him. I have it in for that man of wrath. Listen to the facts, Jeeves, and tell me if I am not justified in planning a hideous vengeance.' I took a sip of tea, for the mere memory of my wrongs had shaken me. 'In spite of the fact that young Tuppy is the nephew of Sir Roderick Glossop, at whose hands, Jeeves, as you are aware, I have suffered much, I fraternized with him freely, both at the Drones Club and elsewhere. I said to myself that a man is not to be blamed for his relations, and that I would hate to have my pals hold my Aunt Agatha, for instance, against me. Broad-minded, Jeeves, I think?'

'Extremely, sir.'

'Well, then, as I say, I sought this Tuppy out, Jeeves, and hobnobbed, and what do you think he did?'

'I could not say, sir.'

'I will tell you. One night after dinner at the Drones he betted me I wouldn't swing myself across the swimming-bath by the ropes and rings. I took him on and was buzzing along in great style until I came to the last ring. And then I found that this fiend in human shape had looped it back against the rail, thus leaving me hanging in the void with no means of getting ashore to my home and loved ones. There was nothing for it but to drop into the water. He told me that he had often caught fellows that way: and what I maintain, Jeeves, is that, if I can't get back at him somehow at Skeldings – with all the vast resources which a country-house affords at my disposal – I am not the man I was.'

'I see, sir.'

There was still something in his manner which told me that even now he lacked complete sympathy and understanding, so, delicate though the subject was, I decided to put all my cards on the table.

'And now, Jeeves, we come to the most important reason why I had to spend Christmas at Skeldings. Jeeves,' I said, diving into the old cup once more for a moment and bringing myself out wreathed in blushes, 'the fact of the matter is, I'm in love.'

'Indeed, sir?'

'You've seen Miss Roberta Wickham?'

'Yes, sir.'

'Very well, then.'

There was a pause, while I let it sink in.

'During your stay here, Jeeves,' I said, 'you will, no doubt, be thrown a good deal together with Miss Wickham's maid. On such occasions, pitch it strong.'

'Sir?'

'You know what I mean. Tell her I'm rather a good chap. Mention my hidden depths. These things get round. Dwell on the fact that I have a kind heart and was runner-up in the Squash Handicap at the Drones this year. A boost is never wasted, Jeeves.'

'Very good, sir. But –'

'But what?'

'Well, sir –'

'I wish you wouldn't say "Well, sir" in that soupy tone of voice. I have had to speak of this before. The habit is one that is growing upon you. Check it. What's on your mind?'

'I hardly like to take the liberty –'

'Carry on, Jeeves. We are always glad to hear from you, always.'

'What I was about to remark, if you will excuse me, sir, was that I would scarcely have thought Miss Wickham a suitable –'

'Jeeves,' I said coldly, 'if you have anything to say against that lady, it had better not be said in my presence.'

'Very good, sir.'

'Or anywhere else, for that matter. What is your kick against Miss Wickham?'

'Oh, really, sir!'

'Jeeves, I insist. This is a time for plain speaking. You have beefed about Miss Wickham. I wish to know why.'

'It merely crossed my mind, sir, that for a gentleman of your description Miss Wickham is not a suitable mate.'

'What do you mean by a gentleman of my description?'

'Well, sir –'

'Jeeves!'

'I beg your pardon, sir. The expression escaped me inadvertently. I was about to observe that I can only asseverate –'

'Only what?'

'I can only say that, as you have invited my opinion –'

'But I didn't.'

'I was under the impression that you desired to canvass my views on the matter, sir.'

'Oh? Well, let's have them, anyway.'

'Very good, sir. Then briefly, if I may say so, sir, though Miss Wickham is a charming young lady –'

'There, Jeeves, you spoke an imperial quart. What eyes!'

'Yes, sir.'

'What hair!'

'Very true, sir.'

'And what *espièglerie*, if that's the word I want.'

'The exact word, sir.'

'All right, then. Carry on.'

'I grant Miss Wickham the possession of all these desirable qualities, sir. Nevertheless, considered as a matrimonial prospect for a gentleman of your description, I cannot look upon her as suitable. In my opinion Miss Wickham lacks seriousness, sir. She is too volatile and frivolous. To qualify as Miss Wickham's husband, a gentleman would need to possess a commanding personality and considerable strength of character.'

'Exactly!'

'I would always hesitate to recommend as a life's companion a young lady with quite such a vivid shade of red hair. Red hair, sir, in my opinion, is dangerous.'

I eyed the blighter squarely.

'Jeeves,' I said, 'you're talking rot.'

'Very good, sir.'

'Absolute drivel.'

'Very good, sir.'

'Pure mashed potatoes.'

'Very good, sir.'

'Very good, sir – I mean very good Jeeves, that will be all,' I said.

And I drank a modicum of tea, with a good deal of hauteur.

It isn't often that I find myself able to prove Jeeves in the wrong, but by dinner-time that night I was in a position to do so, and I did it without delay.

'Touching on that matter we were touching on, Jeeves,' I

said, coming in from the bath and tackling him as he studied the shirt, 'I should be glad if you would give me your careful attention for a moment. I warn you that what I am about to say is going to make you look pretty silly.'

'Indeed, sir?'

'Yes, Jeeves. Pretty dashed silly it's going to make you look. It may lead you to be rather more careful in future about broad-casting these estimates of yours of people's characters. This morning, if I remember rightly, you stated that Miss Wickham was volatile, frivolous and lacking in seriousness. Am I correct?'

'Quite correct, sir.'

'Then what I have to tell you may cause you to alter that opinion. I went for a walk with Miss Wickham this afternoon: and, as we walked, I told her about what young Tuppy Glossop did to me in the swimming-bath at the Drones. She hung upon my words, Jeeves, and was full of sympathy.'

'Indeed, sir?'

'Dripping with it. And that's not all. Almost before I had finished, she was suggesting the ripest, fruitiest, brainiest scheme for bringing young Tuppy's grey hairs in sorrow to the grave that anyone could possibly imagine.'

'That is very gratifying, sir.'

'Gratifying is the word. It appears that at the girls' school where Miss Wickham was educated, Jeeves, it used to become necessary from time to time for the right-thinking element of the community to slip it across certain of the baser sort. Do you know what they did, Jeeves?'

'No, sir.'

'They took a long stick, Jeeves, and – follow me closely here – they tied a darning-needle to the end of it. Then at dead of night, it appears, they sneaked privily into the party of the second part's cubicle and shoved the needle through the bedclothes and punctured her hot-water bottle. Girls are much subtler in these matters than boys, Jeeves. At my old school one would occasionally heave a jug of water over another bloke during the night-watches, but we never thought of effecting the same result in this particularly neat and scientific manner. Well, Jeeves, that was the scheme which Miss Wickham suggested I should work on young Tuppy, and that is the girl you call frivolous and lacking in seriousness. Any girl who can think up a wheeze like that is my idea of a helpmeet. I shall be glad, Jeeves, if by the time I come to bed tonight you have waiting for me in this room a stout stick with a good sharp darning-needle attached.'

'Well, sir –'

I raised my hand.

'Jeeves,' I said. 'Not another word. Stick, one, and needle, darning, good, sharp, one, without fail in this room at eleven-thirty tonight.'

'Very good, sir.'

'Have you any idea where young Tuppy sleeps?'

'I could ascertain, sir.'

'Do so, Jeeves.'

In a few minutes he was back with the necessary informash.

'Mr Glossop is established in the Moat Room, sir.'

'Where's that?'

'The second door on the floor below this, sir.'

'Right ho, Jeeves. Are the studs in my shirt?'

'Yes, sir.'

'And the links also?'

'Yes, sir.'

'Then push me into it.'

The more I thought about this enterprise which a sense of duty and good citizenship had thrust upon me, the better it seemed to me. I am not a vindictive man, but I felt, as anybody would have felt in my place, that if fellows like young Tuppy are allowed to get away with it the whole fabric of Society and Civilization must inevitably crumble. The task to which I had set myself was one that involved hardship and discomfort, for it meant sitting up till well into the small hours and then padding down a cold corridor, but I did not shrink from it. After all, there is a lot to be said for family tradition. We Woosters did our bit in the Crusades.

It being Christmas Eve, there was, as I had foreseen, a good deal of revelry and what not. First, the village choir surged round and sang carols outside the front door, and then somebody suggested a dance, and after that we hung around chatting of this and that, so that it wasn't till past one that I got to my room. Allowing for everything, it didn't seem that it was going to be safe to start my little expedition till half-past two at the earliest: and I'm bound to say that it was only the utmost resolution that kept me from snuggling into the sheets and calling it a day. I'm not much of a lad now for late hours.

However, by half-past two everything appeared to be quiet. I shook off the mists of sleep, grabbed the good old stick-and-needle and toddled off along the corridor. And presently, pausing outside the Moat Room, I turned the handle, found the door wasn't locked, and went in.

I suppose a burglar – I mean a real professional who works at the job six nights a week all the year round – gets so that finding himself standing in the dark in somebody else's bedroom means absolutely nothing to him. But for a bird like me, who has had no previous experience, there's a lot to be said in favour of washing the whole thing out and closing the door gently and popping back to bed again. It was only by summoning up all the old bull-dog courage of the Woosters, and reminding myself that, if I let this opportunity slip another might never occur, that I managed to stick out what you might call the initial minute of the binge. Then the weakness passed, and Bertram was himself again.

At first when I beetled in, the room had seemed as black as a coal-cellar: but after a bit things began to lighten. The curtains weren't quite drawn over the window and I could see a trifle of the scenery here and there. The bed was opposite the window, with the head against the wall and the end where the feet were jutting out towards where I stood, thus rendering it possible after one had sown the seed, so to speak, to make a quick getaway. There only remained now the rather tricky problem of locating the old hot-water bottle. I mean to say, the one thing you can't do if you want to carry a job like this through with secrecy and dispatch is to stand at the end of a fellow's bed, jabbing the blankets at random with a darning-needle. Before proceeding to anything in the nature of definite steps, it is imperative that you locate the bot.

I was a good deal cheered at this juncture to hear a fruity snore from the direction of the pillows. Reason told me that a bloke who could snore like that wasn't going to be awakened by a trifle. I edged forward and ran a hand in a gingerly sort of way over the coverlet. A moment later I had found the bulge. I steered the good old darning-needle on to it, gripped the stick, and shoved. Then, pulling out the weapon, I sidled towards the door, and in another moment would have been outside, buzzing for home and the good night's rest, when suddenly there was a crash that sent my spine shooting up through the top of my head and the contents of the bed sat up like a jack-in-the-box and said:

'Who's that?'

It just shows how your most careful strategic moves can be

the very ones that dish your campaign. In order to facilitate the orderly retreat according to plan I had left the door open, and the beastly thing had slammed like a bomb.

But I wasn't giving much thought to the causes of the explosion, having other things to occupy my mind. What was disturbing me was the discovery that, whoever else the bloke in the bed might be, he was not young Tuppy. Tuppy has one of those high, squeaky voices that sound like the tenor of the village choir failing to hit a high note. This one was something in between the last Trump and a tiger calling for breakfast after being on a diet for a day or two. It was the sort of nasty, rasping voice you hear shouting 'Fore!' when you're one of a slow foursome on the links and are holding up a couple of retired colonels. Among the qualities it lacked were kindliness, suavity and that sort of dove-like cooing note which makes a fellow feel he has found a friend.

I did not linger. Getting swiftly off the mark, I dived for the door-handle and was off and away, banging the door behind me. I may be a chump in many ways, as my Aunt Agatha will freely attest, but I know when and when not to be among those present.

And I was just about to do the stretch of corridor leading to the stairs in a split second under the record time for the course, when something brought me up with a sudden jerk. One moment, I was all dash and fire and speed; the next, an irresistible force had checked me in my stride and was holding me straining at the leash, as it were.

You know, sometimes it seems to me as if Fate were going out of its way to such an extent to snooter you that you wonder if it's worth while continuing to struggle. The night being a trifle chillier than the dickens, I had donned for this expedition a dressing-gown. It was the tail of this infernal garment that had caught in the door and pipped me at the eleventh hour.

The next moment the door had opened, light was streaming through it, and the bloke with the voice had grabbed me by the arm.

It was Sir Roderick Glossop.

The next thing that happened was a bit of a lull in the proceedings. For about three and a quarter seconds or possibly more we just stood there, drinking each other in, so to speak, the old boy still attached with a limpet-like grip to my elbow. If I hadn't been in a dressing-gown and he in pink pyjamas with a blue stripe, and if he hadn't been glaring quite so much as if he were shortly going to commit a murder, the tableau would have looked rather like one of those advertisements you see in the magazines, where the experienced elder is patting the young man's arm, and saying to him, 'My boy, if you subscribe to the Mutt-Jeff Correspondence School of Oswego, Kan., as I did, you may some day, like me, become Third Assistant Vice-President of the Schenectady Consolidated Nail-File and Eyebrow Tweezer Corporation.'

'You!' said Sir Roderick finally. And in this connection I want to state that it's all rot to say you can't hiss a word that hasn't an 's' in it. The way he pushed out that 'You!' sounded like an angry cobra, and I am betraying no secrets when I mention that it did me no good whatsoever.

By rights, I suppose, at this point I ought to have said something. The best I could manage, however, was a faint, soft bleating sound. Even on ordinary social occasions, when meeting this bloke as man to man and with a clear conscience, I could never be completely at my ease: and now those eyebrows seemed to pierce me like a knife.

'Come in here,' he said, lugging me into the room. 'We don't want to wake the whole house. Now,' he said, depositing me on the carpet and closing the door and doing a bit of eyebrow work, 'kindly inform me what is this latest manifestation of insanity?'

It seemed to me that a light and cheery laugh might help the thing along. So I had a pop at one.

'Don't gibber!' said my genial host. And I'm bound to admit that the light and cheery hadn't come out quite as I'd intended.

I pulled myself together with a strong effort.

'Awfully sorry about all this,' I said in a hearty sort of voice. 'The fact is, I thought you were Tuppy.'

'Kindly refrain from inflicting your idiotic slang on me. What do you mean by the adjective "tuppy"?'

'It isn't so much an adjective, don't you know. More of a noun, I should think, if you examine it squarely. What I mean to say is, I thought you were your nephew.'

'You thought I was my nephew? Why should I be my nephew?'

'What I'm driving at is, I thought this was his room.'

'My nephew and I changed rooms. I have a great dislike for sleeping on an upper floor. I am nervous about fire.'

For the first time since this interview had started, I braced up a trifle. The injustice of the whole thing stirred me to such an extent that for a moment I lost that sense of being a toad under the harrow which had been cramping my style up till now. I even went so far as to eye this pink-pyjamaed poltroon with a good deal of contempt and loathing. Just because he had this craven fear of fire and this selfish preference for letting Tuppy be cooked instead of himself should the emergency occur, my nicely-reasoned plans had gone up the spout. I gave him a look, and I think I may even have snorted a bit.

'I should have thought that your man-servant would have informed you,' said Sir Roderick, 'that we contemplated making this change. I met him shortly before luncheon and told him to tell you.'

I reeled. Yes, it is not too much to say that I reeled. This extraordinary statement had taken me amidships without any preparation, and it staggered me. That Jeeves had been aware all along that this old crumb would be the occupant of the bed which I was proposing to prod with darning-needles and had let me rush upon my doom without a word of warning was almost beyond belief. You might say I was aghast. Yes, practically aghast.

'You told Jeeves that you were going to sleep in this room?' I gasped.

'I did. I was aware that you and my nephew were on terms of intimacy, and I wished to spare myself the possibility of a visit from you. I confess that it never occurred to me that such a visit was to be anticipated at three o'clock in the morning. What the devil do you mean,' he barked, suddenly hotting up, 'by prowling about the house at this hour? And what is that thing in your hand?'

I looked down, and found that I was still grasping the stick. I give you my honest word that, what with the maelstrom of emotions into which his revelation about Jeeves had cast me, the discovery came as an absolute surprise.

'This?' I said. 'Oh, yes.'

'What do you mean, "Oh, yes"? What is it?'

'Well, it's a long story –'

'We have the night before us.'

'It's this way. I will ask you to picture me some weeks ago, perfectly peaceful and inoffensive, after dinner at the Drones, smoking a thoughtful cigarette and –'

I broke off. The man wasn't listening. He was goggling in a rapt sort of way at the end of the bed, from which there had now begun to drip on to the carpet a series of drops.

'Good heavens!'

'— thoughtful cigarette and chatting pleasantly of this and that —'

I broke off again. He had lifted the sheets and was gazing at the corpse of the hot-water bottle.

'Did you do this?' he said in a low, strangled sort of voice.

'Er — yes. As a matter of fact, yes. I was just going to tell you —'

'And your aunt tried to persuade me that you were not insane!'

'I'm not. Absolutely not. If you'll just let me explain.'

'I will do nothing of the kind.'

'It all began —'

'Silence!'

'Right-ho.'

He did some deep-breathing exercises through the nose.

'My bed is drenched!'

'The way it all began —'

'Be quiet!' He heaved somewhat for awhile. 'You wretched, miserable idiot,' he said, 'kindly inform me which bedroom you are supposed to be occupying?'

'It's on the floor above. The Clock Room.'

'Thank you. I will find it.'

He gave me the eyebrow.

'I propose,' he said, 'to pass the remainder of the night in your room, where, I presume, there is a bed in a condition to be slept in. You may bestow yourself as comfortably as you can here. I will wish you good-night.'

He buzzed off, leaving me flat.

Well, we Woosters are old campaigners. We can take the rough with the smooth. But to say that I liked the prospect now before me would be paltering with the truth. One glance at the bed told me that any idea of sleeping there was out. A goldfish could have done it, but not Bertram. After a bit of a look round, I decided that the best chance of getting a sort of night's rest was to doss as well as I could in the arm-chair. I pinched a couple of pillows off the bed, shoved the hearth-rug over my knees, and sat down and started counting sheep.

But it wasn't any good. The old lemon was sizzling much too much to admit of anything in the nature of slumber. This hideous revelation of the blackness of Jeeves's treachery kept coming back to me every time I nearly succeeded in dropping off: and, what's more, it seemed to get colder and colder as the long night wore on. I was just wondering if I would ever get to sleep again in this world when a voice at my elbow said 'Good-morning, sir,' and I sat up with a jerk.

I could have sworn I hadn't so much as dozed off for even a minute, but apparently I had. For the curtains were drawn back and daylight was coming in through the window and there was Jeeves standing beside me with a cup of tea on a tray.

'Merry Christmas, sir!'

I reached out a feeble hand for the restoring brew. I swallowed a mouthful or two, and felt a little better. I was aching in every limb and the dome felt like lead, but I was now able to think with a certain amount of clearness, and I fixed the man with a stony eye and prepared to let him have it.

'You think so, do you?' I said. 'Much, let me tell you, depends on what you mean by the adjective "merry". If, moreover, you suppose that it is going to be merry for you, correct that impression. Jeeves,' I said, taking another half-oz of tea and speaking in a cold, measured voice, 'I wish to ask you one question. Did you or did you not know that Sir Roderick Glossop was sleeping in this room last night?'

'Yes, sir.'

'You admit it!'

'Yes, sir.'

'And you didn't tell me!'

'No, sir. I thought it would be more judicious not to do so.'

'Jeeves —'

'If you will allow me to explain, sir.'

'Explain!'

'I was aware that my silence might lead to something in the nature of an embarrassing contretemps, sir —'

'You thought that, did you?'

'Yes, sir.'

'You were a good guesser,' I said, sucking down further Bohea.

'But it seemed to me, sir, that whatever might occur was all for the best.'

I would have put in a crisp word or two here, but he carried on without giving me the opp.

'I thought that possibly, on reflection, sir, your views being what they are, you would prefer your relations with Sir Roderick Glossop and his family to be distant rather than cordial.'

'My views? What do you mean, my views?'

'As regards a matrimonial alliance with Miss Honoria Glossop, sir.'

Something like an electric shock seemed to zip through me. The man had opened up a new line of thought. I suddenly saw what he was driving at, and realized all in a flash that I had been wronging this faithful fellow. All the while I supposed he had been landing me in the soup, he had really been steering me away from it. It was like those stories one used to read as a kid about the traveller going along on a dark night and his dog grabs him by the leg of his trousers and he says 'Down, sir! What are you doing, Rover?' and the dog hangs on and he gets rather hot under the collar and curses a bit but the dog won't let him go and then suddenly the moon shines through the clouds and he finds he's been standing on the edge of a precipice and one more step would have – well, anyway, you get the idea: and what I'm driving at is that much the same sort of thing seemed to have been happening now.

It's perfectly amazing how a fellow will let himself get off his guard and ignore the perils which surround him. I give you my honest word, it had never struck me till this moment that my Aunt Agatha had been scheming to get me in right with Sir Roderick so that I should eventually be received back into the fold, if you see what I mean, and subsequently pushed off on Honoria.

'My God, Jeeves!' I said, paling.

'Precisely, sir.'

'You think there was a risk?'

'I do, sir. A very grave risk.'

A disturbing thought struck me.

'But, Jeeves, on calm reflection won't Sir Roderick have gathered by now that my objective was young Tuppy and that puncturing his hot-water bottle was just one of those things that occur when the Yule-tide spirit is abroad – one of those things that have to be overlooked and taken with the indulgent smile and the fatherly shake of the head? I mean to say, Young Blood and all that sort of thing? What I mean is he'll realize that I wasn't trying to snooter him, and then all the good work will have been wasted.'

'No, sir. I fancy not. That might possibly have been Sir Roderick's mental reaction, had it not been for the second incident.'

'The second incident?'

'During the night, sir, while Sir Roderick was occupying your bed, somebody entered the room, pierced his hot-water bottle with some sharp instrument, and vanished in the darkness.'

I could make nothing of this.

'What! Do you think I walked in my sleep?'

'No, sir. It was young Mr Glossop who did it. I encountered him this morning, sir, shortly before I came here. He was in cheerful spirits and enquired of me how you were feeling about the incident. Not being aware that his victim had been Sir Roderick.'

'But, Jeeves, what an amazing coincidence!'

'Sir?'

'Why, young Tuppy getting exactly the same idea as I did. Or, rather, as Miss Wickham did. You can't say that's not rummy. A miracle, I call it.'

'Not altogether, sir. It appears that he received the suggestion from the young lady.'

'From Miss Wickham?'

'Yes, sir.'

'You mean to say that, after she had put me up to the scheme of puncturing Tuppy's hot-water bottle, she went away and tipped Tuppy off to puncturing mine?'

'Precisely, sir. She is a young lady with a keen sense of humour, sir.'

I sat there, you might say stunned. When I thought how near I had come to offering the heart and hand to a girl capable of double-crossing a strong man's honest love like that, I shivered.

'Are you cold, sir?'

'No, Jeeves. Just shuddering.'

'The occurrence, if I may take the liberty of saying so, sir, will perhaps lend colour to the view which I put forward yesterday that Miss Wickham, though in many respects a charming young lady –'

I raised the hand.

'Say no more, Jeeves,' I replied. 'Love is dead.'

'Very good, sir.'

I brooded for a while.

'You've seen Sir Roderick this morning, then?'

'Yes, sir.'

'How did he seem?'

'A trifle feverish, sir.'

'Feverish?'

'A little emotional, sir. He expressed a strong desire to meet you, sir.'

'What would you advise?'

'If you were to slip out by the back entrance as soon as you are dressed, sir, it would be possible for you to make your way across the field without being observed and reach the village, where you could hire an automobile to take you to London. I could bring on your effects later in your own car.'

'But London, Jeeves? Is any man safe? My Aunt Agatha is in London.'

'Yes, sir.'

'Well, then?'

He regarded me for a moment with a fathomless eye.

'I think the best plan, sir, would be for you to leave England, which is not pleasant at this time of the year, for some little while. I would not take the liberty of dictating your movements, sir, but as you already have accommodation engaged on the Blue Train for Monte Carlo for the day after tomorrow –'

'But you cancelled the booking?'

'No, sir.'

'I thought you had.'

'No, sir.'

'I told you to.'

'Yes, sir. It was remiss of me, but the matter slipped my mind.'

'Oh?'

'Yes, sir.'

'All right, Jeeves. Monte Carlo ho, then.'

'Very good, sir.'

'It's lucky, as things have turned out, that you forgot to cancel that booking.'

'Very fortunate indeed, sir. If you will wait here, sir, I will return to your room and procure a suit of clothes.'

DANCING DAN'S CHRISTMAS *BY* DAMON RUNYON

Alfred Damon Runyon was born on 4 October 1884 in Kansas. He grew up in Colorado and, after a spell in the army, he worked as a journalist and sportswriter. During the First World War he became a war correspondent. He is best known, however, for his colourful and original short stories, which evoked a distinctive era and type of New York society. His first collection was *Guys and Dolls* (1932) – a popular musical with the same title, based on his stories, premiered on Broadway in 1950, with music and lyrics by Frank Loesser. His other collections include *Blue Plate Special* (1934) and *Take It Easy* (1938). Damon Runyon died on 10 December 1946.

N ow one time it comes on Christmas, and in fact it is the
evening before Christmas, and I am in Good Time
Charley Bernstein's little speakeasy in West Forty-seventh
Street, wishing Charley a Merry Christmas and having a few
hot Tom and Jerrys with him.

This hot Tom and Jerry is an old-time drink that is once
used by one and all in this country to celebrate Christmas with,
and in fact it is once so popular that many people think Christmas
is invented only to furnish an excuse for hot Tom and Jerry,
although of course this is by no means true.

But anybody will tell you that there is nothing that brings
out the true holiday spirit like hot Tom and Jerry, and I hear
that since Tom and Jerry goes out of style in the United States,
the holiday spirit is never quite the same.

Well, as Good Time Charley and I are expressing our holiday
sentiments to each other over our hot Tom and Jerry, and I am
trying to think up the poem about the night before Christmas
and all through the house, which I know will interest Charley no
little, all of a sudden there is a big knock at the front door, and
when Charley opens the door, who comes in carrying a large
package under one arm but a guy by the name of Dancing Dan.

This Dancing Dan is a good-looking young guy, who always seems well-dressed, and he is called by the name of Dancing Dan because he is a great hand for dancing around and about with dolls in night clubs, and other spots where there is any dancing. In fact, Dan never seems to be doing anything else, although I hear rumors that when he is not dancing he is carrying on in a most illegal manner at one thing and another. But of course you can always hear rumors in this town about anybody, and personally I am rather fond of Dancing Dan as he always seems to be getting a great belt out of life.

Anybody in town will tell you that Dancing Dan is a guy with no Barnaby whatever in him, and in fact he has about as much gizzard as anybody around, although I wish to say I always question his judgment in dancing so much with Miss Muriel O'Neill, who works in the Half Moon night club. And the reason I question his judgment in this respect is because everybody knows that Miss Muriel O'Neill is a doll who is very well thought of by Heine Schmitz, and Heine Schmitz is not such a guy as will take kindly to anybody dancing more than once and a half with a doll that he thinks well of.

Well, anyway, as Dancing Dan comes in, he weighs up the joint in one quick peek, and then he tosses the package he is carrying into a corner where it goes plunk, as if there is something very heavy in it, and then he steps up to the bar alongside of Charley and me and wishes to know what we are drinking.

Naturally we start boosting hot Tom and Jerry to Dancing Dan, and he says he will take a crack at it with us, and after one crack, Dancing Dan says he will have another crack, and Merry Christmas to us with it, and the first thing anybody knows it is a couple of hours later and we are still having cracks at the hot Tom and Jerry with Dancing Dan, and Dan says he never drinks anything so soothing in his life. In fact, Dancing Dan says he will recommend Tom and Jerry to everybody he knows, only he does not know anybody good enough for Tom and Jerry, except maybe Miss Muriel O'Neill, and she does not drink anything with drugstore rye in it.

Well, several times while we are drinking this Tom and Jerry, customers come to the door of Good Time Charley's little speakeasy and knock, but by now Charley is commencing to be afraid they will wish Tom and Jerry, too, and he does not feel we will have enough for ourselves, so he hangs out a sign which says 'Closed on Account of Christmas', and the only one he will let in is a guy by the name of Ooky, who is nothing but an old rum-dum, and who is going around all week dressed like Santa Claus and carrying a sign advertising Moe Lewinsky's clothing joint around in Sixth Avenue.

This Ooky is still wearing his Santa Claus outfit when Charley lets him in, and the reason Charley permits such a character as Ooky in his joint is because Ooky does the porter work for Charley when he is not Santa Claus for Moe Lewinsky, such as sweeping out, and washing the glasses, and one thing and another.

Well, it is about nine-thirty when Ooky comes in, and his puppies are aching, and he is all petered out generally from walking up and down and here and there with his sign, for any time a guy is Santa Claus for Moe Lewinsky he must earn his dough. In fact, Ooky is so fatigued, and his puppies hurt him so much that Dancing Dan and Good Time Charley and I all feel very sorry for him, and invite him to have a few mugs of hot Tom and Jerry with us, and wish him plenty of Merry Christmas.

But old Ooky is not accustomed to Tom and Jerry and after about the fifth mug he folds up in a chair, and goes right to sleep on us. He is wearing a pretty good Santa Claus make-up, what with a nice red suit trimmed with white cotton, and a wig, and false nose, and long white whiskers, and a big sack stuffed with excelsior on his back, and if I do not know Santa Claus is not apt to be such a guy as will snore loud enough to rattle the windows, I will think Ooky is Santa Claus sure enough.

Well, we forget Ooky and let him sleep, and go on with our hot Tom and Jerry, and in the meantime we try to think up a few songs appropriate to Christmas, and Dancing Dan finally renders *My Dad's Dinner Pail* in a nice baritone and very loud, while I do first rate with *Will You Love Me in December As You Do in May?*

About midnight Dancing Dan wishes to see how he looks as Santa Claus.

So Good Time Charley and I help Dancing Dan pull off Ooky's outfit and put it on Dan, and this is easy as Ooky only has this Santa Claus outfit on over his ordinary clothes, and he does not even wake up when we are undressing him of the Santa Claus uniform.

Well, I wish to say I see many a Santa Claus in my time, but I never see a better looking Santa Claus than Dancing Dan, especially after he gets the wig and white whiskers fixed just right, and we put a sofa pillow that Good Time Charley happens to have around the joint for the cat to sleep on down his pants to give Dancing Dan a nice fat stomach such as Santa Claus is bound to have.

'Well,' Charley finally says, 'it is a great pity we do not know where there are some stockings hung up somewhere, because then,' he says, 'you can go around and stuff things in these stockings, as I always hear this is the main idea of a Santa Claus. But,' Charley says, 'I do not suppose anybody in this section has any stockings hung up, or if they have,' he says, 'the chances are they are so full of holes they will not hold anything. Anyway,' Charley says, 'even if there are any stockings hung up we do not have anything to stuff in them, although person-ally,' he says, 'I will gladly donate a few pints of Scotch.'

Well, I am pointing out that we have no reindeer and that a Santa Claus is bound to look like a terrible sap if he goes around without any reindeer, but Charley's remarks seem to give Dancing Dan an idea, for all of a sudden he speaks as follows:

'Why,' Dancing Dan says, 'I know where a stocking is hung up. It is hung up at Miss Muriel O'Neill's flat over here in West Forty-ninth Street. This stocking is hung up by nobody but a party by the name of Gammer O'Neill, who is Miss Muriel O'Neill's grandmamma,' Dancing Dan says. 'Gammer O'Neill is going on ninety-odd,' he says, 'and Miss Muriel O'Neill tells me she cannot hold out much longer, what with one thing and another, including being a little childish in spots.

'Now,' Dancing Dan says, 'I remember Miss Muriel O'Neill is telling me just the other night how Gammer O'Neill hangs up her stocking on Christmas Eve all her life, and,' he says, 'I judge from what Miss Muriel O'Neill says that the old doll always believes Santa Claus will come along some Christmas and fill the stocking full of beautiful gifts. But,' Dancing Dan says, 'Miss Muriel O'Neill tells me Santa Claus never does this, although Miss Muriel O'Neill personally always takes a few gifts home and pops them into the stocking to make Gammer O'Neill feel better.

'But, of course,' Dancing Dan says, 'these gifts are nothing much because Miss Muriel O'Neill is very poor, and proud, and also good, and will not take a dime off of anybody and I can lick the guy who says she will.

'Now,' Dancing Dan goes on, 'it seems that while Gammer O'Neill is very happy to get whatever she finds in her stocking on Christmas morning, she does not understand why Santa Claus is not more liberal, and,' he says, 'Miss Muriel O'Neill is saying to me that she only wishes she can give Gammer O'Neill one real big Christmas before the old doll puts her checks back in the rack.

'So,' Dancing Dan states, 'here is a job for us. Miss Muriel O'Neill and her grandmamma live all alone in this flat over in West Forty-ninth Street, and,' he says, 'at such an hour as this Miss Muriel O'Neill is bound to be working, and the chances are Gammer O'Neill is sound asleep, and we will just hop over there and Santa Claus will fill up her stocking with beautiful gifts.'

Well, I say, I do not see where we are going to get any beautiful gifts at this time of night, what with all the stores being closed, unless we dash into an all-night drug store and buy a few bottles of perfume and a bum toilet set as guys always do when they forget about their ever-loving wives until after store hours on Christmas Eve, but Dancing Dan says never mind about this, but let us have a few more Tom and Jerrys first.

So we have a few more Tom and Jerrys, and then Dancing Dan picks up the package he heaves into the corner, and dumps most of the excelsior out of Ooky's Santa Claus sack, and puts the bundle in, and Good Time Charley turns out all the lights, but one, and leaves a bottle of Scotch on the table in front of Ooky for a Christmas gift, and away we go.

Personally, I regret very much leaving the hot Tom and Jerry, but then I am also very enthusiastic about going along to help Dancing Dan play Santa Claus, while Good Time Charley is practically overjoyed, as it is the first time in his life Charley is ever mixed up in so much holiday spirit.

As we go up Broadway, headed for Forty-ninth Street, Charley and I see many citizens we know and give them a large hello, and wish them Merry Christmas, and some of these citizens shake hands with Santa Claus, not knowing he is nobody but Dancing Dan, although later I understand there is some gossip among these citizens because they claim a Santa Claus with such a breath on him as our Santa Claus has is a little out of line.

And once we are somewhat embarrassed when a lot of little kids going home with their parents from a late Christmas party somewhere gather about Santa Claus with shouts of childish glee, and some of them wish to climb up Santa Claus' legs. Naturally, Santa Claus gets a little peevish, and calls them a few names, and one of the parents comes up and wishes to know what is the idea of Santa Claus using such language, and Santa Claus takes a punch at the parent, all of which is no doubt astonishing to the little kids who have an idea of Santa Claus as a very kindly old guy.

Well, finally we arrive in front of the place where Dancing Dan says Miss Muriel O'Neill and her grandmamma live, and it is nothing but a tenement house not far back of Madison Square Garden, and furthermore it is a walkup, and at this time there are no lights burning in the joint except a gas jet in the main hall, and by the light of this jet we look at the names on the letter boxes, such as you always find in the hall of these joints, and we see that Miss Muriel O'Neill and her grandmamma live on the fifth floor.

This is the top floor, and personally I do not like the idea of walking up five flights of stairs, and I am willing to let Dancing Dan and Good Time Charley go, but Dancing Dan insists we must all go, and finally I agree because Charley is commencing to argue that the right way for us to do is to get on the roof and let Santa Claus go down a chimney, and is making so much noise I am afraid he will wake somebody up.

So up the stairs we climb and finally we come to a door on the top floor that has a little card in a slot that says O'Neill, so we know we reach our destination. Dancing Dan first tries the knob, and right away the door opens, and we are in a little two- or three-room flat, with not much furniture in it, and what furniture there is, is very poor. One single gas jet is burning near a bed in a room just off the one the door opens into, and by this light we see a very old doll is sleeping on the bed, so we judge this is nobody but Gammer O'Neill.

On her face is a large smile, as if she is dreaming of something very pleasant. On a chair at the head of the bed is hung a long black stocking, and it seems to be such a stocking as is often patched and mended, so I can see that what Miss Muriel O'Neill tells Dancing Dan about her grandmamma hanging up her stocking is really true, although up to this time I have my doubts.

Finally Dancing Dan unslings the sack on his back, and takes out his package, and unties this package, and all of a sudden out pops a raft of big diamond bracelets, and diamond rings, and diamond brooches, and diamond necklaces, and I do not know what else in the way of diamonds, and Dancing Dan and I begin stuffing these diamonds into the stocking and Good Time Charley pitches in and helps us.

There are enough diamonds to fill the stocking to the muzzle, and it is no small stocking, at that, and I judge that Gammer O'Neill has a pretty fair set of bunting sticks when she is young. In fact, there are so many diamonds that we have enough left over to make a nice little pile on the chair after we fill the stocking plumb up, leaving a nice diamond-studded vanity case sticking out the top where we figure it will hit Gammer O'Neill's eye when she wakes up.

And it is not until I get out in the fresh air again that all of a sudden I remember seeing large headlines in the afternoon papers about a five-hundred-G's stickup in the afternoon of one of the biggest diamond merchants in Maiden Lane while he is sitting in his office, and I also recall once hearing rumors that Dancing Dan is one of the best lonehand git-'em-up guys in the world.

Naturally, I commence to wonder if I am in the proper company when I am with Dancing Dan, even if he is Santa Claus. So I leave him on the next corner arguing with Good Time Charley about whether they ought to go and find some more presents somewhere, and look for other stockings to stuff, and I hasten on home and go to bed.

The next day I find I have such a noggin that I do not care to stir around, and in fact I do not stir around much for a couple of weeks.

Then one night I drop around to Good Time Charley's little speakeasy, and ask Charley what is doing.

'Well,' Charley says, 'many things are doing, and personally,' he says, 'I'm greatly surprised I do not see you at Gammer O'Neill's wake. You know Gammer O'Neill leaves this wicked old world a couple of days after Christmas,' Good Time Charley says, 'and,' he says, 'Miss Muriel O'Neill states that Doc Moggs claims it is at least a day after she is entitled to go, but she is sustained,' Charley says, 'by great happiness in finding her stocking filled with beautiful gifts on Christmas morning.

'According to Miss Muriel O'Neill,' Charley says, 'Gammer O'Neill dies practically convinced that there is a Santa Claus, although of course,' he says, 'Miss Muriel O'Neill does not tell her the real owner of the gifts, an all-right guy by the name of Shapiro leaves the gifts with her after Miss Muriel O'Neill notifies him of the finding of same.

'It seems,' Charley says, 'this Shapiro is a tender-hearted guy, who is willing to help keep Gammer O'Neill with us a little longer when Doc Moggs says leaving the gifts with her will do it.

'So,' Charley says, 'everything is quite all right, as the coppers cannot figure anything except that maybe the rascal who takes the gifts from Shapiro gets conscience-stricken, and leaves them the first place he can, and Miss Muriel O'Neill receives a ten-G's reward for finding the gifts and returning them. And,' Charley says, 'I hear Dancing Dan is in San Francisco and is figuring on reforming and becoming a dancing teacher, so he can marry Miss Muriel O'Neill, and of course,' he says, 'we all hope and trust she never learn any details of Dancing Dan's career.'

Well, it is Christmas Eve a year later that I run into a guy by the name of Shotgun Sam, who is mobbed up with Heine Schmitz in Harlem, and who is a very, very obnoxious character indeed.

'Well, well, well,' Shotgun says, 'the last time I see you is another Christmas Eve like this, and you are coming out of Good Time Charley's joint, and,' he says, 'you certainly have your pots on.'

'Well, Shotgun,' I says, 'I am sorry you get such a wrong impression of me, but the truth is,' I say, 'on the occasion you speak of, I am suffering from a dizzy feeling in my head.'

'It is all right with me,' Shotgun says. 'I have a tip this guy Dancing Dan is in Good Time Charley's the night I see you, and Mockie Morgan, and Gunner Jack and me are casing the joint, because,' he says, 'Heine Schmitz is all sored up at Dan over some doll, although of course,' Shotgun says, 'it is all right now as Heine has another doll.

'Anyway,' he says, 'we never get to see Dancing Dan. We watch the joint from six-thirty in the evening until daylight Christmas morning, and nobody goes in all night but old Ooky the Santa Claus guy in his Santa Claus makeup, and,' Shotgun says, 'nobody comes out except you and Good Time Charley and Ooky.

'Well,' Shotgun says, 'it is a great break for Dancing Dan he never goes in or comes out of Good Time Charley's, at that, because,' he says, 'we are waiting for him on the second-floor front of the building across the way with some nice little sawed-offs, and are under orders from Heine not to miss.'

'Well, Shotgun,' I say, 'Merry Christmas.'

'Well, all right,' Shotgun says, 'Merry Christmas.'

CHRISTMAS DIARIES

'MORNING MOST BRILLIANT' *FROM THE* DIARY OF REV FRANCIS KILVERT

Robert Francis Kilvert was born at Hardenhuish, near Chippenham, in Wiltshire on 3 December 1840. He was the second child of the rector of the parish, the Rev Robert Kilvert, and had one brother and four sisters. Francis Kilvert spent his early years at Hardenhuish, was educated privately, went in due course to Wadham College, Oxford, and entered the Church. He became vicar of Bredwardine in Herefordshire in 1877. In 1879 he married Elizabeth Rowland, whom he had met during a visit to Paris. But after little more than a month of marriage, Kilvert died suddenly of peritonitis, aged only thirty-nine. His diaries were discovered many years later, and survive as a charming portrait of nineteenth-century rural Britain.

Sunday, Christmas Day

As I lay awake praying in the early morning I thought I heard a sound of distant bells. It was an intense frost. I sat down in my bath upon a sheet of thick ice which broke in the middle into large pieces whilst sharp points and jagged edges stuck all round the sides of the tub like chevaux de frise, not particularly comforting to the naked thighs and loins, for the keen ice cut like broken glass. The ice water stung and scorched like fire. I had to collect the floating pieces of ice and pile them on a chair before I could use the sponge and then I had to thaw the sponge in my hands for it was a mass of ice. The morning was most brilliant. Walked to the Sunday School with Gibbins and the road sparkled with millions of rainbows, the seven colours gleaming in every glittering point of hoar frost. The Church was very cold in spite of two roaring stove fires. Mr V. preached and went to Bettws.

Monday, 26 December

Much warmer and almost a thaw. Left Clyro at 11 a.m.

At Chippenham my father and John were on the platform. After dinner we opened a hamper of game sent by the Venables, and found in it a pheasant, a hare, a brace of rabbits, a brace of woodcocks, and a turkey. Just like them, and their constant kindness.

Tuesday, 27 December
After dinner drove into Chippenham with Perch and bought a pair of skates at Benk's for 17/6. Across the fields to the Draycot water and the young Awdry ladies chaffed me about my new skates. I had not been on skates since I was here last, 5 years ago, and was very awkward for the first ten minutes, but the knack soon came again. There was a distinguished company on the ice, Lady Dangan, Lord and Lady Royston and Lord George Paget all skating. Also Lord and Lady Sydney and a Mr Calcroft, whom they all of course called the Hangman. I had the honour of being knocked down by Lord Royston, who was coming round suddenly on the outside edge. A large fire of logs burning within an enclosure of wattled hurdles. Harriet Awdry skated beautifully and jumped over a half sunken punt. Arthur Law skating jumped over a chair on its legs.

Wednesday, 28 December
An inch of snow fell last night and as we walked to Draycot to skate the snow storm began again. As we passed Langley Burrell Church we heard the strains of the quadrille band on the ice at Draycot. The afternoon grew murky and when we began to skate the air was thick with falling snow. But it soon stopped and gangs of labourers were at work immediately sweeping away the new fallen snow and skate cuttings of ice. The Lancers was beautifully skated. When it grew dark the ice was lighted with Chinese lanterns, and the intense glare of blue, green, and crimson lights and magnesium riband made the whole place as light as day. Then people skated with torches.

Thursday, 29 December
Skating at Draycot again with Perch. Fewer people on the ice today. No quadrille band, torches or fireworks, but it was very pleasant, cosy and sociable. Yesterday when the Lancers was being skated Lord Royston was directing the figures. Harriet Awdry corrected him in one figure and he was quite wrong. But he immediately left the quadrille and sat down sulking on the bank, saying to one of his friends, 'Those abominable Miss Awdrys have contradicted me about the Lancers'. This was overheard and repeated to Harriet by a mutual friend, and the next time she saw him she said meaningly, 'Lord Royston, sometimes remarks are overheard and repeated', or something to that effect. However soon after he wanted to make it up and asked her to skate up the ice hand in hand with him. 'Certainly *not*, Lord Royston,' she said. Lady Royston skates very nicely and seems very nice. A sledge chair was put on the ice and Lady Royston and Lady Dangan, Margaret, Fanny, Maria, and Harriet Awdry were drawn about in it by turns, Charles Awdry pushing behind and Edmund and Arthur and Walter pulling with ropes. It was a capital team and went at a tremendous pace up and down the ice. A German ladies' maid from Draycot House was skating and making ridiculous antics.

New Year's Day
My Mother, Perch and I sat up last night to watch the old year out and the New Year in. The wind was in the North and the sound of the bells came faintly and muffled over the snow from Chippenham and Kington. We opened the dining room window to 'loose in' the sound of the chimes and 'the New Year' as they say in Wales. It was bitter cold, but we went to the door, Perch and I, to hear better. I was carrying my travelling clock in my hand and as we stood on the terrace just outside the front

door, the little clock struck midnight with its tinkling silvery bell in the keen frost. We thought we could hear three peals of Church bells, Chippenham, St Paul's, and very faintly Kington. 'Ring happy bells across the snow.'

When Perch came back from skating at Draycot last night, he amused us with an account of Friday's and Saturday's doings on the ice. On Friday they had a quadrille band from Malmesbury, skated quadrilles, Lancers, and Sir Roger de Coverley. Then they skated up and down with torches, ladies and gentlemen pairing off and skating arm in arm, each with a torch. There were numbers of Chinese lanterns all round the water, blue, crimson and green lights, magnesium riband, and a fire balloon was sent up. Maria Awdry, forgetting herself and the passage of time, inadvertently spoke to Perch calling him 'Teddy' instead of 'Mr Kilvert'. Having done which she perceived her mistake, turned 'away and smote herself on the mouth', while Perch 'looked at her with a face like a stone'. While people were standing about in groups or skating up and down gently young Spencer skated up suddenly with outstretched arm to shake hands with Teddy. At the critical moment his skate hitched and he lost his balance and made a deep but involuntary obeisance before Perch, describing 'an attenuated arch', with his fingers and toes resting on the ice. People hid their faces, turned and skated away with a sour smile or grinning with repressed laughter. Perch stood still waiting for the 'attenuated arch' to unbind itself and retrieve its erect posture, 'looking on with a face like a stone'. Gradually the 'arch' rose from its deep obeisance. The arch was the arch described by an attenuated tom cat. During the torch skating Harriet Awdry hurled her half-burnt torch ashore. Lord Cowley was walking up and down the path on the bank watching with great impatience the skaters whom he detests. The fiery torch came whirling and flaming through the dark and hit the noble diplomatist sharply across the shins, rebounding from which it lay blazing at the foot of a tree. Lord Cowley was very angry. 'I wish these people wouldn't throw their torches about here at me,' grumbled his lordship. 'Come away and hide behind the island or he'll see you,' said Perch to Harriet. So they glided away and from the cover of the island they watched Lord Cowley angrily beating the blazing torch against the ground to try to put it out. But the more he beat it, the more the torch flamed and showered sparks into his face. Harriet described the incident thus, 'I hit old Cowley such a crack over the shins'.

'A NICE BOY' *FROM* THE DIARY OF A NOBODY *BY* GEORGE & WEEDON GROSSMITH

George and Weedon Grossmith were born in London in 1847 and 1852 respectively to a theatrical family who were friends with Henry Irving and Ellen Terry. George became a popular composer and performer of comic songs as well as a successful actor. Weedon trained as a painter at the Slade and the Royal Academy, but soon turned to acting like his brother. *The Diary of a Nobody* began life as a series of humorous columns about the self-important suburban Londoner Charles Pooter and his family, which the brothers wrote together for *Punch* magazine. The columns were later expanded into a novel, which was published in 1892 to instant acclaim and has remained in print ever since. George died in 1912, followed by his brother in 1919.

December 19

THE ANNUAL invitation came to spend Christmas with Carrie's mother – the usual family festive gathering to which we always look forward. Lupin declined to go. I was astounded, and expressed my surprise and disgust. Lupin then obliged us with the following Radical speech: 'I hate a family gathering at Christmas. What does it mean? Why, someone says: "Ah! we miss poor Uncle James, who was here last year," and we all begin to snivel. Someone else says: "It's two years since poor Aunt Liz used to sit in that corner." Then we all begin to snivel again. Then another gloomy relation says: "Ah! I wonder whose turn it will be next?" Then we all snivel again, and proceed to eat and drink too much; and they don't discover until *I* get up that we have been seated thirteen at dinner.'

December 20

Went to Smirksons', the drapers, in the Strand, who this year have turned out everything in the shop and devoted the whole place to the sale of Christmas cards. Shop crowded with people, who seemed to take up the cards rather roughly, and, after a hurried glance at them, throw them down again. I remarked to one of the young persons serving, that carelessness appeared to be a disease with some purchasers. The observation was scarcely out of my mouth, when my thick coat-sleeve caught against a large pile of expensive cards in boxes one on top of the other, and threw them down. The manager came forward, looking very much annoyed, and picking up several cards from the ground, said to one of the assistants, with a palpable side-glance at me: 'Put these amongst the sixpenny goods; they can't be sold for a shilling now.' The result was, I felt it my duty to buy some of these damaged cards.

I had to buy more and pay more than intended. Unfortunately I did not examine them all, and when I got home I discovered a vulgar card with a picture of a fat nurse with two babies, one black and the other white, and the words: 'We wish Pa a Merry Christmas.' I tore up the card and threw it away. Carrie said the great disadvantage of going out in Society and increasing the number of our friends was, that we should have to send out nearly two dozen cards this year.

December 21
To save the postman a miserable Christmas, we follow the example of all unselfish people, and send out our cards early. Most of the cards had fingermarks, which I did not notice at night. I shall buy all future cards in the daytime. Lupin (who, ever since he has had the appointment with a stock and share broker, does not seem over-scrupulous in his dealings) told me never to rub out the pencilled price on the backs of the cards. I asked him why. Lupin said: 'Suppose your card is marked *9d*. Well, all you have to do is to pencil a 3 – and a long down-stroke after it – in *front* of the ninepence, and people will think you have given five times the price for it.'

In the evening Lupin was very low-spirited, and I reminded him that behind the clouds the sun was shining. He said: 'Ugh! it never shines on me.' I said: 'Stop, Lupin, my boy; you are worried about Daisy Mutlar. Don't think of her any more. You ought to congratulate yourself on having got off a very bad bargain. Her notions are far too grand for our simple tastes.' He jumped up and said: 'I won't allow one word to be uttered against her. She's worth the whole bunch of your friends put together, that inflated sloping-head of a Perkupp included.' I left the room with silent dignity, but caught my foot in the mat.

December 23
I exchanged no words with Lupin in the morning; but as he seemed to be in exuberant spirits in the evening I ventured to ask him where he intended to spend his Christmas. He replied: 'Oh, most likely at the Mutlars.'

In wonderment, I said: 'What! after your engagement has been broken off?'

Lupin said: 'Who said it is off?'

I said: 'You have given us both to understand –'

He interrupted me by saying: 'Well, never mind what I said. *It is on again – there!*'

December 24
I am a poor man, but I would gladly give ten shillings to find out who sent me the insulting Christmas card I received this morning. I never insult people; why should they insult me? The worst part of the transaction is, that I find myself suspecting all my friends. The handwriting on the envelope is evidently disguised, being written sloping the wrong way. I cannot think either Gowing or Cummings would do such a mean thing. Lupin denied all knowledge of it, and I believe him; although I disapprove of his laughing and sympathizing with the offender. Mr Franching would be above such an act; and I don't think any of the Mutlars would descend to such a course. I wonder if

Pitt, that impudent clerk at the office, did it? Or Mrs Birrell, the charwoman, or Burwin-Fosselton? The writing is too good for the former.

Christmas Day

We caught the 10.20 train at Paddington, and spent a pleasant day at Carrie's mother's. The country was quite nice and pleasant, although the roads were sloppy. We dined in the middle of the day, just ten of us, and talked over old times. If everybody had a nice, *un*interfering mother-in-law, such as I have, what a deal of happiness there would be in the world. Being all in good spirits, I proposed her health; and I made, I think, a very good speech.

I concluded, rather neatly, by saying: 'On an occasion like this – whether relatives, friends, or acquaintances – we are all inspired with good feelings towards each other. We are of one mind, and think only of love and friendship. Those who have quarrelled with absent friends should kiss and make it up. Those who happily have *not* fallen out, can kiss all the same.'

I saw the tears in the eyes of both Carrie and her mother, and must say I felt very flattered by the compliment. That dear old Reverend John Panzy Smith, who married us, made a most cheerful and amusing speech, and said he should act on my suggestion respecting the kissing. He then walked round the table and kissed all the ladies, including Carrie. Of course one did not object to this; but I was more than staggered when a young fellow named Moss, who was a stranger to me, and who had scarcely spoken a word through dinner, jumped up suddenly with a sprig of mistletoe, and exclaimed: 'Hulloh! I don't see why I shouldn't be on in this scene.' Before one could realize what he was about to do, he kissed Carrie and the rest of the ladies.

Fortunately the matter was treated as a joke, and we all

laughed; but it was a dangerous experiment, and I felt very uneasy for a moment as to the result. I subsequently referred to the matter to Carrie, but she said: 'Oh, he's not much more than a boy.' I said that he had a very large moustache for a boy. Carrie replied: 'I didn't say he was not a nice boy.'

'I DON'T KNOW WHAT'S HAPPENED TO CHRISTMAS LATELY' *FROM* THE GROWING PAINS OF ADRIAN MOLE *BY* SUE TOWNSEND

Sue Townsend was born in Leicester on 2 April 1946. She left school at fifteen, married a few years later and had three children. In 1978 she joined a Writers Group at the Phoenix Art Centre in Leicester and began writing. *The Secret Diary of Adrian Mole Aged 13¾* and its sequel, *The Growing Pains of Adrian Mole*, were published during the 1980s and became extremely popular bestsellers. Three more Adrian Mole sequels followed. Together the Mole diaries have sold over eight million copies, and have been adapted for radio, television and theatre. Sue Townsend lives in Leicester.

Saturday December 25th
CHRISTMAS DAY

G OT UP at 7.30.
Had a wash and a shave, cleaned teeth, squeezed spots
then went downstairs and put kettle on. I don't know what's
happened to Christmas Day lately, but something has. It's just
not the same as it used to be when I was a kid. My mother
fed and cleaned Rosie, and I did the same to Bert. Then we
went into the lounge and opened our presents. I was dead
disappointed when I saw the shape of my present. I could tell
at a glance that it didn't contain a single microchip. OK a
sheepskin coat is warm but there's nothing you can *do* with
it, except wear it.

In fact after only two hours of wearing it, I got bored and
took it off. However, my mother was ecstatic about her egg
timer; she said, 'Wow, another one for my collection.' Rosie
ignored the chocolate Santa I bought her. That's 79 pence
wasted! *This is what I got:*

3/4 length sheepskin coat (out of Littlewoods catalogue)

Beano Annual (a sad disappointment, this year's is very childish)

Slippers (like Michael Caine wears, although not many people know that)

Swiss army knife (my father is hoping I'll go out into the fresh air and use it)

Tin of humbugs (supposedly from the dog)

Knitted Balaclava helmet (from Grandma Mole. Yuk! Yuk!)

Boys' Book of Sport (from Grandma Sugden: Stanley Matthews on cover)

I was glad when Auntie Susan and her friend Gloria turned up; at 11 o'clock. Their talk is very metropolitan and daring; and Gloria is dead glamorous and sexy. She wears frilly dresses, and lacy tights, and high heels. And she's got an itsy-bitsy voice that makes my stomach go soft. Why she's friends with Auntie Susan, who is a prison warder, smokes Panama cigars and has got hairy fingers, I'll never know.

The turkey was OK. But would have been better if the giblets and the plastic bag had been removed before cooking. Bert made chauvinist remarks during the carving. He leered at Gloria's cleavage and said, 'Give me a nice piece of breast.' Gloria wasn't a bit shocked, but I went dead red, and pretended that I'd dropped my cracker under the table.

When my mother asked me which part of the turkey I wanted, I said, 'A wing please!' I really wanted breast, leg, or thigh. But wing was the only part of the bird without sexual connotations. Rosie had a few spoons of mashed potato and gravy. Her table manners are disgusting, even worse than Bert's.

I was given a glass of Bull's Blood wine and felt dead sensual. I talked brilliantly and with consummate wit for an hour, but then my mother told me to leave the table, saying, 'One sniff of the barmaid's apron and his mouth runs away with him.'

The Queen didn't look very happy when she was giving her speech. Perhaps she got lousy Christmas presents this year, like me. Bert and Auntie Susan had a disagreement about the Royal Family. Bert said he would 'move the whole lot of 'em into council houses in Liverpool'.

Gloria said, 'Oh Bert that's a bit drastic. Milton Keynes would be more suitable. They're not used to roughing it you know.'

In the evening I went round to see Grandma and my father. Grandma forced me to eat four mincepies, and asked me why I wasn't wearing my new Balaclava helmet. My father didn't say anything; he was dead drunk in an armchair.

Sunday December 26th
FIRST AFTER CHRISTMAS

Pandora and I exchanged presents in a candlelit ceremony in my bedroom. I put the solid gold chain round her neck, and she put a 70% wool, 10% cashmere, 20% acrylic scarf round my neck.

A cashmere scarf at fifteen!

I'll make sure the label can be seen by the public at all times.

Pandora went barmy about the solid gold chain. She kept looking at herself in the mirror, she said, 'Thank you, darling, but how on earth can you afford solid gold? It must have cost you at least a hundred pounds!'

I didn't tell her that Woolworth's were selling them cheap at two pounds a go.

Monday December 27th
BOXING DAY, HOLIDAY (UK EXCEPT SCOTLAND). HOLIDAY (CANADA).
BANK HOLIDAY (SCOTLAND). HOLIDAY (REPUBLIC OF IRELAND)

Just had a note handed to me from a kid riding a new BMX.

Dear heart,
I'm awfully sorry but I will have to cancel our trip to the cinema
to see *ET*.
    I woke up this morning with an ugly disfiguring rash around
my neck.
    Yours sincerely,
    Pandora
P.S. I am allergic to non-precious metal.

CHRISTMAS CAROLING

'CAROL BARKING' *FROM* CIDER WITH ROSIE *BY* LAURIE LEE

Laurie Lee was born in Stroud, Gloucestershire, in 1914, and was educated at Slad village school and Stroud Central School. At the age of nineteen he walked to London and then travelled on foot through Spain, where he was trapped by the outbreak of the Civil War. He later returned by crossing the Pyrenees, as described in his book *As I Walked Out One Midsummer Morning*. In 1950 he married Catherine Polge and they had one daughter. Laurie Lee died in May 1997. *Cider With Rosie* is Lee's memoir of childhood in the remote Cotswold village where he grew up. It is a vivid, enchanting evocation of a world that is both immediate and real but also belongs to a now-distant past.

LATER, TOWARDS Christmas, there was heavy snow, which raised the roads to the top of the hedges. There were millions of tons of the lovely stuff, plastic, pure, all-purpose, which nobody owned, which one could carve or tunnel, eat, or just throw about. It covered the hills and cut off the villages, but nobody thought of rescues; for there was hay in the barns and flour in the kitchens, the women baked bread, the cattle were fed and sheltered – we'd been cut off before, after all.

The week before Christmas, when snow seemed to lie thickest, was the moment for carol-singing; and when I think back to those nights it is to the crunch of snow and to the lights of the lanterns on it. Carol-singing in my village was a special tithe for the boys, the girls had little to do with it. Like hay-making, blackberrying, stone-clearing, and wishing-people-a-happy-Easter, it was one of our seasonal perks.

By instinct we knew just when to begin it; a day too soon and we should have been unwelcome, a day too late and we should have received lean looks from people whose bounty was already exhausted. When the true moment came, exactly balanced, we recognized it and were ready.

So as soon as the wood had been stacked in the oven to dry

for the morning fire, we put on our scarves and went out through the streets, calling loudly between our hands, till the various boys who knew the signal ran out from their houses to join us.

One by one they came stumbling over the snow, swinging their lanterns around their heads, shouting and coughing horribly.

'Coming carol-barking then?'

We were the Church Choir, so no answer was necessary. For a year we had praised the Lord out of key, and as a reward for this service – on top of the Outing – we now had the right to visit all the big houses, to sing our carols and collect our tribute.

To work them all in meant a five-mile foot journey over wild and generally snowed-up country. So the first thing we did was to plan our route; a formality, as the route never changed. All the same, we blew on our fingers and argued; and then we chose our Leader. This was not binding, for we all fancied ourselves as Leaders, and he who started the night in that position usually trailed home with a bloody nose.

Eight of us set out that night. There was Sixpence the Tanner, who had never sung in his life (he just worked his mouth in church); the brothers Horace and Boney, who were always fighting everybody and always getting the worst of it; Clergy Green, the preaching maniac; Walt the bully, and my two brothers. As we went down the lane other boys, from other villages, were already about the hills, bawling 'Kingwenslush', and shouting through keyholes 'Knock on the knocker! Ring at the Bell! Give us a penny for singing so well!' They weren't an approved charity as we were, the Choir; but competition was in the air.

Our first call as usual was the house of the Squire, and we trouped nervously down his drive. For light we had candles in marmalade-jars suspended on loops of string, and they threw pale gleams on the towering snowdrifts that stood on each side of the drive. A blizzard was blowing, but we were well wrapped up, with Army puttees on our legs, woollen hats on our heads, and several scarves around our ears.

As we approached the Big House across its white silent lawns, we too grew respectfully silent. The lake near by was stiff and black, the waterfall frozen and still. We arranged ourselves shuffling around the big front door, then knocked and announced the Choir.

A maid bore the tidings of our arrival away into the echoing distances of the house, and while we waited we cleared our throats noisily. Then she came back, and the door was left ajar for us, and we were bidden to begin. We brought no music, the carols were in our heads. 'Let's give 'em "Wild Shepherds",' said Jack. We began in confusion, plunging into a wreckage of keys, of different words and tempo; but we gathered our strength; he who sang loudest took the rest of us with him, and the carol took shape if not sweetness.

This huge stone house, with its ivied walls, was always a mystery to us. What were those gables, those rooms and attics, those narrow windows veiled by the cedar trees. As we sang 'Wild Shepherds' we craned our necks, gaping into that lamplit hall which we had never entered; staring at the muskets and untenanted chairs, the great tapestries furred by dust – until suddenly, on the stairs, we saw the old Squire himself standing and listening with his head on one side.

He didn't move until we'd finished; then slowly he tottered towards us, dropped two coins in our box with a trembling hand, scratched his name in the book we carried, gave us each a long look with his moist blind eyes, then turned away in silence.

As though released from a spell, we took a few sedate steps, then broke into a run for the gate. We didn't stop till we were out of the grounds. Impatient, at last, to discover the extent of his bounty, we squatted by the cowsheds, held our lanterns over the book, and saw that he had written 'Two Shillings'. This was quite a good start. No one of any worth in the district would dare to give us less than the Squire.

So with money in the box, we pushed on up the valley, pouring scorn on each other's performance. Confident now, we began to consider our quality and whether one carol was not better suited to us than another. Horace, Walt said, shouldn't sing at all; his voice was beginning to break. Horace disputed this and there was a brief token battle – they fought as they walked, kicking up divots of snow, then they forgot it, and Horace still sang.

Steadily we worked through the length of the valley, going from house to house, visiting the lesser and the greater gentry – the farmers, the doctors, the merchants, the majors, and other exalted persons. It was freezing hard and blowing too; yet not for a moment did we feel the cold. The snow blew into our faces, into our eyes and mouths, soaked through our puttees, got into our boots, and dripped from our woollen caps. But we did not care. The collecting-box grew heavier, and the list of names in the book longer and more extravagant, each trying to outdo the other.

Mile after mile we went, fighting against the wind, falling into snowdrifts, and navigating by the lights of the houses. And yet we never saw our audience. We called at house after house; we sang in courtyards and porches, outside windows, or in the damp gloom of hallways; we heard voices from hidden rooms; we smelt rich clothes and strange hot food; we saw maids bearing in dishes or carrying away coffee-cups; we received nuts, cakes, figs, preserved ginger, dates, cough-drops, and money; but we never once saw our patrons. We sang as it were at the castle walls, and apart from the Squire, who had shown himself to prove that he was still alive, we never expected it otherwise.

As the night drew on there was trouble with Boney. 'Noël', for instance, had a rousing harmony which Boney persisted in singing, and singing flat. The others forbade him to sing it at all, and Boney said he would fight us. Picking himself up, he agreed we were right, then he disappeared altogether. He just turned away and walked into the snow and wouldn't answer when we called him back. Much later, as we reached a far point up the valley, somebody said 'Hark!' and we stopped to listen. Far away across the fields from the distant village came the sound of a frail voice singing, singing 'Noël', and singing it flat – it was Boney, branching out on his own.

We approached our last house high up on the hill, the place of Joseph the farmer. For him we had chosen a special carol, which was about the other Joseph, so that we always felt that singing it added a spicy cheek to the night. The last stretch of country to reach his farm was perhaps the most difficult of all. In these rough bare lanes, open to all winds, sheep were buried and wagons lost. Huddled together, we tramped in one another's footsteps, powdered snow blew into our screwed-up eyes, the candles burnt low, some blew out altogether, and we talked loudly above the gale.

Crossing, at last, the frozen mill-stream – whose wheel in summer still turned a barren mechanism – we climbed up to Joseph's farm. Sheltered by trees, warm on its bed of snow, it seemed always to be like this. As always it was late; as always this was our final call. The snow had a fine crust upon it, and the old trees sparkled like tinsel.

We grouped ourselves round the farmhouse porch. The sky cleared, and broad streams of stars ran down over the valley and away to Wales. On Slad's white slopes, seen through the black sticks of its woods, some red lamps still burned in the windows.

Everything was quiet; everywhere there was the faint crackling silence of the winter night. We started singing, and we were all moved by the words and the sudden trueness of our voices. Pure, very clear, and breathless we sang:

> As Joseph was a walking
> He heard an angel sing;
> 'This night shall be the birth-time
> Of Christ the Heavenly King.
>
> He neither shall be bornèd
> In Housen nor in hall,
> Nor in a place of paradise
> But in an ox's stall . . .'

And two thousand Christmases became real to us then; the houses, the halls, the places of paradise had all been visited; the stars were bright to guide the Kings through the snow; and across the farmyard we could hear the beasts in their stalls. We were given roast apples and hot mince-pies, in our nostrils were spices like myrrh, and in our wooden box, as we headed back for the village, there were golden gifts for all.

'DULCE DOMUM' *FROM* THE WIND IN THE WILLOWS *BY* KENNETH GRAHAME

Kenneth Grahame was born in Edinburgh on 8 March 1859. He was brought up by his grandmother in Cookham Dene in Berkshire and went to school in Oxford before starting work at the Bank of England. He was unable to go to university because of his family's lack of money. His stories and essays were initially published in periodicals such as the *Yellow Book* and then collected together as *Pagan Papers* (1893). This was followed by *The Golden Age* (1895) and *Dream Days* (1898). *The Wind in the Willows* (1908) is based on letters and stories that Grahame made for his only child, Alistair. The novel's popularity grew slowly over the years and A. A. Milne's dramatisation of the novel as *Toad of Toad Hall* brought it greater success. Kenneth Grahame died on 6 July 1932.

In this extract, Mole, who has been staying at Rat's comfortable house by the river bank, has been overcome by homesickness, and the friends are setting out to find his long-forgotten dwelling.

'WHEREVER ARE you (hic) going to (hic), Ratty?' cried the tearful Mole, looking up in alarm.

'We're going to find that home of yours, old fellow,' replied the Rat pleasantly; 'so you had better come along, for it will take some finding, and we shall want your nose.'

'O, come back, Ratty, do!' cried the Mole, getting up and hurrying after him. 'It's no good, I tell you! It's too late, and too dark, and the place is too far off, and the snow's coming! And – and I never meant to let you know I was feeling that way about it – it was all an accident and a mistake! And think of River Bank, and your supper!'

'Hang River Bank, and supper too!' said the Rat heartily. 'I tell you, I'm going to find this place now, if I stay out all night. So cheer up, old chap, and take my arm, and we'll very soon be back there again.'

Still snuffling, pleading, and reluctant, Mole suffered himself to be dragged back along the road by his imperious companion, who by a flow of cheerful talk and anecdote endeavoured to beguile his spirits back and make the weary way seem shorter. When at last it seemed to the Rat that they must be nearing that part of the road where the Mole had been 'held up', he said, 'Now, no more talking. Business! Use your nose, and give your mind to it.'

They moved on in silence for some little way, when suddenly the Rat was conscious, through his arm that was linked in Mole's, of a faint sort of electric thrill that was passing down that animal's body. Instantly he disengaged himself, fell back a pace, and waited, all attention.

The signals were coming through!

Mole stood a moment rigid, while his uplifted nose, quivering slightly, felt the air.

Then a short, quick run forward – a fault – a check – a try back; and then a slow, steady, confident advance.

The Rat, much excited, kept close to his heels as the Mole, with something of the air of a sleep-walker, crossed a dry ditch, scrambled through a hedge, and nosed his way over a field open and trackless and bare in the faint starlight.

Suddenly, without giving warning, he dived; but the Rat was on the alert, and promptly followed him down the tunnel to which his unerring nose had faithfully led him.

It was close and airless, and the earthy smell was strong, and it seemed a long time to Rat ere the passage ended and he could stand erect and stretch and shake himself. The Mole struck a match, and by its light the Rat saw that they were standing in an open space, neatly swept and sanded underfoot, and directly facing them was Mole's little front door, with 'Mole End' painted, in Gothic lettering, over the bell-pull at the side.

Mole reached down a lantern from a nail on the wall and lit it, and the Rat, looking round him, saw that they were in a sort of fore-court. A garden-seat stood on one side of the door, and on the other, a roller; for the Mole, who was a tidy animal when at home, could not stand having his ground kicked up by other animals into little runs that ended in earth-heaps. On the walls hung wire baskets with ferns in them, alternating with brackets carrying plaster statuary – Garibaldi, and the infant Samuel, and Queen Victoria, and other heroes of modern Italy. Down one side of the fore-court ran a skittle-alley, with benches along it and little wooden tables marked with rings that hinted at beer-mugs. In the middle was a small round pond containing goldfish and surrounded by a cockle-shell border. Out of the centre of the pond rose a fanciful erection clothed in more cockle-shells and topped by a large silvered glass ball that reflected everything all wrong and had a very pleasing effect.

Mole's face beamed at the sight of all these objects so dear to him, and he hurried Rat through the door, lit a lamp in the hall, and took one glance round his old home. He saw the dust lying thick on everything, saw the cheerless, deserted look of the long-neglected house, and its narrow, meagre dimensions, its worn and shabby contents – and collapsed again on a hall-chair, his nose in his paws. 'O, Ratty!' he cried dismally, 'why ever did I do it? Why did I bring you to this poor, cold little place, on a night like this, when you might have been at River Bank by this time, toasting your toes before a blazing fire, with all your own nice things about you!'

The Rat paid no heed to his doleful self-reproaches. He was running here and there, opening doors, inspecting rooms and cupboards, and lighting lamps and candles and sticking them up everywhere. 'What a capital little house this is!' he called out cheerily. 'So compact! So well planned! Everything here and everything in its place! We'll make a jolly night of it. The first thing we want is a good fire; I'll see to that – I always know where to find things. So this is the parlour? Splendid! Your own idea, those little sleeping-bunks in the wall? Capital! Now, I'll fetch the wood and the coals, and you get a duster,

Mole – you'll find one in the drawer of the kitchen table – and try and smarten things up a bit. Bustle about, old chap!'

Encouraged by his inspiriting companion, the Mole roused himself and dusted and polished with energy and heartiness, while the Rat, running to and fro with armfuls of fuel, soon had a cheerful blaze roaring up the chimney. He hailed the Mole to come and warm himself; but Mole promptly had another fit of the blues, dropping down on a couch in dark despair and burying his face in his duster.

'Rat,' he moaned, 'how about your supper, you poor, cold, hungry, weary animal? I've nothing to give you – nothing – not a crumb!'

'What a fellow you are for giving in!' said the Rat reproachfully. 'Why, only just now I saw a sardine-opener on the kitchen dresser, quite distinctly; and everybody knows that means there are sardines about somewhere in the neighbourhood. Rouse yourself! Pull yourself together, and come with me and forage.'

They went and foraged accordingly, hunting through every cupboard and turning out every drawer. The result was not so very depressing after all, though of course it might have been better; a tin of sardines – a box of captain's biscuits, nearly full – and a German sausage encased in silver paper.

'There's a banquet for you!' observed the Rat, as he arranged the table. 'I know some animals who would give their ears to be sitting down to supper with us tonight!'

'No bread!' groaned the Mole dolorously; 'no butter, no –'

'No *pâté de foie gras*, no champagne!' continued the Rat, grinning. 'And that reminds me – what's that little door at the end of the passage? Your cellar, of course! Every luxury in this house! Just you wait a minute.'

He made for the cellar door, and presently reappeared, somewhat dusty, with a bottle of beer in each paw and another under each arm. 'Self-indulgent beggar you seem to be, Mole,' he observed. 'Deny yourself nothing. This is really the jolliest little place I ever was in. Now, wherever did you pick up those prints? Make the place look so home-like, they do. No wonder you're so fond of it, Mole. Tell us all about it, and how you came to make it what it is.'

Then, while the Rat busied himself fetching plates, and knives and forks, and mustard which he mixed in an egg-cup, the Mole, his bosom still heaving with the stress of his recent emotion, related – somewhat shyly at first, but with more freedom as he warmed to his subject – how this was planned, and how that was thought out, and how this was got through a windfall from an aunt, and that was a wonderful find and a bargain, and this other thing was bought out of laborious savings and a certain amount of 'going without'. His spirits finally quite restored, he must needs go and caress his possessions, and take a lamp and show off their points to his visitor, and expatiate on them, quite forgetful of the supper they both so much needed; Rat, who was desperately hungry but strove to conceal it, nodding seriously, examining with a puckered brow, and saying, 'Wonderful', and 'Most remarkable', at intervals, when the chance for an observation was given him.

At last the Rat succeeded in decoying him to the table, and had just got seriously to work with the sardine-opener when sounds were heard from the fore-court without – sounds like the scuffling of small feet in the gravel and a confused murmur of tiny voices, while broken sentences reached them – 'No, all in a line – hold the lantern up a bit, Tommy – clear your throats first – no coughing after I say one, two, three. – Where's young Bill? – Here, come on, do, we're all a-waiting –'

'What's up?' inquired the Rat, pausing in his labours.

'I think it must be the field-mice,' replied the Mole, with a touch of pride in his manner. 'They go round carol-singing regularly at this time of the year. They're quite an institution in these parts. And they never pass me over – they come to Mole End last of all; and I used to give them hot drinks, and supper too sometimes, when I could afford it. It will be like old times to hear them again.'

'Let's have a look at them!' cried the Rat, jumping up and running to the door.

It was a pretty sight, and a seasonable one, that met their eyes when they flung the door open. In the fore-court, lit by the dim rays of a horn lantern, some eight or ten little field-mice stood in a semicircle, red worsted comforters round their throats, their fore-paws thrust deep into their pockets, their feet jigging for warmth. With bright beady eyes they glanced shyly at each other, sniggering a little, sniffing and applying coat-sleeves a good deal. As the door opened, one of the elder ones that carried the lantern was just saying, 'Now then, one, two, three!' and forthwith their shrill little voices uprose on the air, singing one of the old-time carols that their fore-fathers composed in fields that were fallow and held by frost, or when snow-bound in chimney corners, and handed down to be sung in the miry street to lamp-lit windows at Yule-time.

CAROL

Villagers all, this frosty tide,
Let your doors swing open wide,
Though wind may follow, and snow beside,
Yet draw us in by your fire to bide;
    Joy shall be yours in the morning!

Here we stand in the cold and the sleet,
Blowing fingers and stamping feet,
Come from far away you to greet –
You by the fire and we in the street –
    Bidding you joy in the morning!

For ere one half of the night was gone,
Sudden a star has led us on,
Raining bliss and benison –
Bliss tomorrow and more anon,
    Joy for every morning!

Goodman Joseph toiled through the snow –
Saw the star o'er a stable low;
Mary she might not further go –
Welcome thatch, and litter below!
    Joy was hers in the morning!

And then they heard the angels tell
'Who were the first to cry Nowell?
Animals all, as it befell,
In the stable where they did dwell!
    Joy shall be theirs in the morning!'

The voices ceased, the singers, bashful but smiling, exchanged sidelong glances, and silence succeeded – but for a moment only. Then, from up above and far away, down the tunnel they had so lately travelled was borne to their ears in a faint musical hum the sound of distant bells ringing a joyful and clangorous peal.

'Very well sung, boys!' cried the Rat heartily. 'And now come along in, all of you, and warm yourselves by the fire, and have something hot!'

'Yes, come along, field-mice,' cried the Mole eagerly. 'This is quite like old times! Shut the door after you. Pull up that settle to the fire. Now, you just wait a minute, while we – O, Ratty!' he cried in despair, plumping down on a seat, with tears impending. 'Whatever are we doing? We've nothing to give them!'

'You leave all that to me,' said the masterful Rat. 'Here, you with the lantern! Come over this way. I want to talk to you. Now, tell me, are there any shops open at this hour of the night?'

'Why, certainly, sir,' replied the field-mouse respectfully. 'At this time of the year our shops keep open to all sorts of hours.'

'Then look here!' said the Rat. 'You go off at once, you and your lantern, and you get me –'

Here much muttered conversation ensued, and the Mole only heard bits of it, such as –'Fresh, mind! – no, a pound of that will do – see you get Buggins's, for I won't have any other – no, only the best – if you can't get it there, try somewhere else – yes, of course, home-made, no tinned stuff – well then, do the best you can!' Finally, there was a chink of coin passing from paw to paw, the field-mouse was provided with an ample basket for his purchases, and off he hurried, he and his lantern.

The rest of the field-mice, perched in a row on the settle, their small legs swinging, gave themselves up to enjoyment of the fire, and toasted their chilblains till they tingled; while the Mole, failing to draw them into easy conversation, plunged into family history and made each of them recite the names of his numerous brothers, who were too young, it appeared, to be allowed to go out a-carolling this year, but looked forward very shortly to winning the parental consent.

The Rat, meanwhile, was busy examining the label on one of the beer-bottles. 'I perceive this to be Old Burton,' he remarked approvingly. '*Sensible* Mole! The very thing! Now we shall be able to mull some ale! Get the things ready, Mole, while I draw the corks.'

It did not take long to prepare the brew and thrust the tin heater well into the red heart of the fire; and soon every field-mouse was sipping and coughing and choking (for a little mulled ale goes a long way) and wiping his eyes and laughing and forgetting he had ever been cold in all his life.

'They act plays too, these fellows,' the Mole explained to the Rat. 'Make them up all by themselves, and act them afterwards. And very well they do it, too! They gave us a capital one last year, about a field-mouse who was captured at sea by a Barbary corsair, and made to row in a galley; and when he escaped and got home again, his lady-love had gone into a convent. Here, *you*! You were in it, I remember. Get up and recite a bit.'

The field-mouse addressed got up on his legs, giggled shyly, looked round the room, and remained absolutely tongue-tied. His comrades cheered him on, Mole coaxed and encouraged him, and the Rat went so far as to take him by the shoulders and shake him; but nothing could overcome his stage-fright. They were all busily engaged on him like watermen applying the Royal Humane Society's regulations to a case of long submersion, when the latch clicked, the door opened, and the field-mouse with the lantern reappeared, staggering under the weight of his basket.

There was no more talk of play-acting once the very real and solid contents of the basket had been tumbled out on the table. Under the generalship of Rat, everybody was set to do something or to fetch something. In a very few minutes supper was ready, and Mole, as he took the head of the table in a sort of dream, saw a lately barren board set thick with savoury comforts; saw his little friends' faces brighten and beam as they fell to without delay; and then let himself loose – for he was famished indeed – on the provender so magically provided, thinking what a happy home-coming this had turned out, after all. As they ate, they talked of old times, and the field-mice gave him the local gossip up to date, and answered as well as they could the hundred questions he had to ask them. The Rat said little or nothing, only taking care that each guest had what he wanted, and plenty of it, and that Mole had no trouble or anxiety about anything.

They clattered off at last, very grateful and showering wishes of the season, with their jacket pockets stuffed with remembrances for the small brothers and sisters at home. When the door had closed on the last of them and the chink of the lanterns had died away, Mole and Rat kicked the fire up, drew their chairs in, brewed themselves a last nightcap of mulled ale, and discussed the events of the long day. At last the Rat, with a tremendous yawn, said, 'Mole, old chap, I'm ready to drop. Sleepy is simply not the word. That your own bunk over on that side? Very well, then, I'll take this. What a ripping little house this is! Everything so handy!'

He clambered into his bunk and rolled himself well up in the blankets, and slumber gathered him forthwith, as a swath of barley is folded into the arms of the reaping-machine.

The weary Mole also was glad to turn in without delay, and soon had his head on his pillow, in great joy and contentment. But ere he closed his eyes he let them wander round his old room, mellow in the glow of the firelight that played or rested on familiar and friendly things which had long been unconsciously a part of him, and now smilingly received him back, without rancour. He was now in just the frame of mind that the tactful Rat had quietly worked to bring about in him. He saw clearly how plain and simple – how narrow, even – it all was; but clearly, too, how much it all meant to him, and the special value of some such anchorage in one's existence. He did not at all want to abandon the new life and its splendid spaces, to turn his back on sun and air and all they offered him and creep home and stay there; the upper world was all too strong, it called to him still, even down there, and he knew he must return to the larger stage. But it was good to think he had this to come back to, this place which was all his own, these things which were so glad to see him again and could always be counted upon for the same simple welcome.

CHRISTMAS WITH THE FAMILY

'LADY BOBBIN'S CHRISTMAS DAY'
FROM A CHRISTMAS PUDDING *BY*
NANCY MITFORD

Nancy Mitford was born in London on November 28 1904, daughter of the second Baron Redesdale. Her sisters included Lady Diana Mosley; Deborah, Duchess of Devonshire and Jessica, who immortalised the Mitford family in her autobiography *Hons and Rebels*. Nancy contributed columns to *The Lady* and the *Sunday Times*, as well as writing a series of popular novels including *The Pursuit of Love* and *Love in a Cold Climate*, which detailed the high-society affairs of the six Radlett sisters. While working in London during the Blitz, Nancy met and fell in love with Gaston Palewski, General de Gaulle's chief of staff, and eventually moved to Paris to be near him. In the 1950s she began writing historical biographies – her life of Louis XIV, *The Sun King*, became an international bestseller. Nancy completed her last book, *Frederick the Great*, before she died of Hodgkin's disease on 30 June 1973.

CHRISTMAS DAY itself was organized by Lady Bobbin with the thoroughness and attention to detail of a general leading his army into battle. Not one moment of its enjoyment was left to chance or to the ingenuity of her guests; these received on Christmas Eve their marching orders, orders which must be obeyed to the letter on pain of death. Even Lady Bobbin, however, superwoman though she might be, could not prevent the day from being marked by a good deal of crossness, much over-eating, and a series of startling incidents.

The battle opened, as it were, with the Christmas stockings. These, in thickest worsted, bought specially for the occasion, were handed to the guests just before bedtime on Christmas Eve, with instructions that they were to be hung up on their bedposts by means of huge safety pins, which were also distributed. Lady Bobbin and her confederate, Lord Leamington Spa, then allowed a certain time to elapse until, judging that Morpheus would have descended upon the household, they sallied forth together (he arrayed in a white wig, beard and eyebrows and red dressing-gown, she clasping a large basket full of suitable presents) upon a stealthy noctambulation, during the course of which every stocking was neatly filled.

The objects thus distributed were exactly the same every year, a curious and wonderful assortment including a pocket handkerchief, Old Moore's Almanack, a balloon not as yet blown up, a mouth organ, a ball of string, a penknife, an instrument for taking stones out of horses' shoes, a book of jokes, a puzzle, and, deep down in the woolly toe of the stocking, whence it would emerge in a rather hairy condition, a chocolate baby. Alas! Most of Lady Bobbin's guests felt that they would willingly have forgone these delightful but inexpensive objects in return for the night's sleep of which they were thus deprived. Forewarned though they were, the shadowy and terrifying appearance of Lord Leamington Spa fumbling about the foot of their beds in the light of a flickering candle gave most of them such a fearful start that all thoughts of sleep were banished for many hours to come.

For the lucky ones who did manage to doze off a rude shock was presently in store. At about five o'clock in the morning Master Christopher Robin Chadlington made a tour of the bedrooms, and having awoken each occupant in turn with a blast of his mouth organ, announced in a voice fraught with tragedy that Auntie Gloria had forgotten to put a chocolate baby in his stocking. 'Please might I have a bit of yours?' This quaint ruse was only too successful, and Christopher Robin acquired thereby no fewer than fourteen chocolate babies, all of which he ate before breakfast. The consequences, which were appalling, took place under the dining-room table at a moment when everybody else was busily opening the Christmas post. After this, weak but cheerful, young Master Chadlington spent the rest of the day in bed practising on his mouth organ.

By luncheon time any feelings of Christmas goodwill which the day and the religious service, duly attended by all, might have been expected to produce had quite evaporated, and towards the end of that meal the dining-room echoed with sounds of furious argument among the grown-ups.

The afternoon was so wet and foggy, so extremely unseasonable, in fact, that Lady Bobbin was obliged with the utmost reluctance to abandon the paper chase which she had organized. Until four o'clock, therefore, the house party was left to enjoy in peace that exquisite discomfort which can only be produced by overfed slumberings in arm-chairs. At four punctually everybody assembled in the ballroom while for nearly an hour the Woodford school children mummed. It was the Woodford school children's annual burden to mum at Christmas; it was the annual burden of the inhabitants of Compton Bobbin to watch the mumming. Both sides, however, bore this infliction with fortitude, and no further awkwardness took place until after tea, when Lord Leamington Spa, having donned once more his dressing-gown and wig, was distributing gifts from the laden branches of the Christmas Tree. This was the big moment of the day. The tree, of course, immediately caught fire, but this was quite a usual occurrence, and the butler had no difficulty in putting it out. The real crisis occurred when Lady Bobbin opened the largish, square parcel which had 'To darling mummy from her very loving little Bobby' written on it, and which to Lady Bobbin's rage and horror was found to contain a volume entitled *The Sexual Life of Savages in Northern Melanesia*. This classic had been purchased at great expense by poor Bobby as a present for Paul, and had somehow changed places with *Tally Ho! Songs of Horse and Hound*, which was intended for his mother, and which, unluckily, was a volume of very similar size and shape. Bobby, never losing his head for an instant, explained volubly and in tones of utmost distress to his mother and the company in general that the shop must have sent the wrong book by mistake, and this explanation was rather ungraciously accepted. Greatly to Bobby's disgust, however, *The Sexual Life of Savages in Northern Melanesia* was presently consigned to the stokehole flames by Lady Bobbin in person.

The remaining time before dinner, which was early so that the children could come down, was spent by Bobby and Héloïse rushing about the house in a state of wild excitement. Paul suspected, and rightly as it turned out, that this excess of high spirits boded no good to somebody. It was quite obvious to the student of youthful psychology that some practical joke was on hand. He wondered rather nervously where the blow would fall.

It fell during dinner. Captain Chadlington was in the middle of telling Lady Bobbin what the P.M. had said to him about pig-breeding in the West of England when a loud whirring noise was heard under his chair. He looked down, rather startled, turned white to the lips at what he saw, sprang to his feet and said, in a voice of unnatural calm: 'Will the women and children please leave the room immediately. There is an infernal machine under my chair.' A moment of panic ensued. Bobby and Héloïse, almost too swift to apprehend his meaning, rushed to the door shrieking, 'A bomb, a bomb, we shall all be blown up,' while everyone else stood transfixed with horror, looking at the small black box under Captain Chadlington's chair as though uncertain of what they should do next. Paul alone remained perfectly calm. With great presence of mind he advanced towards the box, picked it up and conveyed it to the pantry sink, where he left it with the cold water tap running over it. This golden deed made him, jointly with Captain Chadlington, the hero of the hour. Lady Bobbin shook hands with him and said he was a very plucky young fellow and had saved all their lives, and he was overwhelmed with thanks and praise on every side. Captain

Chadlington, too, was supposed to have shown wonderful fortitude in requesting the women and children to leave the room
before mentioning his own danger. Only Bobby and Héloïse
received no praise from anybody for their behaviour and were,
indeed, more or less, sent to Coventry for the rest of the evening.

Captain Chadlington secretly delighted to think that he was
now of such importance politically that attempts were made on
his life (he never doubted for a moment that this was the doing
of Bolshevik agents) went off to telephone to the police. Bobby
and Héloïse, listening round the corner, heard him say: 'Hullo,
Woodford police? It is Captain Chadlington, M.P., speaking
from Compton Bobbin. Look here, officer, there has just been
an attempt to assassinate me. The Bolsheviks, I suppose. An
infernal machine under my chair at dinner. Would you send
somebody along to examine it at once, please, and inform
Scotland Yard of what has happened?'

Lady Brenda said: 'I have always been afraid of something
like this ever since Charlie made that speech against Bolshevism
at Moreton-in-Marsh. Anyhow, we must be thankful that it was
no worse.'

Lady Bobbin said that perhaps now the Government would
do something about the Bolsheviks at last.

Lord Leamington Spa said that he didn't like it at all, which
was quite true, he didn't, because on Christmas night after
dinner he always sang 'The Mistletoe Bough' with great feeling
and now it looked as though the others would be too busy
talking about the bomb to listen to him.

Michael Lewes and Squibby Almanack dared to wonder
whether it was really an infernal machine at all, but they only
imparted this scepticism to each other.

The duchess said that of course it would be very good
publicity for Charlie Chadlington, and she wondered – but

added that perhaps, on the whole, he was too stupid to think of such a thing.

Captain Chadlington said that public men must expect this sort of thing and that he didn't mind for himself, but that it was just like those cowardly dagoes to attempt to blow up a parcel of women and children as well.

Everybody agreed that the tutor had behaved admirably.

'Where did you get it from?' Paul asked Bobby, whom he presently found giggling in the schoolroom with the inevitable Héloïse.

'A boy in my house made it for me last half; he says nobody will be able to tell that it's not a genuine bomb. In fact, it is a genuine one, practically, that's the beauty of it. Poor old Charlie Chad., he's most awfully pleased about the whole thing, isn't he, fussing about with those policemen like any old turkey cock. Oh! It all went off too, too beautifully, eg I cegouldn't thegink egit fegunnegier, cegould yegou?'

'I think you're an odious child,' said Paul, 'and I've a very good mind to tell your mother about you.'

'That would rather take the gilt off your heroic action, though, wouldn't it, old boy?' said Bobby comfortably.

The local police, as Bobby's friend had truly predicted, were unable to make up their minds as to whether the machine was or was not an infernal one. Until this pretty point should be settled Captain Chadlington was allotted two human bull-dogs who were instructed by Scotland Yard that they must guard his life with their own. A camp bed was immediately made up for one of these trusty fellows in the passage, across the captain's bedroom door, and the other was left to prowl about the house and garden all night, armed to the teeth.

'Darling,' said the Duchess to Bobby, as they went upstairs to bed after this exhausting day, 'have you seen the lovely man who's sleeping just outside my room? I don't know what your mother expects to happen, but one is only made of flesh and blood after all.'

'Well, for goodness sake, try and remember that you're a duchess again now,' said Bobby, kissing his aunt good night.

CHRISTMAS AT COLD COMFORT FARM
BY STELLA GIBBONS

Stella Gibbons was born in London in 1902. She went to the North London Collegiate School and studied journalism at University College, London. She then worked for ten years on various papers, including the *Evening Standard*. Stella Gibbons is the author of twenty-five novels, three volumes of short stories, and four volumes of poetry. Her first publication was a book of poems *The Mountain Beast* (1930) and her first novel *Cold Comfort Farm* (1932) won the Femina Vie Heureuse Prize for 1933. Amongst her works are *Christmas at Cold Comfort Farm* (1940), *Westwood* (1946), *Conference at Cold Comfort Farm* (1959) and *Starlight* (1967). She was elected a Fellow of the Royal Society of Literature in 1950. In 1933 she married the actor and singer Allan Webb. They had one daughter. Stella Gibbons died in 1989.

I T WAS Christmas Eve. Dusk, a filthy mantle, lay over Sussex when the Reverend Silas Hearsay, Vicar of Howling, set out to pay his yearly visit to Cold Comfort Farm. Earlier in the afternoon he had feared he would not be Guided to go there, but then he had seen a crate of British Port-type wine go past the Vicarage on the grocer's boy's bicycle, and it could only be going, by that road, to the farmhouse. Shortly afterwards he was Guided to go, and set out upon his bicycle.

The Starkadders, of Cold Comfort Farm, had never got the hang of Christmas, somehow, and on Boxing Day there was always a run on the Howling Pharmacy for lint, bandages, and boracic powder. So the Vicar was going up there, as he did every year, to show them the ropes a bit. (It must be explained that these events took place some years before the civilizing hand of Flora Poste had softened and reformed the Farm and its rude inhabitants.)

After removing two large heaps of tussocks which blocked the lane leading to the Farm and thereby releasing a flood of muddy, icy water over his ankles, the Vicar wheeled his machine on towards the farmhouse, reflecting that those tussocks had never fallen there from the dung-cart of Nature. It was clear that someone did not want him to come to the place. He pushed his bicycle savagely up the hill, muttering.

The farmhouse was in silence and darkness. He pulled the ancient hell-bell (once used to warn excommunicated persons to stay away from Divine Service) hanging outside the front door, and waited.

For a goodish bit nothing happened. Suddenly a window far above his head was flung open and a voice wailed into the twilight –

'No! No! No!'

And the window slammed shut again.

'You're making a mistake, I'm sure,' shouted the Vicar, peering up into the webby thongs of the darkness. 'It's me. The Rev Silas Hearsay.'

There was a pause. Then –

'Beant you postman?' asked the voice, rather embarrassed.

'No, no, of course not; come, come!' laughed the Vicar, grinding his teeth.

'I be comin',' retorted the voice. 'Thought it were postman after his Christmas Box.' The window slammed again. After a very long time indeed the door suddenly opened and there stood Adam Lambsbreath, oldest of the farm servants, peering up at the Reverend Hearsay by the light of a lonely rushdip (so called because you dipped it in grease and rushed to wherever you were going before it went out).

'Is anyone at home? May I enter?' enquired the Vicar, entering, and staring scornfully round the desolate kitchen, at the dead blue ashes in the grate, the thick dust on hanch and beam, the feathers blowing about like fun everywhere. Yet even here there were signs of Christmas, for a withered branch of holly stood in a shapeless vessel on the table. And Adam himself . . . there was something even more peculiar than usual about him.

'Are you ailing, man?' asked the Vicar irritably, kicking a chair out of the way and perching himself on the edge of the table.

'Nay, Rev, I be niver better,' piped the old man. '*The older the berry, The more it makes merry.*'

'Then why,' thundered the Vicar, sliding off the table and walking on tiptoe towards Adam with his arms held at full length above his head, 'are you wearing three of Mrs Starkadder's red shawls?'

Adam stood his ground.

'I mun have a red courtepy, master. Can't be Santa Claus wi'out a red courtepy,' he said. 'Iverybody knows that. Ay, the hand o' Fate lies heavy on us all, Christmas and all the year round alike, but I thought I'd bedight meself as Santa Claus, so I did, just to please me little Elfine. And this night at midnight I be goin' around fillin' the stockin's, if I'm spared.'

The Vicar laughed contemptuously.

'So that were why I took three o' Mrs Starkadder's red shawls,' concluded Adam.

'I suppose you have never thought of God in terms of Energy? No, it is too much to expect.' The Reverend Hearsay re-seated himself on the table and glanced at his watch. 'Where in Energy's name *is* everybody? I have to be at the Assembly Rooms to read a paper on *The Future of The Father Fixation* at eight, and I've got to feed first. If nobody's coming, I'd rather go.'

'Won't ee have a dram o' swede wine first?' a deep voice asked, and a tall woman stepped over the threshold, followed by a little girl of twelve or so with yellow hair and clear, beautiful features. Judith Starkadder dropped her hat on the floor and leant against the table, staring listlessly at the Vicar.

'No swede wine, I thank you,' snapped the Reverend Hearsay.

He glanced keenly round the kitchen in search of the British Port-type, but there was no sign of it. 'I came up to discuss an article with you and yours. An article in *Home Anthropology*.'

''Twere good of ee, Reverend,' she said tiredly.

'It is called *Christmas: From Religious Festival to Shopping Orgy*. Puts the case for Peace and Good Will very sensibly. Both good for trade. What more can you want?'

'Nothing,' she said, leaning her head on her hand.

'But I see,' the Vicar went on furiously, in a low tone and glaring at Adam, 'that here, as everywhere else, the usual childish wish-fantasies are in possession. Stars, shepherds, mangers, stockings, fir-trees, puddings . . . Energy help you all! I wish you good night, and a prosperous Christmas.'

He stamped out of the kitchen, and slammed the door after him with such violence that he brought a slate down on his back tyre and cut it open, and he had to walk home, arriving there too late for supper before setting out for Godmere.

After he had gone, Judith stared into the fire without speaking, and Adam busied himself with scraping the mould from a jar of mincemeat and picking some things which had fallen into it out of a large crock of pudding which he had made yesterday.

Elfine, meanwhile, was slowly opening a small brown paper parcel which she had been nursing, and at last revealed a small and mean-looking doll dressed in a sleazy silk dress and one under-garment that did not take off. This she gently nursed, talking to it in a low, sweet voice.

'Who gave you that, child?' asked her mother idly.

'I told you, mother. Uncle Micah and Aunt Rennett and Aunt Prue and Uncle Harkaway and Uncle Ezra.'

'Treasure it. You will not get many such.'

'I know, mother; I do. I love her very much, dear, dear Caroline,' and Elfine gently put a kiss on the doll's face.

'Now, missus, have ee got the Year's Luck? Can't make puddens wi'out the Year's Luck,' said Adam, shuffling forward.

'It's somewhere here. I forget –'

She turned her shabby handbag upside down, and there fell out on the table the following objects:

A small coffin-nail.

A menthol cone.

Three bad sixpences.

A doll's cracked looking-glass.

A small roll of sticking-plaster.

Adam collected these objects and ranged them by the pudding basin.

'Ay, them's all there,' he muttered. 'Him as gets the sticking-plaster'll break a limb; the menthol cone means as you'll be blind wi' headache, the bad coins means as you'll lose all yer money, and him as gets the coffin-nail will die afore the New Year. The mirror's seven years' bad luck for someone. Aie! In ye go, curse ye!' and he tossed the objects into the pudding, where they were not easily nor long distinguishable from the main mass.

'Want a stir, missus? Come, Elfine, my popelot, stir long, stir firm, your meat to earn,' and he handed her the butt of an old rifle, once used by Fig Starkadder in the Gordon Riots.

Judith turned from the pudding with what is commonly described as a gesture of loathing, but Elfine took the rifle butt and stirred the mixture once or twice.

'Ay, now tes all mixed,' said the old man, nodding with satisfaction. 'Tomorrer we'll boil un fer a good hour, and un'll be done.'

'Will an hour be enough?' said Elfine. 'Mrs Hawk-Monitor up at Hautcouture Hall boils hers for eight hours, and another four on Christmas Day.'

'How do ee know?' demanded Adam. 'Have ee been runnin' wi' that young goosepick Mus' Richard again?'

'You shut up. He's awfully decent.'

"Tisn't decent to run wi' a young popelot all over the Downs in all weathers.'

'Well, it isn't any of your business, so shut up.'

After an offended pause, Adam said:

'Well, niver fret about puddens. None of 'em here has iver tasted any puddens but mine, and they won't know no different.'

At midnight, when the farmhouse was in darkness save for the faint flame of a nightlight burning steadily beside the bed of Harkaway, who was afraid of bears, a dim shape might have been seen moving stealthily along the corridor from bedroom to bedroom. It wore three red shawls pinned over its torn nightshirt and carried over its shoulder a nose-bag (the property of Viper the gelding), distended with parcels. It was Adam, bent on putting into the stockings of the Starkadders the presents which he had made or bought with his savings. The presents were chiefly swedes, beetroots, mangel-wurzels and turnips, decorated with coloured ribbons and strips of silver paper from tea packets.

'Ay,' muttered the old man, as he opened the door of the room where Meriam, the hired girl, was sleeping over the Christmas week. 'An apple for each will make 'em retch, a couple o' nuts will warm their wits.'

The next instant he stepped back in astonishment. There was a light in the room and there, sitting bolt upright in bed beside her slumbering daughter, was Mrs Beetle.

Mrs Beetle looked steadily at Adam, for a minute or two. Then she observed:

'Some 'opes.'

'Nay, niver say that, soul,' protested Adam, moving to the bedrail where hung a very fully-fashioned salmon-pink silk stocking with ladders all down it. ''Tisn't so. Ee do know well that I looks on the maidy as me own child.'

Mrs Beetle gave a short laugh and adjusted a curler. 'You better not let Agony 'ear you, 'intin' I dunno wot,' said Mrs Beetle. ''Urry up and put yer rubbish in there, I want me sleep out; I got to be up at cock-wake ter-morrer.'

Adam put a swede, an apple and a small pot in the stocking and was tip-toeing away when Mrs Beetle, raising her head from the pillow, inquired:

'Wot's that you've give 'er?'

'Eye-shadow,' whispered Adam hoarsely, turning at the door.

'*Wot?*' hissed Mrs Beetle, inclining her head in an effort to hear. ''Ave you gorn crackers?'

'Eye-shadow. To put on the maidy's eyes. 'Twill give that touch o' glamour as be irresistible; it do say so on pot.'

'Get out of 'ere, you old trouble-maker! Don't she 'ave enough bother resistin' as it is, and then you go and give 'er . . . 'ere, wait till I –' and Mrs Beetle was looking around for something to throw as Adam hastily retreated.

'And I'll lay you ain't got no present fer me, ter make matters worse,' she called after him.

Silently he placed a bright new tin of beetle-killer on the washstand and shuffled away.

His experiences in the apartments of the other Starkadders were no more fortunate, for Seth was busy with a friend and was so furious at being interrupted that he threw his riding-boots at the old man, Luke and Mark had locked their door and could be heard inside roaring with laughter at Adam's discomfiture, and Amos was praying, and did not even get up off his knees or open his eyes as he discharged at Adam the goat-pistol which he kept ever by his bed. And everybody else had such enormous holes in their stockings that the small presents Adam put in them fell through on to the floor along with the big ones, and when the Starkadders got up in the morning and rushed round to the foot of the bed to see what Santa had brought, they stubbed their toes on the turnips and swedes and walked on the smaller presents and smashed them to smithereens.

So what with one thing and another everybody was in an even worse temper than usual when the family assembled round the long table in the kitchen for the Christmas dinner about half-past two the next afternoon. They would all have sooner been in some place else, but Mrs Ada Doom (Grandmother Doom, known as Grummer) insisted on them all being there, and as they did not want her to go mad and bring disgrace on the House of Starkadder, there they had to be.

One by one they came in, the men from the fields with soil on their boots, the women fresh from hennery and duck filch with eggs in their bosoms that they gave to Mrs Beetle who was just making the custard. Everybody had to work as usual on Christmas Day, and no one had troubled to put on anything handsomer than their usual workaday clouts stained with mud and plough-oil. Only Elfine wore a cherry-red jersey over her dark skirt and had pinned a spray of holly on herself. An aunt, a distant aunt named Mrs Poste, who lived in London, had unexpectedly sent her the pretty jersey. Prue and Letty had stuck sixpenny artificial posies in their hair, but they only looked wild and queer.

At last all were seated and waiting for Ada Doom.

'Come, come, mun we stick here like jennets i' the trave?' demanded Micah at last. 'Amos, Reuben, do ee carve the turkey. If so be as we wait much longer, 'twill be shent, and the sausages, too.'

Even as he spoke, heavy footsteps were heard approaching the head of the stairs, and everybody at once rose to their feet and looked towards the door.

The low-ceilinged room was already half in dusk, for it was a cold, still Christmas Day, without much light in the grey sky, and the only other illumination came from the dull fire, half-buried under a tass of damp kindling.

Adam gave a last touch to the pile of presents, wrapped in hay and tied with bast, which he had put round the foot of the withered thorn-branch that was the traditional Starkadder Christmas-tree, hastily rearranged one of the tufts of sheep's-wool that decorated its branches, straightened the raven's skeleton that adorned its highest branch in place of a fairy-doll or star, and shuffled into his place just as Mrs Doom reached the foot of the stairs, leaning on her daughter Judith's arm. Mrs Doom struck at him with her stick in passing as she went slowly to the head of the table.

'Well, well. What are we waiting for? Are you all mishooden?' she demanded impatiently as she seated herself. 'Are you all here? All? Answer me!' banging her stick.

'Ay, Grummer,' rose the low, dreary drone from all sides of the table. 'We be all here.'

'Where's Seth?' demanded the old woman, peering sharply on either side of the long row.

'Gone out,' said Harkaway briefly, shifting a straw in his mouth.

'What for?' demanded Mrs Doom.

There was an ominous silence.

'He said he was going to fetch something, Grandmother,' at last said Elfine.

'Ay. Well, well, no matter, so long as he comes soon. Amos, carve the bird. Ay, would it were a vulture, 'twere more fitting!

Reuben, fling these dogs the fare my bounty provides. Sausages . . . pah! Mince-pies . . . what a black-bitter mockery it all is! Every almond, every raisin, is wrung from the dry, dying soil and paid for with sparse greasy notes grudged alike by bank and buyer. Come, Ezra, pass the ginger wine! Be gay, spawn! Laugh, stuff yourselves, gorge and forget, you rat-heaps! Rot you all!' and she fell back in her chair, gasping and keeping one eye on the British Port-type that was now coming up the table.

'Tes one of her bad days,' said Judith tonelessly. 'Amos, will you pull a cracker wi' me? We were lovers . . . once.'

'Hush, woman.' He shrank back from the proffered treat. 'Tempt me not wi' motters and paper caps. Hell is paved wi' such.' Judith smiled bitterly and fell silent.

Reuben, meanwhile, had seen to it that Elfine got the best bit off the turkey (which is not saying much) and had filled her glass with Port-type wine and well-water.

The turkey gave out before it got to Letty, Prue, Susan, Phoebe, Jane and Rennett, who were huddled together at the foot of the table, and they were making do with brussels-sprouts as hard as bullets drenched with weak gravy, and home-brewed braket. There was silence in the kitchen except for the sough of swallowing, the sudden suck of drinking.

'WHERE IS SETH?' suddenly screamed Mrs Doom, flinging down her turkey-leg and glaring round.

Silence fell; everyone moved uneasily, not daring to speak in case they provoked an outburst. But at that moment the cheerful, if unpleasant, noise of a motor-cycle was heard outside, and in another moment it stopped at the kitchen door. All eyes were turned in that direction, and in another moment in came Seth.

'Well, Grummer! Happen you thought I was lost!' he cried impudently, peeling off his boots and flinging them at Meriam, the hired girl, who cowered by the fire gnawing a sausage skin.

Mrs Doom silently pointed to his empty seat with the turkey-leg, and he sat down.

'She hev had an outhees. Ay, 'twas terrible,' reproved Judith in a low tone as Seth seated himself beside her.

'Niver mind, I ha' something here as will make her chirk like a mellet,' he retorted, and held up a large brown paper parcel. 'I ha' been to the Post Office to get it.'

'Ah, gie it me! Aie, my lost pleasurings! Tes none I get, nowadays; gie it me now!' cried the old woman eagerly.

'Nay, Grummer. Ee must wait till pudden time,' and the young man fell on his turkey ravenously.

When everyone had finished, the women cleared away and poured the pudding into a large dusty dish, which they bore to the table and set before Judith.

'Amos? Pudding?' she asked listlessly. 'In a glass or on a plate?'

'On plate, on plate, woman,' he said feverishly bending forward with a fierce glitter in his eye. 'Tes easier to see the Year's Luck so.'

A stir of excitement now went through the company, for everybody looked forward to seeing everybody else drawing ill-luck from the symbols concealed in the pudding. A fierce, attentive silence fell. It was broken by a wail from Reuben —

'The coin — the coin! Wala wa!' and he broke into deep, heavy sobs. He was saving up to buy a tractor, and the coin meant, of course, that he would lose all his money during the year.

'Never mind, Reuben, dear,' whispered Elfine, slipping an arm round his neck. 'You can have the penny father gave me.'

Shrieks from Letty and Prue now announced that they had received the menthol cone and the sticking-plaster, and a low mutter of approval greeted the discovery by Amos of the broken mirror.

Now there was only the coffin-nail, and a ghoulish silence fell on everybody as they dripped pudding from their spoons in a feverish hunt for it; Ezra was running his through a tea-strainer.

But no one seemed to have got it.

'Who has the coffin-nail? Speak, you draf-saks!' at last demanded Mrs Doom.

'Not I.' 'Nay.' 'Niver sight nor snitch of it,' chorused everybody.

'Adam!' Mrs Doom turned to the old man. 'Did you put the coffin-nail into the pudding?'

'Ay, mistress, that I did – didn't I, Mis' Judith, didn't I, Elfine, my liddle lovesight?'

'He speaks truth for once, mother.'

'Yes, he did, Grandmother. I saw him.'

'*Then where is it?*' Mrs Doom's voice was low and terrible and her gaze moved slowly down the table, first on one side and then the other, in search of signs of guilt, while everyone cowered over their plates.

Everyone, that is, except Mrs Beetle, who continued to eat a sandwich that she had taken out of a cellophane wrapper, with every appearance of enjoyment.

'Carrie Beetle!' shouted Mrs Doom.

'I'm 'ere,' said Mrs Beetle.

'Did you take the coffin-nail out of the pudding?'

'Yes, I did.' Mrs Beetle leisurely finished the last crumb of sandwich and wiped her mouth with a clean handkerchief. 'And will again, if I'm spared till next year.'

'You . . . you . . . you . . .' choked Mrs Doom, rising in her chair and beating the air with her clenched fists. 'For two hundred years . . . Starkadders . . . coffin-nails in puddings . . . and now . . . you . . . dare . . .'

'Well, I 'ad enough of it las' year,' retorted Mrs Beetle. 'That pore old soul Earnest Dolour got it, as well you may remember –'

'That's right. Cousin Earnest,' nodded Mark Dolour. 'Got a job workin' on the oil-field down Henfield way. Good money, too.'

'Thanks to me, if he 'as,' retorted Mrs Beetle. 'If I 'adn't put it up to you, Mark Dolour, you'd 'ave let 'im die. All of you was 'angin' over the pore old soul waitin' for 'im to 'and in 'is dinner pail, and Micah (wot's old enough to know better, 'eaven only knows) askin' 'im could 'e 'ave 'is wrist-watch if anything was to 'appen to 'im . . . it fair got me down. So I says to Mark, why don't yer go down and 'ave a word with Mr Earthdribble the undertaker in Howling and get 'im to tell Earnest it weren't a proper coffin-nail at all, it were a throw-out, so it didn't count. The bother we 'ad! Shall I ever fergit it! Never again, I says to meself. So this year there ain't no coffin-nail. I fished it out o' the pudden meself. Parss the water, please.'

'Where is it?' whispered Mrs Doom, terribly. 'Where is this year's nail, woman?'

'Down the –' Mrs Beetle checked herself, and coughed, 'down the well,' concluded Mrs Beetle firmly.

'Niver fret, Grummer, I'll get it up fer ee! Me and the water voles, we can dive far and deep!' and Urk rushed from the room, laughing wildly.

'There ain't no need,' called Mrs Beetle after him. 'But anything to keep you an' yer rubbishy water voles out of mischief!' And Mrs Beetle went into a cackle of laughter, alternately slapping her knee and Caraway's arm, and muttering, 'Oh, cor, wait till I tell Agony! "Dive far and deep." Oh, cor!'

After a minute's uneasy silence –

'Grummer.' Seth bent winningly towards the old woman, the large brown paper parcel in his hand. 'Will you see your present now?'

'Aye, boy, aye. Let me see it. You're the only one that has thought of me, the only one.'

Seth was undoing the parcel, and now revealed a large book, handsomely bound in red leather with gilt lettering.

'There, Grummer. 'Tis the year's numbers o' *The Milk Producers' Weekly Bulletin and Cowkeepers' Guide*. I collected un for ee, and had un bound. Art pleased?'

'Ay. 'Tis handsome enough. A graceful thought,' muttered the old lady, turning the pages. Most of them were pretty battered, owing to her habit of rolling up the paper and hitting anyone with it who happened to be within reach. ''Tis better so. 'Tis heavier. Now I can *throw* it.'

The Starkadders so seldom saw a clean and handsome object at the farmhouse (for Seth was only handsome) that they now crept round, fascinated, to examine the book with murmurs of awe. Among them came Adam, but no sooner had he bent over the book than he recoiled from it with a piercing scream.

'Aie! . . . aie! aie!'

'What's the matter, dotard?' screamed Mrs Doom, jabbing at him with the volume. 'Speak, you kaynard!'

'Tes calf! Tes bound in calf! And tes our Pointless's calf, as she had last Lammastide, as was sold at Godmere to Farmer Lust!' cried Adam, falling to the floor. At the same instant, Luke hit Micah in the stomach, Harkaway pushed Ezra into the fire, Mrs Doom flung the bound volume of *The Milk Producers' Weekly Bulletin and Cowkeepers' Guide* at the struggling mass, and the Christmas dinner collapsed into indescribable confusion.

In the midst of the uproar, Elfine, who had climbed on to the table, glanced up at the window as though seeking help, and saw a laughing face looking at her, and a hand in a yellow string glove beckoning with a riding-crop. Swiftly she darted down from the table and across the room, and out through the half-open door, slamming it after her.

Dick Hawk-Monitor, a sturdy boy astride a handsome pony, was out in the yard.

'Hallo!' she gasped. 'Oh, Dick, I am glad to see you!'

'I thought you never would see me – what on earth's the matter in there?' he asked curiously.

'Oh, never mind them, they're always like that. Dick, do tell me, what presents did you have?'

'Oh, a rifle, and a new saddle, and a fiver – lots of things. Look here, Elfine, you mustn't mind, but I brought you –'

He bent over the pony's neck and held out a sandwich box, daintily filled with slices of turkey, a piece of pudding, a tiny mince-pie and a crystallized apricot.

'Thought your dinner mightn't be very –' he ended gruffly.

'Oh, Dick, it's lovely! Darling little . . . what is it?'

'Apricot. Crystallized fruit. Look here, let's go up to the usual place, shall we? – and I'll watch you eat it.'

'But you must have some, too.'

'Man! I'm stoked up to the brim now! But I dare say I could manage a bit more. Here, you catch hold of Rob Roy, and he'll help you up the hill.'

He touched the pony with his heels and it trotted on towards the snow-streaked Downs, Elfine's yellow hair flying out like a shower of primroses under the grey sky of winter.

CHRISTMAS GIFTS

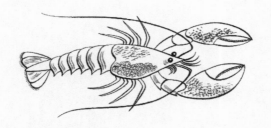

CHRISTMAS IS A SAD SEASON FOR THE POOR *BY* JOHN CHEEVER

John Cheever was born in Quincy, Massachusetts, in 1912, and he went to school at Thayer Academy in South Braintree. He is the author of seven collections of stories and five novels. His first novel, *The Wapshot Chronicle*, won the 1958 National Book Award. In 1965 he received the Howells Medal for Fiction from the National Academy of Arts and Letters and in 1978 he won the National Book Critics Circle Award and the Pulitzer Prize. Shortly before his death in 1982 he was awarded the National Medal for Literature.

CHRISTMAS IS a sad season. The phrase came to Charlie an instant after the alarm clock had waked him, and named for him an amorphous depression that had troubled him all the previous evening. The sky outside his window was black. He sat up in bed and pulled the light chain that hung in front of his nose. Christmas is a very sad day of the year, he thought. Of all the millions of people in New York, I am practically the only one who has to get up in the cold black of 6 a.m. on Christmas Day in the morning; I am practically the only one.

He dressed, and when he went downstairs from the top floor of the rooming house in which he lived, the only sounds he heard were the coarse sounds of sleep; the only lights burning were lights that had been forgotten. Charlie ate some breakfast in an all-night lunchwagon and took an Elevated train uptown. From Third Avenue, he walked over to Park. Park Avenue was dark. House after house put into the shine of the street lights a wall of black windows. Millions and millions were sleeping, and this general loss of consciousness generated an impression of abandonment, as if this were the fall of the city, the end of time. He opened the iron-and-glass doors of the apartment building where he had been working for six months as an elevator operator, and went through the elegant lobby to a locker room at the back. He put on a striped vest with brass buttons, a false ascot, a pair of pants with a light-blue stripe on the seam, and a coat. The night elevator man was dozing on the little bench in the car. Charlie woke him. The night elevator man told him thickly that the day doorman had been taken sick and wouldn't be in that day. With the doorman sick, Charlie wouldn't have any relief for lunch, and a lot of people would expect him to whistle for cabs.

Charlie had been on duty a few minutes when 14 rang – a Mrs Hewing, who, he happened to know, was kind of immoral. Mrs Hewing hadn't been to bed yet, and she got into the elevator wearing a long dress under her fur coat. She was followed by her two funny-looking dogs. He took her down and watched her go out into the dark and take her dogs to the curb. She was outside for only a few minutes. Then she came in and he took her up to 14 again. When she got off the elevator, she said, 'Merry Christmas, Charlie.'

'Well, it isn't much of a holiday for me, Mrs Hewing,' he said. 'I think Christmas is a very sad season of the year. It isn't that people around here ain't generous – I mean I got plenty of tips – but, you see, I live alone in a furnished room and I don't have any family or anything, and Christmas isn't much of a holiday for me.'

'I'm sorry, Charlie,' Mrs Hewing said. 'I don't have any family myself. It is kind of sad when you're alone, isn't it?' She called her dogs and followed them into her apartment. He went down.

It was quiet then, and Charlie lighted a cigarette. The heating plant in the basement encompassed the building at that hour in a regular and profound vibration, and the sullen noises of arriving steam heat began to resound, first in the lobby and then to reverberate up through all the sixteen stories, but this was a mechanical awakening, and it didn't lighten his loneliness or his petulance. The black air outside the glass doors had begun to turn blue, but the blue light seemed to have no source; it appeared in the middle of the air. It was a tearful light, and as it picked out the empty street and the long file of Christmas trees, he wanted to cry. Then a cab drove up, and the Walsers got out, drunk and dressed in evening clothes, and he took them up to their penthouse. The Walsers got him to brooding about the difference between his life in a furnished room and the lives of the people overhead. It was terrible.

Then the early churchgoers began to ring, but there were only three of these that morning. A few more went off to church at eight o'clock, but the majority of the building remained unconscious, although the smell of bacon and coffee had begun to drift into the elevator shaft.

At a little after nine, a nursemaid came down with a child. Both the nursemaid and the child had a deep tan and had just returned, he knew, from Bermuda. He had never been to Bermuda. He, Charlie, was a prisoner, confined eight hours a day to a six-by-eight elevator cage, which was confined, in turn, to a sixteen-story shaft. In one building or another, he had made his living as an elevator operator for ten years. He estimated the average trip at about an eighth of a mile, and when he thought of the thousands of miles he had traveled, when he thought that he might have driven the car through the mists above the Caribbean and set it down on some coral beach in Bermuda, he held the narrowness of his travels against his passengers, as if it were not the nature of the elevator but the pressure of their lives that confined him, as if they had clipped his wings.

He was thinking about this when the DePauls, on 9, rang. They wished him a merry Christmas.

'Well, it's nice of you to think of me,' he said as they descended, 'but it isn't much of a holiday for me. Christmas is a sad season when you're poor. I live alone in a furnished room. I don't have any family.'

'Who do you have dinner with, Charlie?' Mrs DePaul asked.

'I don't have any Christmas dinner,' Charlie said. 'I just get a sandwich.'

'Oh, Charlie!' Mrs DePaul was a stout woman with an impulsive heart, and Charlie's plaint struck at her holiday mood as if she had been caught in a cloudburst. 'I do wish we could share our Christmas dinner with you, you know,' she said. 'I come from Vermont, you know, and when I was a child, you know, we always used to have a great many people at our table. The mailman, you know, and the school-teacher, and just anybody who didn't have any family of their own, you know, and I wish we could share our dinner with you the way we used to, you know, and I don't see any reason why we can't. We can't have you at the table, you know, because you couldn't leave the elevator – could you? – but just as soon as Mr DePaul has carved the goose, I'll give you a ring, and I'll arrange a tray for you, you know, and I want you to come up and at least share our Christmas dinner.'

Charlie thanked them, and their generosity surprised him, but he wondered if, with the arrival of friends and relatives, they wouldn't forget their offer.

Then old Mrs Gadshill rang, and when she wished him a merry Christmas, he hung his head.

'It isn't much of a holiday for me, Mrs Gadshill,' he said. 'Christmas is a sad season if you're poor. You see, I don't have any family. I live alone in a furnished room.'

'I don't have any family either, Charlie,' Mrs Gadshill said. She spoke with a pointed lack of petulance, but her grace was forced. 'That is, I don't have any children with me today. I have three children and seven grandchildren, but none of them can see their way to coming East for Christmas with me. Of course, I understand their problems. I know that it's difficult to travel with children during the holidays, although I always seemed to manage it when I was their age, but people feel differently, and we mustn't condemn them for the things we can't understand. But I know how you feel, Charlie. I haven't any family either. I'm just as lonely as you.'

Mrs Gadshill's speech didn't move him. Maybe she was lonely, but she had a ten-room apartment and three servants and bucks and bucks and diamonds and diamonds, and there were plenty of poor kids in the slums who would be happy at a chance at the food her cook threw away. Then he thought about poor kids. He sat down on a chair in the lobby and thought about them.

They got the worst of it. Beginning in the fall, there was all this excitement about Christmas and how it was a day for them. After Thanksgiving, they couldn't miss it. It was fixed so they couldn't miss it. The wreaths and decorations everywhere, and bells ringing, and trees in the park, and Santa Clauses on every corner and pictures in the magazines and newspapers and on every wall and window in the city told them that if they were good, they would get what they wanted. Even if they couldn't read, they couldn't miss it. They couldn't miss it even if they were blind. It got into the air the poor kids inhaled. Every time they took a walk, they'd see all the expensive toys in the store windows, and they'd write letters to Santa Claus, and their mothers and fathers would promise to mail them, and after the kids had gone to sleep, they'd burn the letters in the stove. And when it came Christmas morning, how could you explain it, how could you tell them that Santa Claus only visited the rich, that he didn't know about the good? How could you face them when all you had to give them was a balloon or a lollipop?

On the way home from work a few nights earlier, Charlie had seen a woman and a little girl going down Fifty-ninth Street. The little girl was crying. He guessed she was crying, he knew she was crying, because she'd seen all the things in the toy-store windows and couldn't understand why none of them were for her. Her mother did housework, he guessed, or maybe was a waitress, and he saw them going back to a room like his, with green walls and no heat, on Christmas Eve, to eat a can of soup. And he saw the little girl hang up her ragged stocking and fall asleep, and he saw the mother looking through her purse for something to put into the stocking – This reverie was interrupted by a bell on 11. He went up, and Mr and Mrs Fuller were waiting. When they wished him a merry Christmas, he said, 'Well, it isn't much of a holiday for me, Mrs Fuller. Christmas is a sad season when you're poor.'

'Do you have any children, Charlie?' Mrs Fuller asked.

'Four living,' he said. 'Two in the grave.' The majesty of his lie overwhelmed him. 'Mrs Leary's a cripple,' he added.

'How sad, Charlie,' Mrs Fuller said. She started out of the elevator when it reached the lobby, and then she turned. 'I want to give your children some presents, Charlie,' she said. 'Mr Fuller and I are going to pay a call now, but when we come back, I want to give you some things for your children.'

He thanked her. Then the bell rang on 4, and he went up to get the Westons.

'It isn't much of a holiday for me,' he told them when they wished him a merry Christmas. 'Christmas is a sad season when you're poor. You see, I live alone in a furnished room.'

'Poor Charlie,' Mrs Weston said. 'I know just how you feel. During the war, when Mr Weston was away, I was all alone at Christmas. I didn't have any Christmas dinner or a tree or anything. I just scrambled myself some eggs and sat there and cried.' Mr Weston, who had gone into the lobby, called impatiently to his wife. 'I know just how you feel, Charlie,' Mrs Weston said.

By noon, the climate in the elevator shaft had changed from bacon and coffee to poultry and game, and the house, like an enormous and complex homestead, was absorbed in the preparations for a domestic feast. The children and their nursemaids had all returned from the Park. Grandmothers and aunts were arriving in limousines. Most of the people who came through the lobby were carrying packages wrapped in colored paper, and were wearing their best furs and new clothes. Charlie continued to complain to most of the tenants when they wished him a merry Christmas, changing his story from the lonely bachelor to the poor father, and back again, as his mood changed, but this outpouring of melancholy, and the sympathy it aroused, didn't make him feel any better.

At half past one, 9 rang, and when he went up, Mr DePaul was standing in the door of their apartment holding a cocktail shaker and a glass. 'Here's a little Christmas cheer, Charlie,' he said, and he poured Charlie a drink. Then a maid appeared with a tray of covered dishes, and Mrs DePaul came out of the living room. 'Merry Christmas, Charlie,' she said. 'I had Mr DePaul carve the goose early, so that you could have some, you know. I didn't want to put the dessert on the tray, because I was afraid it would melt, you know, so when we have our dessert, we'll call you.'

'And what is Christmas without presents?' Mr DePaul said,

and he brought a large, flat box from the hall and laid it on top of the covered dishes.

'You people make it seem like a real Christmas to me,' Charlie said. Tears started into his eyes. 'Thank you, thank you.'

'Merry Christmas! Merry Christmas!' they called, and they watched him carry his dinner and his present into the elevator. He took the tray and the box into the locker room when he got down. On the tray, there was a soup, some kind of creamed fish, and a serving of goose. The bell rang again, but before he answered it, he tore open the DePauls' box and saw that it held a dressing gown. Their generosity and their cocktail had begun to work on his brain, and he went jubilantly up to 12. Mrs Gadshill's maid was standing in the door with a tray, and Mrs Gadshill stood behind her. 'Merry Christmas, Charlie!' she said. He thanked her, and tears came into his eyes again. On the way down, he drank off the glass of sherry on Mrs Gadshill's tray. Mrs Gadshill's contribution was a mixed grill. He ate the lamb chop with his fingers. The bell was ringing again, and he wiped his face with a paper towel and went up to 11. 'Merry Christmas, Charlie,' Mrs Fuller said, and she was standing in the door with her arms full of packages wrapped in silver paper, just like a picture in an advertisement, and Mr Fuller was beside her with an arm around her, and they both looked as if they were going to cry. 'Here are some things I want you to take home to your children,' Mrs Fuller said. 'And here's something for Mrs Leary and here's something for you. And if you want to take these things out to the elevator, we'll have your dinner ready for you in a minute.' He carried the things into the elevator and came back for the tray. 'Merry Christmas, Charlie!' both of the Fullers called after him as he closed the door. He took their dinner and their presents into the locker room and tore open the box that was marked for him.

There was an alligator wallet in it, with Mr Fuller's initials in the corner. Their dinner was also goose, and he ate a piece of the meat with his fingers and was washing it down with a cocktail when the bell rang. He went up again. This time it was the Westons. 'Merry Christmas, Charlie!' they said, and they gave him a cup of eggnog, a turkey dinner, and a present. Their gift was also a dressing gown. Then 7 rang, and when he went up, there was another dinner and some more toys. Then 14 rang, and when he went up, Mrs Hewing was standing in the hall, in a kind of negligee, holding a pair of riding boots in one hand and some neckties in the other. She had been crying and drinking. 'Merry Christmas, Charlie,' she said tenderly. 'I wanted to give you something, and I've been thinking about you all morning, and I've been all over the apartment, and these are the only things I could find that a man might want. These are the only things that Mr Brewer left. I don't suppose you'd have any use for the riding boots, but wouldn't you like the neckties?' Charlie took the neckties and thanked her and hurried back to the car, for the elevator bell had rung three times.

By three o'clock, Charlie had fourteen dinners spread on the table and the floor of the locker room, and the bell kept ringing. Just as he started to eat one, he would have to go up and get another, and he was in the middle of the Parsons' roast beef when he had to go up and get the DePauls' dessert. He kept the door of the locker room closed, for he sensed that the quality of charity is exclusive and that his friends would have been disappointed to find that they were not the only ones to try to lessen his loneliness. There were goose, turkey, chicken, pheasant, grouse, and pigeon. There were trout and salmon, creamed scallops and oysters, lobster, crabmeat, whitebait, and clams. There were plum puddings, mince pies, mousses, puddles of melted ice cream, layer cakes, *Torten*, éclairs, and two slices of Bavarian cream. He had dressing gowns, neckties, cuff links, socks, and handkerchiefs, and one of the tenants had asked for his neck size and then given him three green shirts. There were a glass teapot filled, the label said, with jasmine honey, four bottles of aftershave lotion, some alabaster bookends, and a dozen steak knives. The avalanche of charity he had precipitated filled the locker room and made him hesitant, now and then, as if he had touched some wellspring in the female heart that would bury him alive in food and dressing gowns. He had made almost no headway on the food, for all the servings were preternaturally large, as if loneliness had been counted on to generate in him a brutish appetite. Nor had he opened any of the presents that had been given to him for his imaginary children, but he had drunk everything they sent down, and around him were the dregs of Martinis, Manhattans, Old-Fashioneds, champagne-and-raspberry shrub cocktails, eggnogs, Bronxes, and Side Cars.

His face was blazing. He loved the world, and the world loved him. When he thought back over his life, it appeared to him in a rich and wonderful light, full of astonishing experiences and unusual friends. He thought that his job as an elevator operator – cruising up and down through hundreds of feet of perilous space – demanded the nerve and the intellect of a birdman. All the constraints of his life – the green walls of his room and the months of unemployment – dissolved. No one was ringing, but he got into the elevator and shot it at full speed up to the penthouse and down again, up and down, to test his wonderful mastery of space.

A bell rang on 12 while he was cruising, and he stopped in his flight long enough to pick up Mrs Gadshill. As the car started to fall, he took his hands off the controls in a paroxysm of joy and shouted, 'Strap on your safety belt, Mrs Gadshill! We're going to make a loop-the-loop!' Mrs Gadshill shrieked. Then, for some reason, she sat down on the floor of the elevator. Why was her face so pale, he wondered; why was she sitting on the floor? She shrieked again. He grounded the car gently, and cleverly, he thought, and opened the door. 'I'm sorry if I scared you, Mrs Gadshill,' he said meekly. 'I was only fooling.' She shrieked again. Then she ran out into the lobby, screaming for the superintendent.

The superintendent fired Charlie and took over the elevator himself. The news that he was out of work stung Charlie for a minute. It was his first contact with human meanness that day. He sat down in the locker room and gnawed on a drumstick. His drinks were beginning to let him down, and while it had not reached him yet, he felt a miserable soberness in the offing. The excess of food and presents around him began to make him feel guilty and unworthy. He regretted bitterly the lie he had told about his children. He was a single man with simple needs. He had abused the goodness of the people upstairs. He was unworthy.

Then up through this drunken train of thought surged the sharp figure of his landlady and her three skinny children. He thought of them sitting in their basement room. The cheer of Christmas had passed them by. This image got him to his feet. The realization that he was in a position to give, that he could bring happiness easily to someone else, sobered him. He took a big burlap sack, which was used for collecting waste, and began to stuff it, first with his presents and then with the presents for his imaginary children. He worked with the haste of a man whose train is approaching the station, for he could hardly wait to see those long faces light up when he came in the door. He changed his clothes, and, fired by a wonderful and unfamiliar sense of power, he slung his bag over his shoulder like a regular Santa Claus, went out the back way, and took a taxi to the lower East Side.

The landlady and her children had just finished off a turkey, which had been sent to them by the local Democratic Club, and they were stuffed and uncomfortable when Charlie began pounding on the door, shouting 'Merry Christmas!' He dragged the bag in after him and dumped the presents for the children onto the floor. There were dolls and musical toys, blocks, sewing kits, an Indian suit, and a loom, and it appeared to him that, as he had hoped, his arrival in the basement dispelled its gloom. When half the presents had been opened, he gave the landlady a bathrobe and went upstairs to look over the things he had been given for himself.

Now, the landlady's children had already received so many presents by the time Charlie arrived that they were confused with receiving, and it was only the landlady's intuitive grasp of the nature of charity that made her allow the children to open some of the presents while Charlie was still in the room, but as soon as he had gone, she stood between the children and the presents that were still unopened. 'Now, you kids have had enough already,' she said. 'You kids have got your share. Just look at the things you got there. Why, you ain't even played with the half of them. Mary Anne, you ain't even looked at that doll the Fire Department give you. Now, a nice thing to do would be to take all this stuff that's left over to those poor people on Hudson Street – them Deckkers. They ain't got nothing.' A beatific light came into her face when she realized that she could give, that she could bring cheer, that she could put a healing finger on a case needier than hers, and – like Mrs DePaul and Mrs Weston, like Charlie himself and like Mrs Deckker, when Mrs Deckker was to think, subsequently, of the poor Shannons – first love, then charity, and then a sense of power drove her. 'Now, you kids help me get all this stuff together. Hurry, hurry, hurry,' she said, for it was dark then, and she knew that we are bound, one to another, in licentious benevolence for only a single day, and that day was nearly over. She was tired, but she couldn't rest, she couldn't rest.

THE GIFT OF THE MAGI *BY* O. HENRY

William Sydney Porter was born in North Carolina on 11 September 1862. He left school at fifteen and moved to Texas several years later, where he married and worked as a journalist. In 1897 he was convicted of embezzling money, and he began a five-year sentence at Columbus, Ohio the following year. He began to write short stories while in prison, to raise money to support his family. Porter changed his name to O. Henry on his release from prison in 1901 and continued to write. His first collection of stories, *Cabbages and Kings*, was published three years later, followed by another nine collections and over six hundred stories. O. Henry died of cirrhosis of the liver on 5 June 1910 in New York.

ONE DOLLAR and eighty-seven cents. That was all. And sixty cents of it was in pennies. Pennies saved one and two at a time by bulldozing the grocer and the vegetable man and the butcher until one's cheeks burned with the silent imputation of parsimony that such close dealing implied. Three times Della counted it. One dollar and eighty-seven cents. And the next day would be Christmas.

There was clearly nothing left to do but flop down on the shabby little couch and howl. So Della did it. Which instigates the moral reflection that life is made up of sobs, sniffles, and smiles, with sniffles predominating.

While the mistress of the home is gradually subsiding from the first stage to the second, take a look at the home. A furnished flat at $8 per week. It did not exactly beggar description, but it certainly had that word on the look-out for the mendicancy squad.

In the vestibule below was a letter-box into which no letter would go, and an electric button from which no mortal finger could coax a ring. Also appertaining thereunto was a card bearing the name 'Mr James Dillingham Young.'

The 'Dillingham' had been flung to the breeze during a

former period of prosperity when its possessor was being paid $30 per week. Now, when the income was shrunk to $20, the letters of 'Dillingham' looked blurred, as though they were thinking seriously of contracting to a modest and unassuming D. But whenever Mr James Dillingham Young came home and reached his flat above he was called 'Jim' and greatly hugged by Mrs James Dillingham Young, already introduced to you as Della. Which is all very good.

Della finished her cry and attended to her cheeks with the powder rag. She stood by the window and looked out dully at a gray cat walking a gray fence in a gray backyard. Tomorrow would be Christmas Day, and she had only $1.87 with which to buy Jim a present. She had been saving every penny she could for months, with this result. Twenty dollars a week doesn't go far. Expenses had been greater than she had calculated. They always are. Only $1.87 to buy a present for Jim. Her Jim. Many a happy hour she had spent planning for something nice for him. Something fine and rare and sterling – something just a little bit near to being worthy of the honour of being owned by Jim.

There was a pier-glass between the windows of the room. Perhaps you have seen a pier-glass in an $8 flat. A very thin and very agile person may, by observing his reflection in a rapid sequence of longitudinal strips, obtain a fairly accurate conception of his looks. Della, being slender, had mastered the art.

Suddenly she whirled from the window and stood before the glass. Her eyes were shining brilliantly, but her face had lost its color within twenty seconds. Rapidly she pulled down her hair and let it fall to its full length.

Now, there were two possessions of the James Dillingham Youngs in which they both took a mighty pride. One was Jim's gold watch that had been his father's and his grandfather's. The other was Della's hair. Had the Queen of Sheba lived in the flat across the airshaft, Della would have let her hair hang out of the window some day to dry just to depreciate Her Majesty's jewels and gifts. Had King Solomon been the janitor, with all his treasures piled up in the basement, Jim would have pulled out his watch every time he passed, just to see him pluck at his beard from envy.

So now Della's beautiful hair fell about her, rippling and shining like a cascade of brown waters. It reached below her knee and made itself almost a garment for her. And then she did it up again nervously and quickly. Once she faltered for a minute and stood still while a tear or two splashed on the worn red carpet.

On went her old brown jacket; on went her old brown hat. With a whirl of skirts and with the brilliant sparkle still in her eyes, she cluttered out of the door and down the stairs to the street.

Where she stopped the sign read: 'Mme Sofronie. Hair Goods of All Kinds.' One Eight up Della ran, and collected herself, panting. Madame, large, too white, chilly, hardly looked the 'Sofronie.'

'Will you buy my hair?' asked Della.

'I buy hair,' said Madame. 'Take yer hat off and let's have a sight at the looks of it.'

Down rippled the brown cascade.

'Twenty dollars,' said Madame, lifting the mass with a practised hand.

'Give it to me quick,' said Della.

Oh, and the next two hours tripped by on rosy wings. Forget the hashed metaphor. She was ransacking the stores for Jim's present.

She found it at last. It surely had been made for Jim and no one else. There was no other like it in any of the stores, and she had turned all of them inside out. It was a platinum fob chain simple and chaste in design, properly proclaiming its value by substance alone and not by meretricious ornamentation – as all good things should do. It was even worthy of The Watch. As soon as she saw it she knew that it must be Jim's. It was like him. Quietness and value – the description applied to both. Twenty-one dollars they took from her for it, and she hurried home with the 78 cents. With that chain on his watch Jim might be properly anxious about the time in any company. Grand as the watch was, he sometimes looked at it on the sly on account of the old leather strap that he used in place of a chain.

When Della reached home her intoxication gave way a little to prudence and reason. She got out her curling irons and lighted the gas and went to work repairing the ravages made by generosity added to love. Which is always a tremendous task, dear friends – a mammoth task.

Within forty minutes her head was covered with tiny, close-lying curls that made her look wonderfully like a truant schoolboy. She looked at her reflection in the mirror long, carefully, and critically.

'If Jim doesn't kill me,' she said to herself, 'before he takes a second look at me, he'll say I look like a Coney Island chorus girl. But what could I do – oh! what could I do with a dollar and eighty-seven cents?'

At 7 o'clock the coffee was made and the frying-pan was on the back of the stove hot and ready to cook the chops.

Jim was never late. Della doubled the fob chain in her hand and sat on the corner of the table near the door that he always entered. Then she heard his step on the stair away down on the first flight, and she turned white for just a moment. She had a habit of saying little silent prayers about the simplest everyday things, and now she whispered: 'Please, God, make him think I am still pretty.'

The door opened and Jim stepped in and closed it. He looked thin and very serious. Poor fellow, he was only twenty-two — and to be burdened with a family! He needed a new overcoat and he was without gloves.

Jim stepped inside the door, as immovable as a setter at the scent of quail. His eyes were fixed upon Della, and there was an expression in them that she could not read, and it terrified her. It was not anger, nor surprise, nor disapproval, nor horror, nor any of the sentiments that she had been prepared for. He simply stared at her fixedly with that peculiar expression on his face.

Della wriggled off the table and went for him.

'Jim, darling,' she cried, 'don't look at me that way. I had my hair cut off and sold it because I couldn't have lived through Christmas without giving you a present. It'll grow out again — you won't mind, will you? I just had to do it. My hair grows awfully fast. Say "Merry Christmas!" Jim, and let's be happy. You don't know what a nice — what a beautiful, nice gift I've got for you.'

'You've cut off your hair?' asked Jim, laboriously, as if he had not arrived at that patent fact yet, even after the hardest mental labour.

'Cut it off and sold it,' said Della. 'Don't you like me just as well, anyhow? I'm me without my hair, ain't I?'

Jim looked about the room curiously.

'You say your hair is gone?' he said, with an air almost of idiocy.

'You needn't look for it,' said Della. 'It's sold, I tell you — sold and gone, too. It's Christmas Eve, boy. Be good to me, for it went for you. Maybe the hairs of my head were numbered,' she went on with a sudden serious sweetness, 'but nobody could ever count my love for you. Shall I put the chops on, Jim?'

Out of his trance Jim seemed quickly to wake. He enfolded his Della. For ten seconds let us regard with discreet scrutiny some inconsequential object in the other direction. Eight dollars a week or a million a year – what is the difference? A mathematician or a wit would give you the wrong answer. The magi brought valuable gifts, but that was not among them. This dark assertion will be illuminated later on.

Jim drew a package from his overcoat pocket and threw it upon the table.

'Don't make any mistake, Dell,' he said, 'about me. I don't think there's anything in the way of a haircut or a shave or a shampoo that could make me like my girl any less. But if you'll unwrap that package you may see why you had me going a while at first.'

White fingers and nimble tore at the string and paper. And then an ecstatic scream of joy; and then, alas! a quick feminine change to hysterical tears and wails, necessitating the immediate employment of all the comforting powers of the lord of the flat.

For there lay The Combs – the set of combs, side and back, that Della had worshipped for long in a Broadway window. Beautiful combs, pure tortoise-shell, with jewelled rims – just the shade to wear in the beautiful vanished hair. They were expensive combs, she knew, and her heart had simply craved and yearned over them without the least hope of possession. And now, they were hers, but the tresses that should have adorned the coveted adornments were gone.

But she hugged them to her bosom, and at length she was able to look up with dim eyes and a smile and say: 'My hair grows so fast, Jim!'

And then Della leaped up like a little singed cat and cried, 'Oh, oh!'

Jim had not yet seen his beautiful present. She held it out to him eagerly upon her open palm. The dull precious metal seemed to flash with a reflection of her bright and ardent spirit.

'Isn't it a dandy, Jim? I hunted all over town to find it. You'll have to look at the time a hundred times a day now. Give me your watch. I want to see how it looks on it.'

Instead of obeying, Jim tumbled down on the couch and put his hands under the back of his head and smiled.

'Dell,' said he, 'let's put our Christmas presents away and keep 'em a while. They're too nice to use just at present. I sold the watch to get the money to buy your combs. And now suppose you put the chops on.'

The magi, as you know, were wise men – wonderfully wise men – who brought gifts to the Babe in the manger. They invented the art of giving Christmas presents. Being wise, their gifts were no doubt wise ones, possibly bearing the privilege of exchange in case of duplication. And here I have lamely related to you the uneventful chronicle of two foolish children in a flat who most unwisely sacrificed for each other the greatest treasures of their house. But in a last word to the wise of these days let it be said that of all who give gifts these two were the wisest. Of all who give and receive gifts, such as they are wisest. Everywhere they are wisest. They are the magi.

CHRISTMAS DINNERS

'THERE NEVER WAS SUCH A GOOSE' *FROM* A CHRISTMAS CAROL *BY* CHARLES DICKENS

Charles Dickens was born in Hampshire on 7 February 1812. His father was a clerk in the navy pay office, who was well paid but often ended up in financial troubles. When Dickens was twelve years old he was sent to work in a shoe polish factory because his family had been taken to the debtors' prison. His career as a writer of fiction started in 1833 when his short stories and essays began to appear in periodicals. *The Pickwick Papers*, his first commercial success, was published in 1836. In the same year he married the daughter of his friend George Hogarth, Catherine Hogarth. *Oliver Twist* and many other novels followed. *The Old Curiosity Shop* brought Dickens international fame and he became a celebrity in America as well as Britain. He separated from his wife in 1858. Charles Dickens died on 9 June 1870, leaving his last novel, *The Mystery of Edwin Drood*, unfinished. He is buried in Westminster Abbey.

In this extract from Dickens' short novel *A Christmas Carol*, the Ghost of Christmas Present has conducted the miser Scrooge to the home of his poor clerk, Bob Cratchit, where, invisible, they observe the Cratchit family's celebrations.

THEN UP rose Mrs Cratchit, Cratchit's wife, dressed out but poorly in a twice-turned gown, but brave in ribbons, which are cheap and make a goodly show for sixpence; and she laid the cloth, assisted by Belinda Cratchit, second of her daughters, also brave in ribbons; while Master Peter Cratchit plunged a fork into the saucepan of potatoes, and getting the corners of his monstrous shirt-collar (Bob's private property, conferred upon his son and heir in honour of the day) into his mouth, rejoiced to find himself so gallantly attired, and yearned to show his linen in the fashionable Parks. And now two smaller Cratchits, boy and girl, came tearing in, screaming that outside the baker's they had smelt the goose, and known it for their own; and basking in luxurious thoughts of sage and onion, these young Cratchits danced about the table, and exalted Master Peter Cratchit to the skies, while he (not proud, although his collars nearly choked him) blew the fire, until the slow potatoes bubbling up, knocked loudly at the saucepan-lid to be let out and peeled.

'What has ever got your precious father then,' said Mrs Cratchit. 'And your brother, Tiny Tim; and Martha warn't as late last Christmas Day by half-an-hour!'

'Here's Martha, mother!' said a girl, appearing as she spoke.

'Here's Martha, mother!' cried the two young Cratchits. 'Hurrah! There's *such* a goose, Martha!'

'Why, bless your heart alive, my dear, how late you are!' said Mrs Cratchit, kissing her a dozen times, and taking off her shawl and bonnet for her, with officious zeal.

'We'd a deal of work to finish up last night,' replied the girl, 'and had to clear away this morning, mother!'

'Well! Never mind so long as you are come,' said Mrs Cratchit. 'Sit ye down before the fire, my dear, and have a warm, Lord bless ye!'

'No no! There's father coming,' cried the two young Cratchits, who were everywhere at once. 'Hide Martha, hide!'

So Martha hid herself, and in came little Bob, the father, with at least three feet of comforter exclusive of the fringe, hanging down before him; and his thread-bare clothes darned up and brushed, to look seasonable; and Tiny Tim upon his shoulder. Alas for Tiny Tim, he bore a little crutch, and had his limbs supported by an iron frame!

'Why, where's our Martha?' cried Bob Cratchit looking round.

'Not coming,' said Mrs Cratchit.

'Not coming!' said Bob, with a sudden declension in his high spirits; for he had been Tim's blood horse all the way from church, and had come home rampant. 'Not coming upon Christmas Day!'

Martha didn't like to see him disappointed, if it were only in joke; so she came out prematurely from behind the closet door, and ran into his arms, while the two young Cratchits hustled Tiny Tim, and bore him off into the wash-house, that he might hear the pudding singing in the copper.

'And how did little Tim behave?' asked Mrs Cratchit, when

she had rallied Bob on his credulity and Bob had hugged his daughter to his heart's content.

'As good as gold,' said Bob, 'and better. Somehow he gets thoughtful sitting by himself so much, and thinks the strangest things you ever heard. He told me, coming home, that he hoped the people saw him in the church, because he was a cripple, and it might be pleasant to them to remember upon Christmas Day, who made lame beggars walk and blind men see.'

Bob's voice was tremulous when he told them this, and trembled more when he said that Tiny Tim was growing strong and hearty.

His active little crutch was heard upon the floor, and back came Tiny Tim before another word was spoken, escorted by his brother and sister to his stool before the fire; and while Bob, turning up his cuffs – as if, poor fellow, they were capable of being made more shabby – compounded some hot mixture in a jug with gin and lemons, and stirred it round and round and put it on the hob to simmer; Master Peter, and the two ubiquitous young Cratchits went to fetch the goose, with which they soon returned in high procession.

Such a bustle ensued that you might have thought a goose the rarest of all birds; a feathered phenomenon, to which a black swan was a matter of course; and in truth it was something very like it in that house. Mrs Cratchit made the gravy (ready beforehand in a little saucepan) hissing hot; Master Peter mashed the potatoes with incredible vigour; Miss Belinda sweetened up the apple-sauce; Martha dusted the hot plates; Bob took Tiny Tim beside him in a tiny corner at the table; the two young Cratchits set chairs for everybody, not forgetting themselves, and mounting guard upon their posts, crammed spoons into their mouths, lest they should shriek for goose before their turn came to be helped. At last the dishes were set on, and grace was said. It was succeeded by a breathless pause, as Mrs Cratchit, looking slowly all along the carving-knife, prepared to plunge it in the breast; but when she did, and when the long expected gush of stuffing issued forth, one murmur of delight arose all round the board, and even Tiny Tim, excited by the two young Cratchits, beat on the table with the handle of his knife, and feebly cried Hurrah!

There never was such a goose. Bob said he didn't believe there ever was such a goose cooked. Its tenderness and flavour, size and cheapness, were the themes of universal admiration. Eked out by the apple-sauce and mashed potatoes, it was a sufficient dinner for the whole family; indeed, as Mrs Cratchit said with great delight (surveying one small atom of a bone upon the dish), they hadn't ate it all at last! Yet every one had had enough, and the youngest Cratchits in particular, were steeped in sage and onion to the eyebrows! But now, the plates being changed by Miss Belinda, Mrs Cratchit left the room alone – too nervous to bear witnesses – to take the pudding up, and bring it in.

Suppose it should not be done enough! Suppose it should break in turning out! Suppose somebody should have got over the wall of the backyard, and stolen it, while they were merry with the goose: a supposition at which the two young Cratchits became livid! All sorts of horrors were supposed.

Hallo! A great deal of steam! The pudding was out of the copper. A smell like a washing-day! That was the cloth. A smell like an eating-house, and a pastry cook's next door to each other, with a laundress's next door to that! That was the pudding. In half a minute Mrs Cratchit entered: flushed, but smiling proudly: with the pudding, like a speckled cannon-ball, so hard and firm, blazing in half of half-a-quartern of ignited brandy, and bedight with Christmas holly stuck into the top.

Oh, a wonderful pudding! Bob Cratchit said, and calmly too,

that he regarded it as the greatest success achieved by Mrs Cratchit since their marriage. Mrs Cratchit said that now the weight was off her mind, she would confess she had had her doubts about the quantity of flour. Everybody had something to say about it, but nobody said or thought it was at all a small pudding for a large family. It would have been flat heresy to do so. Any Cratchit would have blushed to hint at such a thing.

At last the dinner was all done, the cloth was cleared, the hearth swept, and the fire made up. The compound in the jug being tasted, and considered perfect, apples and oranges were put upon the table, and a shovel-full of chestnuts on the fire. Then all the Cratchit family drew round the hearth, in what Bob Cratchit called a circle, meaning half a one; and at Bob Cratchit's elbow stood the family display of glass; two tumblers, and a custard-cup without a handle.

These held the hot stuff from the jug, however, as well as golden goblets would have done; and Bob served it out with beaming looks, while the chestnuts on the fire sputtered and crackled noisily. Then Bob proposed:

'A Merry Christmas to us all, my dears. God bless us!'

Which all the family re-echoed.

'God bless us every one!' said Tiny Tim, the last of all.

He sat very close to his father's side, upon his little stool. Bob held his withered little hand in his, as if he loved the child, and wished to keep him by his side, and dreaded that he might be taken from him.

'Spirit,' said Scrooge, with an interest he had never felt before, 'tell me if Tiny Tim will live.'

'I see a vacant seat,' replied the Ghost, 'in the poor chimney corner, and a crutch without an owner, carefully preserved. If these shadows remain unaltered by the Future, the child will die.'

'No, no,' said Scrooge. 'Oh no, kind Spirit! say he will be spared.'

'If these shadows remain unaltered by the Future, none other of my race,' returned the Ghost, 'will find him here. What then? If he be like to die, he had better do it, and decrease the surplus population.'

Scrooge hung his head to hear his own words quoted by the Spirit, and was overcome with penitence and grief.

'Man,' said the Ghost, 'if man you be in heart, not adamant, forbear that wicked cant until you have discovered What the surplus is, and Where it is. Will you decide what men shall live, what men shall die? It may be, that in the sight of Heaven, you are more worthless and less fit to live than millions like this poor man's child. Oh God! to hear the Insect on the leaf pronouncing on the too much life among his hungry brothers in the dust!'

Scrooge bent before the Ghost's rebuke, and trembling cast his eyes upon the ground. But he raised them speedily, on hearing his own name.

'Mr Scrooge!' said Bob; 'I'll give you Mr Scrooge, the Founder of the Feast!'

'The Founder of the Feast indeed!' cried Mrs Cratchit, reddening. 'I wish I had him here. I'd give him a piece of my mind to feast upon, and I hope he'd have a good appetite for it.'

'My dear,' said Bob, 'the children; Christmas Day.'

'It should be Christmas Day, I am sure,' said she, 'on which one drinks the health of such an odious, stingy, hard, unfeeling man as Mr Scrooge. You know he is, Robert! Nobody knows it better than you do, poor fellow!'

'My dear,' was Bob's mild answer, 'Christmas Day.'

'I'll drink his health for your sake and the Day's,' said Mrs

Cratchit, 'not for his. Long life to him! A merry Christmas and a happy new year! – he'll be very merry and very happy, I have no doubt!'

The children drank the toast after her. It was the first of their proceedings which had no heartiness in it. Tiny Tim drank it last of all, but he didn't care twopence for it. Scrooge was the Ogre of the family. The mention of his name cast a dark shadow on the party, which was not dispelled for full five minutes.

After it had passed away, they were ten times merrier than before, from the mere relief of Scrooge the Baleful being done with. Bob Cratchit told them how he had a situation in his eye for Master Peter, which would bring in, if obtained, full five-and-sixpence weekly. The two young Cratchits laughed tremendously at the idea of Peter's being a man of business; and Peter himself looked thoughtfully at the fire from between his collars, as if he were deliberating what particular investments he should favour when he came into the receipt of that bewildering income. Martha, who was a poor apprentice at a milliner's, then told them what kind of work she had to do, and how many hours she worked at a stretch, and how she meant to lie a-bed tomorrow morning for a good long rest; tomorrow being a holiday she passed at home. Also how she had seen a countess and a lord some days before, and how the lord 'was much about as tall as Peter'; at which Peter pulled up his collars so high that you couldn't have seen his head if you had been there. All this time the chestnuts and the jug went round and round; and bye and bye they had a song, about a lost child travelling in the snow, from Tiny Tim; who had a plaintive little voice, and sang it very well indeed.

There was nothing of high mark in this. They were not a handsome family; they were not well dressed; their shoes were far from being water-proof; their clothes were scanty; and Peter might have known, and very likely did, the inside of a pawn-broker's. But they were happy, grateful, pleased with one another, and contented with the time; and when they faded, and looked happier yet in the bright sprinklings of the Spirit's torch at parting, Scrooge had his eye upon them, and especially on Tiny Tim, until the last.

'A CONSCIENCE PUDDING' *FROM* THE NEW TREASURE SEEKERS *BY* E. NESBIT

Edith Nesbit was born in 1858. Her father died when she was only three and her impoverished family moved continually all over England. As a young married woman with small children, she sold stories and poems to supplement the family income. Her first children's book, *The Treasure Seekers*, was published in 1899. She also wrote *Five Children and It* but her most famous story, *The Railway Children*, was first published in 1905 and has never been out of print. Edith Nesbit died in 1924.

IT WAS Christmas, nearly a year after Mother died. I cannot write about Mother – but I will just say one thing. If she had only been away for a little while, and not for always, we shouldn't have been so keen on having a Christmas. I didn't understand this then, but I am much older now, and I think it was just because everything was so different and horrid we felt we *must* do something; and perhaps we were not particular enough *what*. Things make you much more unhappy when you loaf about than when you are doing events.

Father had to go away just about Christmas. He had heard that his wicked partner, who ran away with his money, was in France, and he thought he could catch him, but really he was in Spain, where catching criminals is never practised. We did not know this till afterwards.

Before Father went away he took Dora and Oswald into his study, and said –

'I'm awfully sorry I've got to go away, but it is very serious business, and I must go. You'll be good while I'm away, kiddies, won't you?'

We promised faithfully. Then he said –

'There are reasons – you wouldn't understand if I tried to

tell you – but you can't have much of a Christmas this year. But I've told Matilda to make you a good plain pudding. Perhaps next Christmas will be brighter.'

(It was; for the next Christmas saw us the affluent nephews and nieces of an Indian uncle – but that is quite another story, as good old Kipling says.)

When Father had been seen off at Lewisham Station with his bags, and a plaid rug in a strap, we came home again, and it was horrid. There were papers and things littered all over his room where he had packed. We tidied the room up – it was the only thing we could do for him. It was Dicky who accidentally broke his shaving-glass, and H.O. made a paper boat out of a letter we found out afterwards Father particularly wanted to keep. This took us some time, and when we went into the nursery the fire was black out, and we could not get it alight again, even with the whole *Daily Chronicle*. Matilda, who was our general then, was out, as well as the fire, so we went and sat in the kitchen. There is always a good fire in kitchens. The kitchen hearthrug was not nice to sit on, so we spread newspapers on it.

It was sitting in the kitchen, I think, that brought to our minds my Father's parting words – about the pudding, I mean.

Oswald said, 'Father said we couldn't have much of a Christmas for secret reasons, and he said he had told Matilda to make us a plain pudding.'

The plain pudding instantly cast its shadow over the deepening gloom of our young minds.

'I wonder *how* plain she'll make it?' Dicky said.

'As plain as plain, you may depend,' said Oswald. 'A here-am-I-where-are-you pudding – that's her sort.'

The others groaned, and we gathered closer round the fire till the newspapers rustled madly.

'I believe I could make a pudding that *wasn't* plain, if I tried,' Alice said. 'Why shouldn't we?'

'No chink,' said Oswald, with brief sadness.

'How much would it cost?' Noël asked, and added that Dora had twopence and H.O. had a French halfpenny.

Dora got the cookery-book out of the dresser drawer, where it lay doubled up among clothes-pegs, dirty dusters, scallop shells, string, penny novelettes, and the dining-room corkscrew. The general we had then – it seemed as if she did all the cooking on the cookery-book instead of on the baking-board, there were traces of so many bygone meals upon its pages.

'It doesn't say Christmas pudding at all,' said Dora.

'Try plum,' the resourceful Oswald instantly counselled.

Dora turned the greasy pages anxiously.

'"Plum-pudding, 518.

'"A rich, with flour, 517.

'"Christmas, 517.

'"Cold brandy sauce for, 241."

'We shouldn't care about that, so it's no use looking.

'"Good without eggs, 518.

'"Plain, 518."

'We don't want *that* anyhow. "Christmas, 517" – that's the one.'

It took her a long time to find the page. Oswald got a shovel of coals and made up the fire. It blazed up like the devouring elephant the *Daily Telegraph* always calls it. Then Dora read –

'"Christmas plum-pudding. Time six hours."'

'To eat it in?' said H.O.

'No, silly! to make it.'

'Forge ahead, Dora,' Dicky replied.

Dora went on –

'"2072. One pound and a half of raisins; half a pound of

currants; three-quarters of a pound of breadcrumbs; half a pound of flour; three-quarters of a pound of beef suet; nine eggs; one wine glassful of brandy; half a pound of citron and orange peel; half a nutmeg; and a little ground ginger." I wonder *how* little ground ginger.'

'A teacupful would be enough, I think,' Alice said; 'we must not be extravagant.'

'We haven't got anything yet to be extravagant *with*,' said Oswald, who had toothache that day. 'What would you do with the things if you'd got them?'

'You'd "chop the suet as fine as possible" – I wonder how fine that is?' replied Dora and the book together – '"and mix it with the breadcrumbs and flour; add the currants washed and dried."'

'Not starched, then,' said Alice.

'"The citron and orange peel cut into thin slices" – I wonder what they call thin? Matilda's thin bread-and-butter is quite different from what I mean by it – "and the raisins stoned and divided." How many heaps would you divide them into?'

'Seven, I suppose,' said Alice; 'one for each person and one for the pot – I mean pudding.'

'"Mix it all well together with the grated nutmeg and ginger. Then stir in nine eggs well beaten, and the brandy" – we'll leave that out, I think – "and again mix it thoroughly together that every ingredient may be moistened; put it into a buttered mould, tie over tightly, and boil for six hours. Serve it ornamented with holly and brandy poured over it."'

'I should think holly and brandy poured over it would be simply beastly,' said Dicky.

'I expect the book knows. I daresay holly and water would do as well though. "This pudding may be made a month before" – it's no use reading about that though, because we've only got four days to Christmas.'

'It's no use reading about any of it,' said Oswald, with thoughtful repeatedness, 'because we haven't got the things, and we haven't got the coin to get them.'

'We might get the tin somehow,' said Dicky.

'There must be lots of kind people who would subscribe to a Christmas pudding for poor children who hadn't any,' Noël said.

'Well, I'm going skating at Penn's,' said Oswald. 'It's no use thinking about puddings. We must put up with it plain.'

So he went, and Dicky went with him.

When they returned to their home in the evening the fire had been lighted again in the nursery, and the others were just having tea. We toasted our bread-and-butter on the bare side, and it gets a little warm among the butter. This is called French toast. 'I like English better, but it is more expensive,' Alice said –

'Matilda is in a frightful rage about your putting those coals on the kitchen fire, Oswald. She says we shan't have enough to last over Christmas as it is. And Father gave her a talking to before he went about them – asked her if she ate them, she says – but I don't believe he did. Anyway, she's locked the coal-cellar door, and she's got the key in her pocket. I don't see how we can boil the pudding.'

'What pudding?' said Oswald dreamily. He was thinking of a chap he had seen at Penn's who had cut the date 1899 on the ice with four strokes.

'*The* pudding,' Alice said. 'Oh, we've had such a time, Oswald! First Dora and I went to the shops to find out exactly what the pudding would cost – it's only two and elevenpence halfpenny, counting in the holly.'

'It's no good,' Oswald repeated; he is very patient and will say the same thing any number of times. 'It's no good. You know we've got no tin.'

234 ROUND THE CHRISTMAS FIRE

'Ah,' said Alice, 'but Noël and I went out, and we called at some of the houses in Granville Park and Dartmouth Hill – and we got a lot of sixpences and shillings, besides pennies, and one old gentleman gave us half-a-crown. He was so nice. Quite bald, with a knitted red and blue waistcoat. We've got eight-and-sevenpence.'

Oswald did not feel quite sure Father would like us to go asking for shillings and sixpences, or even half-crowns from strangers, but he did not say so. The money had been asked for and got, and it couldn't be helped – and perhaps he wanted the pudding – I am not able to remember exactly why he did not speak up and say, 'This is wrong,' but anyway he didn't.

Alice and Dora went out and bought the things next morning. They bought double quantities, so that it came to five shillings and elevenpence, and was enough to make a noble pudding. There was a lot of holly left over for decorations. We used very little for the sauce. The money that was left we spent very anxiously in other things to eat, such as dates and figs and toffee.

We did not tell Matilda about it. She was a red-haired girl, and apt to turn shirty at the least thing.

Concealed under our jackets and overcoats we carried the parcels up to the nursery, and hid them in the treasure-chest we had there. It was the bureau drawer. It was locked up afterwards because the treacle got all over the green baize and the little drawers inside it while we were waiting to begin to make the pudding. It was the grocer told us we ought to put treacle in the pudding, and also about not so much ginger as a teacupful.

When Matilda had begun to pretend to scrub the floor (she pretended this three times a week so as to have an excuse not to let us in the kitchen, but I know she used to read novelettes most of the time, because Alice and I had a squint through the window more than once), we barricaded the nursery door and set to work. We were very careful to be quite clean. We washed our hands as well as the currants. I have sometimes thought we did not get all the soap off the currants. The pudding smelt like a washing-day when the time came to cut it open. And we washed a corner of the table to chop the suet on. Chopping suet looks easy till you try.

Father's machine he weighs letters with did to weigh out the things. We did this very carefully, in case the grocer had not done so. Everything was right except the raisins. H.O. had carried them home. He was very young then, and there was a hole in the corner of the paper bag and his mouth was sticky.

Lots of people have been hanged to a gibbet in chains on evidence no worse than that, and we told H.O. so till he cried. This was good for him. It was not unkindness to H.O., but part of our duty.

Chopping suet as fine as possible is much harder than any one would think, as I said before. So is crumbling bread – especially if your loaf is new, like ours was. When we had done them the breadcrumbs and the suet were both very large and lumpy, and of a dingy grey colour, something like pale slate pencil.

They looked a better colour when we had mixed them with the flour. The girls had washed the currants with Brown Windsor soap and the sponge. Some of the currants got inside the sponge and kept coming out in the bath for days afterwards. I see now that this was not quite nice. We cut the candied peel as thin as we wish people would cut our bread-and-butter. We tried to take the stones out of the raisins, but they were too sticky, so we just divided them up in seven lots. Then we mixed the other things in the wash-hand basin from the spare bedroom that was always spare. We each put in our own lot of raisins and turned it all into a pudding-basin, and tied it up in one of Alice's pinafores, which was the nearest thing to a proper pudding-cloth we could find – at any rate clean. What was left sticking to the wash-hand basin did not taste so bad.

'It's a little bit soapy,' Alice said, 'but perhaps that will boil out; like stains in table-cloths.'

It was a difficult question how to boil the pudding. Matilda proved furious when asked to let us, just because someone had happened to knock her hat off the scullery door and Pincher had got it and done for it. However, part of the embassy nicked a saucepan while the others were being told what Matilda thought about the hat, and we got hot water out of the bath-room and made it boil over our nursery fire. We put the pudding in – it was now getting on towards the hour of tea – and let it boil. With some exceptions – owing to the fire going down, and Matilda not hurrying up with coals – it boiled for an hour and a quarter. Then Matilda came suddenly in and said, 'I'm not going to have you messing about in here with my saucepans'; and she tried to take it off the fire. You will see that we couldn't stand this; it was not likely. I do not remember who it was that told her to mind her own business, and I think I have forgotten who caught hold of her first to make her chuck it. I am sure no needless violence was used. Anyway, while the struggle progressed, Alice and Dora took the saucepan away and put it in the boot-cupboard under the stairs and put the key in their pocket.

This sharp encounter made every one very hot and cross. We got over it before Matilda did, but we brought her round before bedtime. Quarrels should always be made up before bedtime. It says so in the Bible. If this simple rule was followed there would not be so many wars and martyrs and law suits and inquisitions and bloody deaths at the stake.

All the house was still. The gas was out all over the house except on the first landing, when several darkly-shrouded figures might have been observed creeping downstairs to the kitchen.

On the way, with superior precaution, we got out our saucepan. The kitchen fire was red, but low; the coal-cellar was locked, and there was nothing in the scuttle but a little coal-dust and the piece of brown paper that is put in to keep the coals from tumbling out through the bottom where the hole is. We put the saucepan on the fire and plied it with fuel – two *Chronicles*, a *Telegraph*, and two *Family Herald* novelettes were burned in vain. I am almost sure the pudding did not boil at all that night.

'Never mind,' Alice said. 'We can each nick a piece of coal every time we go into the kitchen tomorrow.'

This daring scheme was faithfully performed, and by night we had nearly half a waste-paper basket of coal, coke, and cinders. And in the depth of night once more we might have been observed, this time with our collier-like waste-paper basket in our guarded hands.

There was more fire left in the grate that night, and we fed it with the fuel we had collected. This time the fire blazed up, and the pudding boiled like mad. This was the time it boiled two hours – at least I think it was about that, but we dropped asleep on the kitchen tables and dresser. You dare not be lowly in the night in the kitchen, because of the beetles. We were aroused by a horrible smell. It was the pudding-cloth burning. All the water had secretly boiled itself away. We filled it up at once with cold, and the saucepan cracked. So we cleaned it and put it back on the shelf and took another and went to bed. You see what a lot of trouble we had over the pudding. Every evening till Christmas, which had now become only the day after tomorrow, we sneaked down in the inky midnight and boiled that pudding for as long as it would.

On Christmas morning we chopped the holly for the sauce, but we put hot water (instead of brandy) and moist sugar. Some of them said it was not so bad. Oswald was not one of these.

Then came the moment when the plain pudding Father had ordered smoked upon the board. Matilda brought it in and went away at once. She had a cousin out of Woolwich Arsenal to see her that day, I remember. Those far-off days are quite distinct in memory's recollection still.

Then we got out our own pudding from its hiding-place and gave it one last hurried boil – only seven minutes, because of the general impatience which Oswald and Dora could not cope with.

We had found means to secrete a dish, and we now tried to dish the pudding up, but it stuck to the basin, and had to be dislodged with the chisel. The pudding was horribly pale. We poured the holly sauce over it, and Dora took up the knife and was just cutting it when a few simple words from H.O. turned us from happy and triumphing cookery artists to persons in despair.

He said: 'How pleased all those kind ladies and gentlemen would be if they knew *we* were the poor children they gave the shillings and sixpences and things for!'

We all said, '*What?*' It was no moment for politeness.

'I say,' H.O. said, 'they'd be glad if they knew it was us was enjoying the pudding, and not dirty little, really poor children.'

'You should say "you were," not "you was,"' said Dora, but it was as in a dream and only from habit.

'Do you mean to say' – Oswald spoke firmly, yet not angrily – 'that you and Alice went and begged for money for poor children, and then *kept* it?'

'We didn't keep it,' said H.O., 'we spent it.'

'We've kept the *things*, you little duffer!' said Dicky, looking at the pudding sitting alone and uncared for on its dish. 'You begged for money for poor children, and then *kept* it. It's stealing, that's what it is. I don't say so much about you – you're only a silly kid – but Alice knew better. Why did you do it?'

He turned to Alice, but she was now too deep in tears to get a word out.

H.O. looked a bit frightened, but he answered the question. We have taught him this. He said –

'I thought they'd give us more if I said poor children than if I said just us.'

'*That's* cheating,' said Dicky, 'downright beastly, mean, low cheating.'

'I'm not,' said H.O.; 'and you're another.' Then he began to cry too. I do not know how the others felt, but I understand from Oswald that he felt that now the honour of the house of Bastable had been stamped on in the dust, and it didn't matter what happened. He looked at the beastly holly that had been left over from the sauce and was stuck up over the pictures. It now appeared hollow and disgusting, though it had got quite a lot of berries, and some of it was the varied kind – green and white. The figs and dates and toffee were set out in the doll's dinner service. The very sight of it all made Oswald blush sickly. He owns he would have liked to cuff H.O., and, if he did for a moment wish to shake Alice, the author, for one, can make allowances.

Now Alice choked and spluttered, and wiped her eyes fiercely, and said, 'It's no use ragging H.O. It's my fault. I'm older than he is.'

H.O. said, 'It couldn't be Alice's fault. I don't see as it was wrong.'

'That, not as,' murmured Dora, putting her arm round the sinner who had brought this degrading blight upon our family tree, but such is girls' undetermined and affectionate silliness. 'Tell sister all about it, H.O. dear. Why couldn't it be Alice's fault?'

H.O. cuddled up to Dora and said snufflingly in his nose –

'Because she hadn't got nothing to do with it. I collected it all. She never went into one of the houses. She didn't want to.'

'And then took all the credit of getting the money,' said Dicky savagely.

Oswald said, 'Not much *credit*,' in scornful tones.

'Oh, you are *beastly*, the whole lot of you, except Dora!' Alice said, stamping her foot in rage and despair. 'I tore my frock on a nail going out, and I didn't want to go back, and I got H.O. to go to the houses alone, and I waited for him outside. And I asked him not to say anything because I didn't want Dora to know about the frock – it's my best. And I don't know what he said inside. He never told me. But I'll bet anything he didn't *mean* to cheat.'

'You *said* lots of kind people would be ready to give money to get pudding for poor children. So I asked them to.'

Oswald, with his strong right hand, waved a wave of passing things over.

'We'll talk about that another time,' he said; 'just now we've got weightier things to deal with.'

He pointed to the pudding, which had grown cold during the conversation to which I have alluded. H.O. stopped crying, but Alice went on with it. Oswald now said –

'We're a base and outcast family. Until that pudding's out of the house we shan't be able to look any one in the face. We must see that that pudding goes to poor children – not grisling, grumpy, whiney-piney, pretending poor children – but real poor ones, just as poor as they can stick.'

'And the figs too – and the dates,' said Noël, with regretting tones.

'Every fig,' said Dicky sternly. 'Oswald is quite right.'

This honourable resolution made us feel a bit better. We hastily put on our best things, and washed ourselves a bit, and hurried out to find some really poor people to give the pudding to. We cut it in slices ready, and put it in a basket with the figs and dates and toffee. We would not let H.O. come with us at first because he wanted to. And Alice would not come because of him. So at last we had to let him. The excitement of tearing into your best things heals the hurt that wounded honour feels, as the poetry writer said – or at any rate it makes the hurt feel better.

We went out into the streets. They were pretty quiet – nearly everybody was eating its Christmas dessert. But presently we met a woman in an apron. Oswald said very politely –

'Please, are you a poor person?' And she told us to get along with us.

The next we met was a shabby man with a hole in his left boot.

Again Oswald said, 'Please, are you a poor person, and have you any poor little children?'

The man told us not to come any of our games with him, or we should laugh on the wrong side of our faces. We went on sadly. We had no heart to stop and explain to him that we had no games to come.

The next was a young man near the Obelisk. Dora tried this time.

She said, 'Oh, if you please we've got some Christmas pudding in this basket, and if you're a poor person you can have some.'

'Poor as Job,' said the young man in a hoarse voice, and he had to come up out of a red comforter to say it.

We gave him a slice of the pudding, and he bit into it without thanks or delay. The next minute he had thrown the pudding slap in Dora's face, and was clutching Dicky by the collar.

'Blime if I don't chuck ye in the river, the whole bloomin' lot of you!' he exclaimed.

The girls screamed, the boys shouted, and though Oswald threw himself on the insulter of his sister with all his manly vigour, yet but for a friend of Oswald's, who is in the police, passing at that instant, the author shudders to think what might have happened, for he was a strong young man, and Oswald is not yet come to his full strength, and the Quaggy runs all too near.

Our policeman led our assailant aside, and we waited anxiously, as he told us to. After long uncertain moments the young man in the comforter loafed off grumbling, and our policeman turned to us.

'Said you give him a dollop o' pudding, and it tasted of soap and hair-oil.'

I suppose the hair-oil must have been the Brown Windsoriness of the soap coming out. We were sorry, but it was still our duty to get rid of the pudding. The Quaggy was handy, it is true, but when you have collected money to feed poor children and spent it on pudding it is not right to throw that pudding in the river. People do not subscribe shillings and sixpences and half-crowns to feed a hungry flood with Christmas pudding.

Yet we shrank from asking any more people whether they were poor persons, or about their families, and still more from offering the pudding to chance people who might bite into it and taste the soap before we had time to get away.

It was Alice, the most paralysed with disgrace of all of us, who thought of the best idea.

She said, 'Let's take it to the workhouse. At any rate they're all poor people there, and they mayn't go out without leave, so they can't run after us to do anything to us after the pudding. No one would give them leave to go out to pursue people who had brought them pudding, and wreck vengeance on them, and at any rate we shall get rid of the conscience-pudding – it's a sort of conscience-money, you know – only it isn't money but pudding.'

The workhouse is a good way, but we stuck to it, though

very cold, and hungrier than we thought possible when we started, for we had been so agitated we had not even stayed to eat the plain pudding our good Father had so kindly and thoughtfully ordered for our Christmas dinner.

The big bell at the workhouse made a man open the door to us, when we rang it. Oswald said (and he spoke because he is next eldest to Dora, and she had had jolly well enough of saying anything about pudding) – he said –

'Please we've brought some pudding for the poor people.'

He looked us up and down, and he looked at our basket, then he said: 'You'd better see the Matron.'

We waited in a hall, feeling more and more uncomfy, and less and less like Christmas. We were very cold indeed, especially our hands and our noses. And we felt less and less able to face the Matron if she was horrid, and one of us at least wished we had chosen the Quaggy for the pudding's long home, and made it up to the robbed poor in some other way afterwards.

Just as Alice was saying earnestly in the burning cold ear of Oswald, 'Let's put down the basket and make a bolt for it. Oh, Oswald, *let's!*' a lady came along the passage. She was very upright, and she had eyes that went through you like blue gimlets. I should not like to be obliged to thwart that lady if she had any design, and mine was opposite. I am glad this is not likely to occur.

She said, 'What's all this about a pudding?'

H.O. said at once, before we could stop him, 'They say I've stolen the pudding, so we've brought it here for the poor people.'

'No, we didn't!' 'That wasn't why!' 'The money was given!' 'It was meant for the poor!' 'Shut up, H.O.!' said the rest of us all at once.

Then there was an awful silence. The lady gimleted us again one by one with her blue eyes.

Then she said: 'Come into my room. You all look frozen.'

She took us into a very jolly room with velvet curtains and a big fire, and the gas lighted, because now it was almost dark, even out of doors. She gave us chairs, and Oswald felt as if his was a dock, he felt so criminal, and the lady looked so Judgular.

Then she took the arm-chair by the fire herself, and said, 'Who's the eldest?'

'I am,' said Dora, looking more like a frightened white rabbit than I've ever seen her.

'Then tell me all about it.'

Dora looked at Alice and began to cry. That slab of pudding in the face had totally unnerved the gentle girl. Alice's eyes were red, and her face was puffy with crying; but she spoke up for Dora and said –

'Oh, please let Oswald tell. Dora can't. She's tired with the long walk. And a young man threw a piece of it in her face, and –'

The lady nodded and Oswald began. He told the story from the very beginning, as he has always been taught to, though he hated to lay bare the family honour's wound before a stranger, however judgelike and gimlet-eyed. He told all – not concealing the pudding-throwing, nor what the young man said about soap.

'So,' he ended, 'we want to give the conscience-pudding to you. It's like conscience-money – you know what that is, don't you? But if you really think it is soapy and not just the young man's horridness, perhaps you'd better not let them eat it. But the figs and things are all right.'

When he had done the lady said, for most of us were crying more or less –

'Come, cheer up! It's Christmas-time, and he's very little – your brother, I mean. And I think the rest of you seem pretty well able to take care of the honour of the family. I'll take the conscience-pudding off your minds. Where are you going now?'

'Home, I suppose,' Oswald said. And he thought how nasty and dark and dull it would be. The fire out most likely and Father away.

'And your Father's not at home, you say,' the blue-gimlet lady went on. 'What do you say to having tea with me, and then seeing the entertainment we have got up for our old people?'

Then the lady smiled and the blue gimlets looked quite merry.

The room was so warm and comfortable and the invitation was the last thing we expected. It was jolly of her, I do think.

No one thought quite at first of saying how pleased we should be to accept her kind invitation. Instead we all just said 'Oh!' but in a tone which must have told her we meant 'Yes, please,' very deeply.

Oswald (this has more than once happened) was the first to restore his manners. He made a proper bow like he has been taught, and said –

'Thank you very much. We should like it very much. It is very much nicer than going home. Thank you very much.'

I need not tell the reader that Oswald could have made up a much better speech if he had had more time to make it up in, or if he had not been so filled with mixed flusteredness and furification by the shameful events of the day.

We washed our faces and hands and had a first-rate muffin and crumpet tea, with slices of cold meats, and many nice jams and cakes. A lot of other people were there, most of them people who were giving the entertainment to the aged poor.

After tea it was the entertainment. Songs and conjuring and a play called 'Box and Cox,' very amusing, and a lot of throwing things about in it – bacon and chops and things – and minstrels. We clapped till our hands were sore.

When it was over we said goodbye. In between the songs

and things Oswald had had time to make up a speech of thanks to the lady.

He said –

'We all thank you heartily for your goodness. The entertainment was beautiful. We shall never forget your kindness and hospitableness.'

The lady laughed, and said she had been very pleased to have us. A fat gentleman said –

'And your teas? I hope you enjoyed those – eh?'

Oswald had not had time to make up an answer to that, so he answered straight from the heart, and said –

'Ra – *ther!*'

And everyone laughed and slapped us boys on the back and kissed the girls, and the gentleman who played the bones in the minstrels saw us home. We ate the cold pudding that night, and H.O. dreamed that something came to eat him, like it advises you to in the advertisements on the hoardings. The grown-ups said it was the pudding, but I don't think it could have been that, because, as I have said more than once, it was so very plain.

Some of H.O.'s brothers and sisters thought it was a judgment on him for pretending about who the poor children were he was collecting the money for. Oswald does not believe such a little boy as H.O. would have a real judgment made just for him and nobody else, whatever he did.

But it certainly is odd. H.O. was the only one who had bad dreams, and he was also the only one who got any of the things we bought with that ill-gotten money, because, you remember, he picked a hole in the raisin-paper as he was bringing the parcel home. The rest of us had nothing, unless you count the scrapings of the pudding-basin, and those don't really count at all.

LAST CHRISTMAS

A CHILD'S CHRISTMAS IN WALES *BY* DYLAN THOMAS

Dylan Thomas was born on 27 October 1914, in Swansea, Wales. His first poems were published while he was still at school and he quickly won acclaim and popularity. Reading tours, stories, radio broadcasts such as *A Child's Christmas in Wales*, and plays such as *Under Milk Wood*, made him a well-known name in Britain and the US. Some of his best-known poems include 'Do not go gentle into that good night' and 'Fern Hill'. Dylan Thomas died in New York on 9 November 1953, and is buried in Wales.

ONE CHRISTMAS was so much like another, in those years around the sea-town corner now and out of all sound except the distant speaking of the voices I sometimes hear a moment before sleep, that I can never remember whether it snowed for six days and six nights when I was twelve or whether it snowed for twelve days and twelve nights when I was six.

All the Christmases roll down towards the two-tongued sea, like a cold and headlong moon bundling down the sky that was our street; and they stop at the rim of the ice-edged, fish-freezing waves, and I plunge my hands in the snow and bring out whatever I can find. In goes my hand into that wool-white bell-tongued ball of holidays resting at the rim of the carol-singing sea, and out come Mrs Prothero and the firemen.

It was on the afternoon of the day of Christmas Eve, and I was in Mrs Prothero's garden, waiting for cats, with her son Jim. It was snowing. It was always snowing at Christmas. December, in my memory, is white as Lapland, though there were no reindeers. But there were cats. Patient, cold and callous, our hands wrapped in socks, we waited to snowball the cats. Sleek and long as jaguars and horrible-whiskered, spitting and snarling, they would slink and sidle over the white back-garden walls, and the lynx-eyed hunters, Jim and I, fur-capped and moccasined trappers from Hudson Bay, off Mumbles Road, would hurl our deadly snowballs at the green of their eyes.

The wise cats never appeared. We were so still, Eskimo-footed arctic marksmen in the muffling silence of the eternal snows – eternal, ever since Wednesday – that we never heard Mrs Prothero's first cry from her igloo at the bottom of the garden. Or, if we heard it at all, it was, to us, like the far-off challenge of our enemy and prey, the neighbour's polar cat. But soon the voice grew louder. 'Fire!' cried Mrs Prothero, and she beat the dinner-gong.

And we ran down the garden, with the snowballs in our arms, towards the house; and smoke, indeed, was pouring out of the dining-room, and the gong was bombilating, and Mrs Prothero was announcing ruin like a town crier in Pompeii. This was better than all the cats in Wales standing on the wall in a row. We bounded into the house, laden with snowballs, and stopped at the open door of the smoke-filled room.

Something was burning all right; perhaps it was Mr Prothero, who always slept there after midday dinner with a newspaper over his face. But he was standing in the middle of the room, saying, 'A fine Christmas!' and smacking at the smoke with a slipper. 'Call the fire brigade,' cried Mrs Prothero as she beat the gong.

'They won't be there,' said Mr Prothero, 'it's Christmas.'

There was no fire to be seen, only clouds of smoke and Mr Prothero standing in the middle of them, waving his slipper as though he were conducting.

'Do something,' he said.

And we threw all our snowballs into the smoke – I think we missed Mr Prothero – and ran out of the house to the telephone box.

'Let's call the police as well,' Jim said.

'And the ambulance.'

'And Ernie Jenkins, he likes fires.'

But we only called the fire brigade, and soon the fire engine came and three tall men in helmets brought a hose into the house and Mr Prothero got out just in time before they turned it on. Nobody could have had a noisier Christmas Eve. And when the firemen turned off the hose and were standing in the wet, smoky room, Jim's aunt, Miss Prothero, came downstairs and peered in at them. Jim and I waited, very quietly, to hear what she would say to them. She said the right thing, always. She looked at the three tall firemen in their shining helmets, standing among the smoke and cinders and dissolving snowballs, and she said: 'Would you like anything to read?'

Years and years and years ago, when I was a boy, when there were wolves in Wales, and birds the colour of red-flannel petticoats whisked past the harp-shaped hills, when we sang and wallowed all night and day in caves that smelt like Sunday afternoons in damp front farmhouse parlours and we chased, with the jawbones of deacons, the English and the bears, before the motor-car, before the wheel, before the duchess-faced horse, when we rode the daft and happy hills bareback, it snowed and it snowed. But here a small boy says: 'It snowed last year, too. I made a snowman and my brother knocked it down and I knocked my brother down and then we had tea.'

'But that was not the same snow,' I say. 'Our snow was not only shaken from whitewash buckets down the sky, it came shawling out of the ground and swam and drifted out of the arms and hands and bodies of the trees; snow grew overnight on the roofs of the houses like a pure and grandfather moss, minutely white-ivied the walls and settled on the postman, opening the gate, like a dumb, numb thunderstorm of white, torn Christmas cards.'

'Were there postmen then, too?'

'With sprinkling eyes and wind-cherried noses, on spread, frozen feet they crunched up to the doors and mittened on them manfully. But all that the children could hear was a ringing of bells.'

'You mean that the postman went rat-a-tat-tat and the doors rang?'

'I mean that the bells that the children could hear were inside them.'

'I only hear thunder sometimes, never bells.'

'There were church bells, too.'

'Inside them?'

'No, no, no, in the bat-black, snow-white belfries, tugged by bishops and storks. And they rang their tidings over the band-aged town, over the frozen foam of the powder and ice-cream hills, over the crackling sea. It seemed that all the churches boomed for joy under my window; and the weathercocks crew for Christmas, on our fence.'

'Get back to the postmen.'

'They were just ordinary postmen, fond of walking and dogs and Christmas and the snow. They knocked on the doors with blue knuckles . . .'

'Ours has got a black knocker . . .'

'And then they stood on the white Welcome mat in the little, drifted porches and huffed and puffed, making ghosts with their breath, and jogged from foot to foot like small boys wanting to go out.'

'And then the Presents?'

'And then the Presents, after the Christmas box. And the cold postman, with a rose on his button-nose, tingled down the tea-tray-slithered run of the chilly glinting hill. He went in his ice-bound boots like a man on fishmonger's slabs. He wagged his bag like a frozen camel's hump, dizzily turned the corner on one foot, and, by God, he was gone.'

'Get back to the Presents.'

'There were the Useful Presents: engulfing mufflers of the old coach days, and mittens made for giant sloths; zebra scarfs of a substance like silky gum that could be tug-o'-warred down to the galoshes; blinding tam-o'-shanters like patchwork tea-cosies and bunny-suited busbies and balaclavas for victims of head-shrinking tribes; from aunts who always wore wool next to the skin there were moustached and rasping vests that made you wonder why the aunts had any skin left at all; and once I had a little crocheted nose bag from an aunt now, alas, no longer whinnying with us. And pictureless books in which small boys, though warned with quotations not to, *would* skate on Farmer Giles' pond and did and drowned; and books that told me everything about the wasp, except why.'

'Go on to the Useless Presents.'

'Bags of moist and many-coloured jelly babies and a folded flag and a false nose and a tram-conductor's cap and a machine that punched tickets and rang a bell; never a catapult; once, by mistake that no one could explain, a little hatchet; and a cellu-loid duck that made, when you pressed it, a most unducklike sound, a mewing moo that an ambitious cat might make who wished to be a cow; and a painting book in which I could make the grass, the trees, the sea and the animals any colour I pleased, and still the dazzling sky-blue sheep are grazing in the red field under the rainbow-billed and pea-green birds.

'Hardboileds, toffee, fudge and allsorts, crunches, cracknels, humbugs, glaciers, marzipan, and butterwelsh for the Welsh. And troops of bright tin soldiers who, if they could not fight, could always run. And Snakes-and-Families and Happy Ladders. And Easy Hobbi-Games for Little Engineers, complete with instructions.

'Oh, easy for Leonardo! And a whistle to make the dogs bark to wake up the old man next door to make him beat on the wall with his stick to shake our picture off the wall.

'And a packet of cigarettes; you put one in your mouth and you stood at the corner of the street and you waited for hours, in vain, for an old lady to scold you for smoking a cigarette, and then with a smirk you ate it. And then it was breakfast under the balloons.'

'Were there Uncles like in our house?'

'There are always Uncles at Christmas.

'The same Uncles. And on Christmas mornings, with dog-disturbing whistle and sugar fags, I would scour the swatched town for the news of the little world, and find always a dead bird by the white Post Office or by the deserted swings; perhaps a robin, all but one of his fires out. Men and women wading or scooping back from chapel, with taproom noses and wind-bussed cheeks, all albinos, huddled their stiff black jarring feathers against the irreligious snow.

'Mistletoe hung from the gas brackets in all the front parlours; there was sherry and walnuts and bottled beer and crackers by the dessertspoons; and cats in their fur-abouts watched the fires; and the high-heaped fire spat, all ready for the chestnuts and the mulling pokers.

'Some few large men sat in the front parlours, without their collars, Uncles almost certainly, trying their new cigars, holding them out judiciously at arms' length, returning them to their mouths, coughing, then holding them out again as though waiting for the explosion; and some few small Aunts, not wanted in the kitchen, nor anywhere else for that matter, sat on the very edges of their chairs, poised and brittle, afraid to break, like faded cups and saucers.'

Not many those mornings trod the piling streets: an old man

always, fawn-bowlered, yellow-gloved and, at this time of year, with spats of snow, would take his constitutional to the white bowling green and back, as he would take it wet or fine on Christmas Day or Doomsday; sometimes two hale young men, with big pipes blazing, no overcoats and wind-blown scarfs, would trudge, unspeaking, down to the forlorn sea, to work up an appetite, to blow away the fumes, who knows, to walk into the waves until nothing of them was left but the two curling smoke clouds of their inextinguishable briars. Then I would be slap-dashing home, the gravy smell of the dinners of others, the bird smell, the brandy, the pudding and mince, coiling up to my nostrils, when out of a snow-clogged side lane would come a boy the spit of myself, with a pink-tipped cigarette and the violet past of a black eye, cocky as a bullfinch, leering all to himself.

I hated him on sight and sound, and would be about to put my dog whistle to my lips and blow him off the face of Christmas when suddenly he, with a violet wink, put *his* whistle to *his* lips and blew so stridently, so high, so exquisitely loud, that gobbling faces, their cheeks bulged with goose, would press against their tinselled windows, the whole length of the white echoing street. For dinner we had turkey and blazing pudding, and after dinner the Uncles sat in front of the fire, loosened all buttons, put their large moist hands over their watch chains, groaned a little and slept. Mothers, aunts and sisters scuttled to and fro, bearing tureens. Auntie Bessie, who had already been frightened, twice, by a clock-work mouse, whimpered at the sideboard and had some elderberry wine. The dog was sick. Auntie Dosie had to have three aspirins, but Auntie Hannah, who liked port, stood in the middle of the snowbound back yard, singing like a big-bosomed thrush. I would blow up balloons to see how big they would blow up to; and, when they burst, which they all did, the Uncles jumped and rumbled. In the rich and heavy afternoon, the Uncles breathing like dolphins and the snow descending, I would sit among festoons and Chinese lanterns and nibble dates and try to make a model man-o'-war, following the Instructions for Little Engineers, and produce what might be mistaken for a sea-going tramcar.

Or I would go out, my bright new boots squeaking, into the white world, on to the seaward hill, to call on Jim and Dan and Jack and to pad through the still streets, leaving huge deep footprints on the hidden pavements.

'I bet people will think there's been hippos.'

'What would you do if you saw a hippo coming down our street?'

'I'd go like this, bang! I'd throw him over the railings and roll him down the hill and then I'd tickle him under the ear and he'd wag his tail.'

'What would you do if you saw *two* hippos?'

Iron-flanked and bellowing he-hippos clanked and battered through the scudding snow towards us as we passed Mr Daniel's house.

'Let's post Mr Daniel a snowball through his letter-box.'

'Let's write things in the snow.'

'Let's write, "Mr Daniel looks like a spaniel" all over his lawn.'

Or we walked on the white shore.

'Can the fishes see it's snowing?'

The silent one-clouded heavens drifted on to the sea. Now we were snow-blind travellers lost on the north hills, and vast dewlapped dogs, with flasks round their necks, ambled and shambled up to us, baying 'Excelsior'. We returned home through the poor streets where only a few children fumbled with bare red fingers in the wheel-rutted snow and cat-called after us, their voices fading away, as we trudged uphill, into the cries of the dock birds and the hooting of ships out in the whirling bay. And then, at tea the recovered Uncles would be jolly; and the ice cake loomed in the centre of the table like a marble grave. Auntie Hannah laced her tea with rum, because it was only once a year.

Bring out the tall tales now that we told by the fire as the gaslight bubbled like a diver. Ghosts whooed like owls in the long nights when I dared not look over my shoulder; animals lurked in the cubbyhole under the stairs where the gas meter ticked. And I remember that we went singing carols once, when there wasn't the shaving of a moon to light the flying streets. At the end of a long road was a drive that led to a large house, and we stumbled up the darkness of the drive that night, each one of us afraid, each one holding a stone in his hand in case, and all of us too brave to say a word. The wind through the trees made noises as of old and unpleasant and maybe webfooted men wheezing in caves. We reached the black bulk of the house.

'What shall we give them? Hark the Herald?'

'No,' Jack said, 'Good King Wenceslas. I'll count three.'

One, two, three, and we began to sing, our voices high and seemingly distant in the snow-felted darkness round the house that was occupied by nobody we knew. We stood close together, near the dark door.

Good King Wenceslas looked out
On the Feast of Stephen . . .

And then a small, dry voice, like the voice of someone who has not spoken for a long time, joined our singing: a small, dry, eggshell voice from the other side of the door: a small dry voice through the keyhole. And when we stopped running we were outside *our* house; the front room was lovely; balloons floated under the hot-water-bottle-gulping gas; everything was good again and shone over the town.

'Perhaps it was a ghost,' Jim said.

'Perhaps it was trolls,' Dan said, who was always reading.

'Let's go in and see if there's any jelly left,' Jack said. And we did that.

Always on Christmas night there was music. An uncle played the fiddle, a cousin sang 'Cherry Ripe', and another uncle sang 'Drake's Drum'. It was very warm in the little house.

Auntie Hannah, who had got on to the parsnip wine, sang a song about Bleeding Hearts and Death, and then another in which she said her heart was like a Bird's Nest; and then everybody laughed again; and then I went to bed. Looking through my bedroom window, out into the moonlight and the unending smoke-coloured snow, I could see the lights in the windows of all the other houses on our hill and hear the music rising from them up the long, steadily falling night. I turned the gas down, I got into bed. I said some words to the close and holy darkness, and then I slept.

A CHRISTMAS MEMORY
BY TRUMAN CAPOTE

Truman Capote was born on 30 September 1925 in New Orleans. He was a childhood friend of the novelist Harper Lee, who based a character in her famous novel *To Kill a Mockingbird* on Capote. He began writing at fourteen, and left school shortly after. He worked at the *New Yorker* and travelled widely. His books include *Other Voices, Other Rooms* (1948), *Breakfast at Tiffany's* (1958) – which inspired the iconic film starring Audrey Hepburn – and the controversial, ground-breaking journalistic work *In Cold Blood* (1965). Truman Capote died on 25 August 1984.

IMAGINE A morning in late November. A coming of winter morning more than twenty years ago. Consider the kitchen of a spreading old house in a country town. A great black stove is its main feature; but there is also a big round table and a fireplace with two rocking chairs placed in front of it. Just today the fireplace commenced its seasonal roar.

A woman with shorn white hair is standing at the kitchen window. She is wearing tennis shoes and a shapeless gray sweater over a summery calico dress. She is small and sprightly, like a bantam hen; but, due to a long youthful illness, her shoulders are pitifully hunched. Her face is remarkable – not unlike Lincoln's, craggy like that, and tinted by sun and wind; but it is delicate too, finely boned, and her eyes are sherry-colored and timid. 'Oh my,' she exclaims, her breath smoking the windowpane, 'it's fruitcake weather!'

The person to whom she is speaking is myself. I am seven; she is sixty-something. We are cousins, very distant ones, and we have lived together – well, as long as I can remember. Other people inhabit the house, relatives; and though they have power over us, and frequently make us cry, we are not, on the whole, too much aware of them. We are each other's best friend. She calls me Buddy, in memory of a boy who was formerly her best friend. The other Buddy died in the 1880's, when she was still a child. She is still a child.

'I knew it before I got out of bed,' she says, turning away from the window with a purposeful excitement in her eyes. 'The courthouse bell sounded so cold and clear. And there were no birds singing; they've gone to warmer country, yes indeed. Oh, Buddy, stop stuffing biscuit and fetch our buggy. Help me find my hat. We've thirty cakes to bake.'

It's always the same: a morning arrives in November, and my friend, as though officially inaugurating the Christmas time of year that exhilarates her imagination and fuels the blaze of her heart, announces: 'It's fruitcake weather! Fetch our buggy. Help me find my hat.'

The hat is found, a straw cartwheel corsaged with velvet roses out-of-doors has faded: it once belonged to a more fashionable relative. Together, we guide our buggy, a dilapidated baby carriage, out to the garden and into a grove of pecan trees. The buggy is mine; that is, it was bought for me when I was born. It is made of wicker, rather unraveled, and the wheels wobble like a drunkard's legs. But it is a faithful object; springtimes, we take it to the woods and fill it with flowers, herbs, wild fern for our porch pots; in the summer, we pile it with picnic paraphernalia and sugar-cane fishing poles and roll it down to the edge of a creek; it has its winter uses, too: as a truck for hauling firewood from the yard to the kitchen, as a warm bed for Queenie, our tough little orange and white rat terrier who has survived distemper and two rattlesnake bites. Queenie is trotting beside it now.

Three hours later we are back in the kitchen hulling a heaping buggyload of windfall pecans. Our backs hurt from gathering them: how hard they were to find (the main crop having been shaken off the trees and sold by the orchard's owners, who are not us) among the concealing leaves, the frosted, deceiving grass. Caarackle! A cheery crunch, scraps of miniature thunder sound as the shells collapse and the golden mound of sweet oily ivory meat mounts in the milk-glass bowl. Queenie begs to taste, and now and again my friend sneaks her a mite, though insisting we deprive ourselves. 'We mustn't, Buddy. If we start, we won't stop. And there's scarcely enough as there is. For thirty cakes.' The kitchen is growing dark. Dusk turns the window into a mirror: our reflections mingle with the rising moon as we work by the fireside in the firelight. At last, when the moon is quite high, we toss the final hull into the fire and, with joined sighs, watch it catch flame. The buggy is empty, the bowl is brimful.

We eat our supper (cold biscuits, bacon, blackberry jam) and discuss tomorrow. Tomorrow the kind of work I like best begins: buying. Cherries and citron, ginger and vanilla and canned Hawaiian pineapple, rinds and raisins and walnuts and whiskey and oh, so much flour, butter, so many eggs, spices, flavorings: why, we'll need a pony to pull the buggy home.

But before these purchases can be made, there is the question of money. Neither of us has any. Except for skinflint sums persons in the house occasionally provide (a dime is considered very big money); or what we earn ourselves from various activities: holding rummage sales, selling buckets of hand-picked blackberries, jars of homemade jam and apple jelly and peach preserves, rounding up flowers for funerals and weddings. Once we won seventy-ninth prize, five dollars, in a national football contest. Not that we know a fool thing about football. It's just that we enter any contest we hear about: at the moment our hopes are centered on the fifty-thousand-dollar Grand Prize being offered to name a new brand of coffee (we suggested

266   ROUND THE CHRISTMAS FIRE

'A.M.'; and, after some hesitation, for my friend thought it perhaps sacrilegious, the slogan 'A.M.! Amen!'). To tell the truth, our only *really* profitable enterprise was the Fun and Freak Museum we conducted in a back-yard woodshed two summers ago. The Fun was a stereopticon with slide views of Washington and New York lent us by a relative who had been to those places (she was furious when she discovered why we'd borrowed it); the Freak was a three-legged biddy chicken hatched by one of our own hens. Everybody hereabouts wanted to see that biddy: we charged grownups a nickel, kids two cents. And took in a good twenty dollars before the museum shut down due to the decease of the main attraction.

But one way and another we do each year accumulate Christmas savings, a Fruitcake Fund. These moneys we keep hidden in an ancient bead purse under a loose board under the floor under a chamber pot under my friend's bed. The purse is seldom removed from this safe location except to make a deposit, or, as happens every Saturday, a withdrawal; for on Saturdays I am allowed ten cents to go to the picture show. My friend has never been to a picture show, nor does she intend to: 'I'd rather hear you tell the story, Buddy. That way I can imagine it more. Besides, a person my age shouldn't squander their eyes. When the Lord comes, let me see him clear.' In addition to never having seen a movie, she has never: eaten in a restaurant, traveled more than five miles from home, received or sent a telegram, read anything except funny papers and the Bible, worn cosmetics, cursed, wished someone harm, told a lie on purpose, let a hungry dog go hungry. Here are a few things she has done, does do: killed with a hoe the biggest rattlesnake ever seen in this county (sixteen rattles), dip snuff (secretly), tame humming-birds (just try it) till they balance on her finger, tell ghost stories (we both believe in ghosts) so tingling they chill you in July, talk to herself, take walks in the rain, grow the prettiest japonicas in town, know the recipe for every sort of old-time Indian cure, including a magical wart-remover.

Now, with supper finished, we retire to the room in a faraway part of the house where my friend sleeps in a scrap-quilt-covered iron bed painted rose pink, her favorite color. Silently, wallowing in the pleasures of conspiracy, we take the bead purse from its secret place and spill its contents on the scrap quilt. Dollar bills, tightly rolled and green as May buds. Somber fifty-cent pieces, heavy enough to weight a dead man's eyes. Lovely dimes, the liveliest coin, the one that really jingles. Nickels and quarters, worn smooth as creek pebbles. But mostly a hateful heap of bitter-odored pennies. Last summer others in the house contracted to pay us a penny for every twenty-five flies we killed. Oh, the carnage of August: the flies that flew to heaven! Yet it was not work in which we took pride. And, as we sit counting pennies, it is as though we were back tabulating dead flies. Neither of us has a head for figures; we count slowly, lose track, start again. According to her calculations we have $12.73. According to mine, exactly $13. 'I do hope you're wrong, Buddy. We can't mess around with thirteen. The cakes will fall. Or put somebody in the cemetery. Why, I wouldn't dream of getting out of bed on the thirteenth.' This is true: she always spends thirteenths in bed. So, to be on the safe side, we subtract a penny and toss it out the window.

Of the ingredients that go into our fruitcakes, whiskey is the most expensive, as well as the hardest to obtain: State laws forbid its sale. But everybody knows you can buy a bottle from Mr Haha Jones. And the next day, having completed our more prosaic shopping, we set out for Mr Haha's business address, a 'sinful' (to quote public opinion) fish-fry and dancing café down by the river. We've been there before, and on the same errand;

but in previous years our dealings have been with Haha's wife, an iodine-dark Indian woman with brazzy peroxided hair and a dead-tired disposition. Actually, we've never laid eyes on her husband, though we've heard that he's an Indian too. A giant with razor scars across his cheeks. They call him Haha because he's so gloomy, a man who never laughs. As we approach his café (a large log cabin festooned inside and out with chains of garish-gay naked lightbulbs and standing by the river's muddy edge under the shade of river trees where moss drifts through the branches like gray mist) our steps slow down. Even Queenie stops prancing and sticks close by. People have been murdered in Haha's café. Cut to pieces. Hit on the head. There's a case coming up in court next month. Naturally these goings-on happen at night when the colored lights cast crazy patterns and the victrola wails. In the daytime Haha's is shabby and deserted. I knock at the door, Queenie barks, my friend calls: 'Mrs Haha, ma'am? Anyone to home?'

Footsteps. The door opens. Our hearts overturn. It's Mr Haha Jones himself! And he *is* a giant; he *does* have scars; he *doesn't* smile. No, he glowers at us through Satan-tilted eyes and demands to know: 'What you want with Haha?'

For a moment we are too paralyzed to tell. Presently my friend half-finds her voice, a whispery voice at best: 'If you please, Mr Haha, we'd like a quart of your finest whiskey.'

His eyes tilt more. Would you believe it? Haha is smiling! Laughing, too. 'Which one of you is a drinkin' man?'

'It's for making fruitcakes, Mr Haha. Cooking.'

This sobers him. He frowns. 'That's no way to waste good whiskey.' Nevertheless, he retreats into the shadowed café and seconds later appears carrying a bottle of daisy yellow unlabeled liquor. He demonstrates its sparkle in the sunlight and says: 'Two dollars.'

We pay him with nickels and dimes and pennies. Suddenly, jangling the coins in his hand like a fistful of dice, his face softens. 'Tell you what,' he proposes, pouring the money back into our bead purse, 'just send me one of them fruitcakes instead.'

'Well,' my friend remarks on our way home, 'there's a lovely man. We'll put an extra cup of raisins in *his* cake.'

The black stove, stoked with coal and firewood, glows like a lighted pumpkin. Eggbeaters whirl, spoons spin round in bowls of butter and sugar, vanilla sweetens the air, ginger spices it; melting, nose-tingling odors saturate the kitchen, suffuse the house, drift out to the world on puffs of chimney smoke. In four days our work is done. Thirty-one cakes, dampened with whiskey, bask on window sills and shelves.

Who are they for?

Friends. Not necessarily neighbor friends: indeed, the larger share are intended for persons we've met maybe once, perhaps not at all. People who've struck our fancy. Like President Roosevelt. Like the Reverend and Mrs J. C. Lucey, Baptist missionaries to Borneo who lectured here last winter. Or the little knife grinder who comes through town twice a year. Or Abner Packer, the driver of the six o'clock bus from Mobile, who exchanges waves with us every day as he passes in a dust-cloud whoosh. Or the young Wistons, a California couple whose car one afternoon broke down outside the house and who spent a pleasant hour chatting with us on the porch (young Mr Wiston snapped our picture, the only one we've ever had taken). Is it because my friend is shy with everyone *except* strangers that these strangers, and merest acquaintances, seem to us our truest friends? I think yes. Also, the scrapbooks we keep of thank-you's on White House stationery, time-to-time communications from California and Borneo, the knife grinder's penny post cards, make us feel connected to eventful worlds beyond the kitchen with its view of a sky that stops.

Now a nude December fig branch grates against the window. The kitchen is empty, the cakes are gone; yesterday we carted the last of them to the post office, where the cost of stamps turned our purse inside out. We're broke. That rather depresses me, but my friend insists on celebrating with two inches of whiskey left in Haha's bottle. Queenie has a spoonful in a bowl of coffee (she likes her coffee chicory-flavored and strong). The rest we divide between a pair of jelly glasses. We're both quite awed at the prospect of drinking straight whiskey; the taste of it brings screwed-up expressions and sour shudders. But by and by we begin to sing, the two of us singing different songs simultaneously. I don't know the words to mine, just: *Come on along, come on along, to the dark-town strutters' ball.* But I can dance: that's what I mean to be, a tap dancer in the movies. My dancing shadow rollicks on the walls; our voices rock the chinaware; we giggle: as if unseen hands were tickling us. Queenie rolls on her back, her paws plow the air, something like a grin stretches her black lips. Inside myself I feel warm and sparky as those crumbling logs, carefree as the wind in the chimney. My friend waltzes round the stove, the hem of her poor calico skirt pinched between her fingers as though it were a party dress: *Show me the way to go home,* she sings, her tennis shoes squeaking on the floor. *Show me the way to go home.*

Enter: two relatives. Very angry. Potent with eyes that scold, tongues that scald. Listen to what they have to say, the words tumbling together into a wrathful tune: 'A child of seven! whiskey on his breath! are you out of your mind? feeding a child of seven! must be loony! road to ruination! remember Cousin Kate? Uncle Charlie? Uncle Charlie's brother-in-law? shame! scandal! humiliation! kneel, pray, beg the Lord!'

Queenie sneaks under the stove. My friend gazes at her shoes, her chin quivers, she lifts her skirt and blows her nose and runs to her room. Long after the town has gone to sleep and the house is silent except for the chimings of clocks and the sputter of fading fires, she is weeping into a pillow already as wet as a widow's handkerchief.

'Don't cry,' I say, sitting at the bottom of her bed and shivering despite my flannel nightgown that smells of last winter's cough syrup, 'don't cry,' I beg, teasing her toes, tickling her feet, 'you're too old for that.'

'It's because,' she hiccups, 'I *am* too old. Old and funny.'

'Not funny. Fun. More fun than anybody. Listen. If you don't stop crying you'll be so tired tomorrow we can't go cut a tree.'

She straightens up. Queenie jumps on the bed (where Queenie is not allowed) to lick her cheeks. 'I know where we'll find pretty trees, Buddy. And holly, too. With berries big as your eyes. It's way off in the woods. Farther than we've ever been. Papa used to bring us Christmas trees from there: carry them on his shoulder. That's fifty years ago. Well, now: I can't wait for morning.'

Morning. Frozen rime lusters the grass; the sun, round as an orange and orange as hot-weather moons, balances on the horizon, burnishes the silvered winter woods. A wild turkey calls. A renegade hog grunts in the undergrowth. Soon, by the edge of knee-deep, rapid-running water, we have to abandon the buggy. Queenie wades the stream first, paddles across barking complaints at the swiftness of the current, the pneumonia-making coldness of it. We follow, holding our shoes and equipment (a hatchet, a burlap sack) above our heads. A mile more: of chastising thorns, burs and briers that catch at our clothes; of rusty pine needles brilliant with gaudy fungus and molted feathers. Here, there, a flash, a flutter, an ecstasy of shrillings remind us that not all the birds have flown south. Always, the path unwinds through lemony sun pools and pitch vine tunnels. Another creek to cross: a disturbed armada of speckled trout froths the water round us, and frogs the size of plates practice belly flops; beaver workmen are building a dam. On the farther shore, Queenie shakes herself and trembles. My friend shivers, too: not with cold but enthusiasm. One of her hat's ragged roses sheds a petal as she lifts her head and inhales the pine-heavy air. 'We're almost there; can you smell it, Buddy?' she says, as though we were approaching an ocean.

And, indeed, it is a kind of ocean. Scented acres of holiday trees, prickly-leafed holly. Red berries shiny as Chinese bells: black crows swoop upon them screaming. Having stuffed our burlap sacks with enough greenery and crimson to garland a dozen windows, we set about choosing a tree. 'It should be,' muses my friend, 'twice as tall as a boy. So a boy can't steal the star.' The one we pick is twice as tall as me. A brave handsome brute that survives thirty hatchet strokes before it keels with a creaking rending cry. Lugging it like a kill, we commence the long trek out. Every few yards we abandon the struggle, sit down and pant. But we have the strength of triumphant huntsmen; that and the tree's virile, icy perfume revive us, goad us on. Many compliments accompany our sunset return along the red clay road to town; but my friend is sly and noncommittal when passers-by praise the treasure perched on our buggy: what a fine tree and where did it come from? 'Yonderways,' she murmurs vaguely. Once a car stops and the rich mill owner's lazy wife leans out and whines: 'Giveya two-bits cash for that ol tree.' Ordinarily my friend is afraid of saying no; but on this occasion she promptly shakes her head: 'We wouldn't take a dollar.' The mill owner's wife persists. 'A dollar, my foot! Fifty cents. That's my last offer. Goodness, woman, you can get another one.' In answer, my friend gently reflects: 'I doubt it. There's never two of anything.'

Home: Queenie slumps by the fire and sleeps till tomorrow, snoring loud as a human.

A trunk in the attic contains: a shoebox of ermine tails (off the opera cape of a curious lady who once rented a room in the house), coils of frazzled tinsel gone gold with age, one silver star, a brief rope of dilapidated, undoubtedly dangerous candy-like light bulbs. Excellent decorations, as far as they go, which isn't far enough: my friend wants our tree to blaze 'like a Baptist window', droop with weighty snows of ornament. But we can't afford the made-in-Japan splendors at the five-and-dime. So we do what we've always done: sit for days at the kitchen table with scissors and crayons and stacks of colored paper. I make sketches and my friend cuts them out: lots of cats, fish too (because they're easy to draw), some apples, some watermelons, a few winged angels devised from saved-up sheets of Hershey-bar tin foil. We use safety pins to attach these creations to the tree; as a final touch, we sprinkle the branches with shredded cotton (picked in August for this purpose). My friend, surveying the effect, clasps her hands together. 'Now honest, Buddy. Doesn't it look good enough to eat?' Queenie tries to eat an angel.

After weaving and ribboning holly wreaths for all the front windows, our next project is the fashioning of family gifts. Tie-dye scarves for the ladies, for the men a home-brewed lemon and licorice and aspirin syrup to be taken 'at the first Symptoms of a Cold and after Hunting'. But when it comes time for making each other's gift, my friend and I separate to work secretly. I would like to buy her a pearl-handled knife, a radio, a whole pound of chocolate-covered cherries (we tasted some once, and she always swears: 'I could live on them, Buddy,

Lord yes I could – and that's not taking His name in vain').
Instead, I am building her a kite. She would like to give me a
bicycle (she's said so on several million occasions: 'If only I
could, Buddy. It's bad enough in life to do without something
you want; but confound it, what gets my goat is not being able
to give somebody something you want *them* to have. Only one
of these days I will, Buddy. Locate you a bike. Don't ask how.
Steal it, maybe'). Instead, I'm fairly certain that she is building
me a kite – the same as last year, and the year before: the year
before that we exchanged slingshots. All of which is fine by
me. For we are champion kite-fliers who study the wind like
sailors; my friend, more accomplished than I, can get a kite aloft
when there isn't enough breeze to carry clouds.

Christmas Eve afternoon we scrape together a nickel and go
to the butcher's to buy Queenie's traditional gift, a good gnaw-
able beef bone. The bone, wrapped in funny paper, is placed
high in the tree near the silver star. Queenie knows it's there.
She squats at the foot of the tree staring up in a trance of greed:
when bedtime arrives she refuses to budge. Her excitement is
equaled by my own. I kick the covers and turn my pillow as
though it were a scorching summer's night. Somewhere a rooster
crows: falsely, for the sun is still on the other side of the world.

'Buddy, are you awake?' It is my friend, calling from her
room, which is next to mine; and an instant later she is sitting
on my bed holding a candle. 'Well, I can't sleep a hoot,' she
declares. 'My mind's jumping like a jack rabbit. Buddy, do you
think Mrs Roosevelt will serve our cake at dinner?' We huddle
in the bed, and she squeezes my hand I-love-you. 'Seems like
your hand used to be so much smaller. I guess I hate to see you
grow up. When you're grown up, will we still be friends?' I say
always. 'But I feel so bad, Buddy. I wanted so bad to give you
a bike. I tried to sell my cameo Papa gave me. Buddy' – she

hesitates, as though embarrassed – 'I made you another kite.'
Then I confess that I made her one, too; and we laugh. The
candle burns too short to hold. Out it goes, exposing the starlight, the stars spinning at the window like a visible caroling
that slowly, slowly daybreak silences. Possibly we doze; but the
beginnings of dawn splash us like cold water: we're up, wide-
eyed and wandering while we wait for others to waken. Quite
deliberately my friend drops a kettle on the kitchen floor. I
tap-dance in front of closed doors. One by one the household
emerges, looking as though they'd like to kill us both; but it's
Christmas, so they can't. First, a gorgeous breakfast: just everything you can imagine – from flapjacks and fried squirrel to
hominy grits and honey-in-the-comb. Which puts everyone in
a good humor except my friend and I. Frankly, we're so impatient to get at the presents we can't eat a mouthful.

Well, I'm disappointed. Who wouldn't be? With socks, a
Sunday school shirt, some handkerchiefs, a hand-me-down
sweater and a year's subscription to a religious magazine for
children. *The Little Shepherd*. It makes me boil. It really does.

My friend has a better haul. A sack of Satsumas, that's her
best present. She is proudest, however, of a white wool shawl
knitted by her married sister. But she *says* her favorite gift is
the kite I built her. And it *is* very beautiful; though not as
beautiful as the one she made me, which is blue and scattered
with gold and green Good Conduct stars; moreover, my name
is painted on it, 'Buddy'.

'Buddy, the wind is blowing.'

The wind is blowing, and nothing will do till we've run to
a pasture below the house where Queenie has scooted to bury
her bone (and where, a winter hence, Queenie will be buried,
too). There, plunging through the healthy waist-high grass, we
unreel our kites, feel them twitching at the string like sky fish

as they swim into the wind. Satisfied, sun-warmed, we sprawl in the grass and peel Satsumas and watch our kites cavort. Soon I forget the socks and hand-me-down sweater. I'm as happy as if we'd already won the fifty-thousand-dollar Grand Prize in that coffee-naming contest.

'My, how foolish I am!' my friend cries, suddenly alert, like a woman remembering too late she has biscuits in the oven. 'You know what I've always thought?' she asks in a tone of discovery, and not smiling at me but a point beyond. 'I've always thought a body would have to be sick and dying before they saw the Lord. And I imagined that when He came it would be like looking at the Baptist window: pretty as colored glass with the sun pouring through, such a shine you don't know it's getting dark. And it's been a comfort: to think of that shine taking away all the spooky feeling. But I'll wager it never happens. I'll wager at the very end a body realizes the Lord has already shown Himself. That things as they are' – her hand circles in a gesture that gathers clouds and kites and grass and Queenie pawing earth over her bone – 'just what they've always seen, was seeing Him. As for me, I could leave the world with today in my eyes.'

This is our last Christmas together.

Life separates us. Those who Know Best decide that I belong in a military school. And so follows a miserable succession of bugle-blowing prisons, grim reveille-ridden summer camps. I have a new home too. But it doesn't count. Home is where my friend is, and there I never go.

And there she remains, puttering around the kitchen. Alone with Queenie. Then alone. ('Buddy dear,' she writes in her wild hard-to-read script, 'yesterday Jim Macy's horse kicked Queenie bad. Be thankful she didn't feel much. I wrapped her in a Fine

Linen sheet and rode her in the buggy down to Simpson's pasture where she can be with all her Bones . . .') For a few Novembers she continues to bake her fruitcakes single-handed; not as many, but some: and, of course, she always sends me 'the best of the batch'. Also, in every letter she encloses a dime wadded in toilet paper: 'See a picture show and write me the story.' But gradually in her letters she tends to confuse me with her other friend, the Buddy who died in the 1880's; more and more thirteenths are not the only days she stays in bed: a morning arrives in November, a leafless birdless coming of winter morning, when she cannot rouse herself to exclaim: 'Oh my, it's fruitcake weather!'

And when that happens, I know it. A message saying so merely confirms a piece of news some secret vein had already received, severing from me an irreplaceable part of myself, letting it loose like a kite on a broken string. That is why, walking across a school campus on this particular December morning, I keep searching the sky. As if I expected to see, rather like hearts, a lost pair of kites hurrying toward heaven.

ACKNOWLEDGMENTS

Every effort has been made to trace and contact all copyright holders. If there are any inadvertent omissions or errors we will be pleased to correct them at the earliest opportunity.

Vintage Classics gratefully acknowledges permission to reprint copyright material as follows:

Truman Capote: 'A Christmas Memory' from *The Complete Stories of Truman Capote* (Penguin, 2005). Copyright © Truman Capote 1956. Reproduced by kind permission of Penguin Books Ltd.

John Cheever: 'Christmas Is a Sad Season for the Poor' from *The Stories of John Cheever* (1978) by John Cheever. Copyright © John Cheever 1978. Published by Vintage Books. Reprinted by permission of The Random House Group Limited.

Stella Gibbons: 'Christmas at Cold Comfort Farm' from *Christmas at Cold Comfort Farm* (1940) by Stella Gibbons. Copyright © Stella Gibbons 1940. Reproduced with permission of Curtis Brown Group Ltd, London on behalf of The Estate of Stella Gibbons.

Laurie Lee: 'Carol Barking' extract from *Cider with Rosie* by Laurie Lee (1959). Copyright © Laurie Lee 1959. First published by Hogarth Press. Reprinted by permission of The Random House Group Limited.

Nancy Mitford: extract from *Christmas Pudding* (1932) by Nancy Mitford. Copyright © Nancy Mitford 1932. Reproduced by permission of the author c/o Rogers, Coleridge and White Ltd., 2 Powis Mews, London W11 1JN. Reprinted by kind permission of Rogers, Coleridge and White Ltd.

Damon Runyon: 'Dancing Dan's Christmas' from *On Broadway* (1950) by Damon Runyon. Copyright © Damon Runyon 1950. Reproduced by kind permission of Constable & Robinson.

Dylan Thomas: extract from *A Child's Christmas in Wales* (1978) by Dylan Thomas. Copyright © The Trustees for the copyright of the late Dylan Thomas 1978. Reproduced by kind permission of David Higham Associates and Orion Books.

Sue Townsend: extract from *The Growing Pains of Adrian Mole* (1984) by Sue Townsend. Copyright © Sue Townsend 1984. First published by Methuen Publishing. Reprinted by permission of The Random House Group Limited.

P. G. Wodehouse: 'Jeeves and the Yule-Tide Spirit' from *Very Good, Jeeves* (1930) by P. G. Wodehouse. Copyright © The Trustees of the Wodehouse Estate. First published by Herbert Jenkins Ltd. Reprinted by permission of The Random House Group Limited.